EX LIBRIS

VINTAGE **CLASSICS**

TALES FROM A MASTER'S NOTEBOOK

Tales from a Master's Notebook

Stories Henry James Never Wrote

EDITED AND INTRODUCED BY

Philip Horne

WITH A FOREWORD BY

Michael Wood

VINTAGE

1 3 5 7 9 10 8 6 4 2

Vintage Classics, an imprint of Vintage,
20 Vauxhall Bridge Road,
London SW1V 2SA

Vintage Classics is part of the Penguin Random House group of companies
whose addresses can be found at global.penguinrandomhouse.com.

This collection first published in Great Britain by Vintage Classics in 2018

penguin.co.uk/vintage

A CIP catalogue record for this book is available from the British Library

ISBN 9781784871475 (Hardback)
ISBN 9781784871499 (Trade Paperback)

Typset in 12.5/15 pt Fournier MT by Jouve (UK), Milton Keynes
Printed and bound by Clays Ltd, St Ives plc

Penguin Random House is committed to a sustainable future for our business, our readers and our planet. This book is made from Forest Stewardship Council® certified paper.

For "Anecdotes":

1) "The Sketches" – some little drama, situation, complication, fantasy; to be worked into small Rye-figure of woman working away (on my doorstep & elsewhere.)

2/ The Coward – le Brave.
The man who by a fluke has done a great bravery in the past; knows he can't do it again & lives in terror of the occasion that shall put him to the test. Dies of that terror.

A page from James's *Notebooks*, from 1899, showing two of James's ideas, under the heading 'Anecdotes' (as if that might have been the title of a collection), for stories that he didn't ever write. The first, 'The Sketches', no one has ever picked up; the second, 'The coward', is the basis of Giles Foden's 'The Road to Gabon'. A transcription of the second can be found in the Appendix (see p. 245); the first reads thus: '1) "The Sketches" – some little drama, situation, complication, fantasy, to be worked into small Rye-figure of woman working away (on my doorstep & elsewhere.)' (MS Am 1094 (2221a) vol. 6, Houghton Library, Harvard University)

CONTENTS

FOREWORD

Henry James's *Notebooks* are full of what he liked to call 'little ideas', some of which he turned into long and famous novels. Many became short stories and novellas, others remained notes only, possibilities abandoned or not even picked up. The ideas took the form of what James thought of as, to quote words used in the appendix to this book, 'notions, subjects, incidents, fantasies, themes, situations'. 'I have my head, thank God, full of visions', he said in 1895. 'One has never too many – one has never enough.' There is something alluring about this plenitude, especially when we think of the visions that were never seen again, and remember perhaps James's own marvellous description of the set-up for his story *The Beast in the Jungle* in August 1901: '*That* was what might have happened, and what *has* happened is that it didn't.'

Sometimes James's jottings take us quite a way into the resulting work, as with this prelude to *The Turn of the Screw*: 'Note here the ghost-story told me at Addington (evening of Thursday 10th) by the Archbishop of Canterbury.' That tale begins with the mention of two ghost-stories being told at a country house and continues with the telling of a third – the framing being crucial to the narrative. I mention the tale also because James was later rather dismissive of it in a way that is wonderfully instructive – he thought he could manage something 'less grossly and merely apparitional' – and because this present volume, *Tales from a Master's Notebook*, is full of ghosts, if we think of them as matter that cannot die. I don't wish to suggest the eleven remarkable stories presented here are narrowly focused, or that James wrote only about the undead. James wrote about many things, and our contemporary writers are different from him and from each other in their tone, theme, setting and much more. But James's ambition for a more refined type of haunting, of a non-apparitional or not merely apparitional ghost, allows us to connect some very varied preoccupations.

Here, briefly described in the light of this thought, are instances you will find in this book of states between life and death: a memory that returns, with real difficulty, as a literal ghost, not seen but heard; a conversation that will never be reported; a secret enemy; a secret life; a test of courage that is also a test of worldliness; a dream of the past as a rich, untouchable fantasy; a waiting for what will live only as long as it is waited for, not consummated. There are also evocations of the clumsiness of failed misbehavior; of the double fear of being found out and of leaving no trace; of an attempted rescue of a life that may not have needed rescuing; of deep and shallow interpretations, perhaps both correct, of a dead man's collection of objects.

The settings of the stories range from Arizona to Norfolk, and from Calcutta to Gabon. The voices are witty, distant, knowing, baffled, confident, the literary strategies very varied. In no instance do we feel the contemporary writer has done what James might have done, so there is, as Philip Horne says, no element of pastiche or even of homage here. This is what the little word 'from' means in the title. We are closest to what James himself thinks – or a persuasive version of what James himself thinks – in Colm Tóibín's story in this volume. James tells Lady Gregory that he often

> noted down something interesting that had been said to him, and on occasion the germ of a story had come to him from a most unlikely source, and other times, of course, from a most obvious and welcome one. He liked to imagine his characters, he said, but he also liked that they might have lived already, to some small extent perhaps, before he painted a new background for them and created a new scenario.

This offers an image of what all the authors here are doing, with the emphasis on the repeated word 'new'. The relation of idea to story is very subtle, and conceptually similar to that other kind of haunting James aspired to with his non-apparitional ghost. Real, historical people inhabit many of the anecdotes that are told to James. Although they have already lived, they do not become James's characters until he has found a new background and scenario for them. Only then do they become the people James likes to think may have already lived, with all the entangled possibilities of a fictional existence now lying in wait for them.

The life of all the stories in this volume begins, in a sense, with the first sentence of each. They have no past. Or more precisely they had no past until their authors chose one – or were chosen by one – and went on to do something with it. In that process each of these stories too seems to live, to occupy a world the author already knows, either through their experience or imagination. This feature connects them with Henry James not simply through lineage or debt but through a common practice of the art of fiction, a passion for which, as he said in *The Future of the Novel* in 1899, is only 'written in the air' – for the illusive, 'the record of what, in any particular case, has *not* been'. These notebook entries are in their own way records of 'what . . . has *not* been', what was never even fully imagined. Now they have taken on a reality that only the imagination can provide: these contemporary authors have given them further fictional life, or half-life, tracing the work of memory, fear, fantasy, assumption, expectation and other ghostly agents and agencies, in a way James might have appreciated.

Michael Wood, 2018

INTRODUCTION

Where do stories come from? What makes an idea work as a story – for a reader or, not quite the same thing, for a writer? Readers are always asking writers, 'Where do you get your ideas?' – and although in one way there are easy answers (from the newspapers, from experience, from friends) it is hard to put one's finger on what makes an idea *click*. How can one tell the difference between a good or workable idea and a bad, or between one that will only work for one writer and one that could work for many? How do stories grow? If they're left too long, do they lose their potency – as some old packet of seeds may have, found at the back of a potting shed – or can they still, in new earth, give rise to fresh life?

Questions like these have always been at the back of my mind during a professional life much of which has been focused on the astonishingly varied career and output of Henry James, who between his birth in New York in 1843 and his death in London early in 1916 made himself one of the greatest writers of the modern period – in fiction and criticism, in autobiography and letters. He knew or met Dickens and George Eliot, Flaubert and Turgenev, Woolf and Pound, Oscar Wilde and Theodore Roosevelt; but more importantly, he drew on his rich experiences of the world for ideas that would drive fictions, and restlessly experimented with the possibilities of tale, novella and novel. Across the decades, from *The Portrait of a Lady*, his first masterpiece of 1881, to *The Ambassadors* of 1903, from 'Daisy Miller' of 1878 through 'The Aspern Papers' of 1888 and 'The Turn of the Screw' of 1898 to 'The Jolly Corner' of 1908, he maintained a dazzling flow of fresh invention – which we can follow by seeing him play with innumerable ideas in his fascinating notebooks.

The questions of where stories come from and what makes them work have been given a new urgency for me by the process of re-editing these notebooks from scratch for a new scholarly edition by Cambridge University Press, still some way off – which involves transcribing the texts afresh from James's often execrable handwriting, annotating to a new level of detail, correcting old errors – and doubtless, though as little as possible, introducing some new ones. James struggled to acquire the habit of the notebook – but it became his way both of working ideas out under the pressure of pen on paper (for him 'expression' meant squeezing things out) and of preserving them, dropping them to mature into what he calls in the 1907 Preface to *The American* 'the deep well of unconscious cerebration', an obscurity in which rich and strange transformations could take place. The notebooks are fascinating, private documents in which we see James's intimate practice of his art. Here the inner logic of the material is gradually seen emerging, so that for instance we see the end of *The Portrait of a Lady* take its present form, or what James first considers 'a real little situation for a short tale' can swell into a novel of 130,000 words like *The Awkward Age* (1899). The notebooks are also, more generally, exemplary, heroic texts for anyone interested in the workings of the creative imagination. They were a refuge for James, in which he could commune with himself and his art; and in them he would give himself the encouragement that the critics often withheld, as when, in January 1894, he told himself that the more he went on the more he found

> that the only balm and the only refuge, the real solution of the pressing question of life, are in this frequent, fruitful, intimate battle with the particular idea, with the subject, the possibility, the place.

In other words, for James the problems of life were only solved in art – by plunging into work.

There are only nine surviving notebooks in the Houghton Library at Harvard – they have recently been put up online if you want to look at them and see James's original hieroglyphics. What survives is just a small fraction of the mountain of volumes he must have filled, most of which doubtless perished in one or other of the great bonfires of letters and documents whose smoke, in his last years, drifted from the garden of the author's home near the Sussex coast as he sorted and purged his archive. The earliest entry dates from 1878, two years after James published his first novel in book form, the last from 1911, five years before his death. They all show him following his own dictum in his great 1884 essay 'The Art of Fiction': 'Try to be one of the people on whom nothing is lost!' Some entries record bare formulas for possible stories, 'germs' as he often calls them (meaning seeds), gathered from the newspapers, or dinner party conversations, or from observation; others set down autobiographical memories and reflections; yet others plot out narrative developments and approaches, sometimes in painstaking, chapter-by-chapter detail. Why these particular volumes survive and the rest were chucked into the flames at Lamb House is something of a puzzle. The theory I find most persuasive is that James preserved notebooks containing either ideas he hadn't yet used and to which he thought he might return, or autobiographical passages like the deeply moving account of his visit to the graves of his parents and sister and a brother in Cambridge, Massachusetts in November 1904: 'Everything was there; everything *came*; the recognition, stillness, the strangeness, the pity & the sanctity & the terror, the breath-catching passion & the divine relief of tears'. At any rate, one fact that came to preoccupy me was the survival in the notebooks of over sixty subjects for fictions that James never got so far as writing – sometimes, no doubt, for lack of time, sometimes apparently because he couldn't find the right turns for the narrative, or the subject somehow lost its interest for him.

The train of thought which has led to this book is mysterious in origin: as James says about *The Tragic Muse* in its Preface, 'I fail to recover my precious first moment of consciousness of the idea to which it was to give form'. I have no memory of where it came from – an idle thought while browsing in the notebooks, perhaps, or a conversation with someone. It's possible that I heard of the never-translated 2009 Spanish volume *After Henry James*, edited by Javier Montes, for which various contributors, mostly Spanish but including Colm Tóibín, wrote stories based on unused 'germs'. (The original English version of the story appeared in his collection *The Empty Family* (2010), and I am very grateful to him for permission to reprint it here.)

Whatever the original stimulus, for me the central prompting – James in his notebooks (sketching the story that Joseph O'Neill has taken on) says that 'I hate to touch things only to leave them' – has been the thought that rather than going to waste, these seeds might grow into something, albeit through a kind of surrogacy, and in the soil of other imaginations than James's own. In the process some serious writers could come together to demonstrate the continuing life of his idea of the liberty of the novel – and of the tale: his idea in 'The Art of Fiction' that 'the good health of an art which undertakes so immediately to reproduce life must demand that it be perfectly free'.

These are not James stories, of course. They show, rather, the truth of James's notion, in the 1908 Preface to *The Portrait of a Lady*, of the multiple aspects of the 'house of fiction': 'The house of fiction has . . . not one window, but a million . . . every one of which has been pierced, or is still pierceable, in its vast front, by the need of the individual vision and by the pressure of the individual will . . . At each of them stands a figure with a pair of eyes, or at least with a field-glass, which forms, again and again, for observation, a unique instrument, insuring to the person making use of it an impression distinct from every other.' In other words, the authors in this book, as I hoped, have taken James's hint and made it their own, have written stories which give their *own* 'impression of life' – not Jamesian pastiches.

James has made a number of appearances in recent fiction, under various guises. As a subject of study in Alan Hollinghurst's *The Line of Beauty* (2004); as a detective, working alongside his brother William and sister Alice to track down Jack the Ripper in *What Alice Knew: A Most Curious Tale of Henry James & Jack the Ripper* (2010) by Paula Marantz Cohen; as a melancholy, unfulfilled homosexual writer struggling towards supreme achievement in Colm Tóibín's *The Master* (2004); as a ruefully sensitive professional man of letters, and friend to George du Maurier, in David Lodge's *Author, Author* (2004); or as the employer of a brilliant young woman (fictionalised as Frieda Wroth but close to the actual Theodora Bosanquet) in Michiel Heyns's *The Typewriter's Tale* (2005). One should also mention *Felony: The Private History of 'The Aspern Papers'* (2002) by Emma Tennant, where James maltreats Constance Fenimore Woolson, who is in love with him; or Cynthia Ozick's long short story *Dictation* (2008), where Theodora

Bosanquet plots mischievously behind James's back; or 'The Master at St. Bartholomew's Hospital, 1914–1916' (2008) by Joyce Carol Oates, where the elderly James becomes the prey of homoerotic fantasies as he visits wounded soldiers; or Joan Aiken's *The Haunting of Lamb House* (1991), where James sees ghosts in his Sussex home. Nor is it a direct continuation of James's own fiction, like John Banville's daring *Mrs Osmond* (2017), a sequel to *The Portrait of a Lady* (1881). In its way, though, it more directly than any of these picks up the dropped baton of James's own strivings in the field of fiction.

The book obviously has a double aspect, but it is organised very simply. The stories are presented in sequence, with no apparatus, so that they can be read first, straightforwardly, as the work of their authors. For those who are interested, an Appendix presents the notebook passages that have been their inspiration, so that readers can compare starting points and finishing lines; then, if they like, going back to reread the stories and trace the continuities and deviations. The subjects, it will be apparent, are in very various states. Some are long and full – sometimes returned to repeatedly over a period of months or years. Others are short, either pithy or (occasionally) nebulous or gnomic – jotted down as an *aide-mémoire* that evidently meant more to James than it can to us. Sometimes, as with the subject from which Giles Foden has evolved 'The Road to Gabon', James just puts down a rough diamond with no attempt at analysing its facets or giving it a setting. (The manuscript notebook page on which it occurs is reproduced as the frontispiece.) In other cases, he pursues one or more apparently false scents, takes what seem to be wrong turns that overcomplicate or end in an impasse. (I haven't always presented these at full length, wanting to show mainly where authors have picked up from James.) Some subjects seem recorded rather dutifully after someone has pressed an anecdote on the famous author at dinner. Others are inspired by James's own half-alienated or ironic observation of how the world wags. Sometimes, one must say, of how it *wagged* – for the topics occasionally feel dated, and after more than a century things have moved on – but even then, contemporary equivalents can usually be found.

I should briefly comment on the title. While these tales start 'from' entries in the notebooks, they mostly move a considerable distance *from* their points of origin. And anything but slavish, they are freely inventive. In the title, also, it is 'a Master' rather than '*the* Master'; partly because there are numerous 'masters' (male and female) besides James, and partly because James maintained a distinctly ironic attitude to the term. In his great novella 'The Lesson of the Master' (1888), the 'Master' of the title is a famous writer, possibly an untrustworthy hypocrite, who has squandered his talent through commercial overproduction; in his tale 'The Tree of Knowledge' (1900) it's the title claimed by a dreadful sculptor whose family have seen through him but have to indulge his pretensions. James can use it to praise writers he admires, as when he speaks (in his lecture 'The Lesson of Balzac') of 'the great interesting art of which Balzac remains the greatest master'; but it's always an unstable notion for him, because as an honorific title it implies a fixed hierarchy, and James knew mastery was always provisional – a writer being only as good as her or his last story, or indeed, *next* story.

I urged myself on from the start with the thought of Takashi Shimura assembling the *Seven Samurai* for a noble, possibly quixotic enterprise in Kurosawa's great film. Recruiting my crew of contributors – seeking fine writers with a real connection to the subject and an excitement about the idea – has indeed been an interesting process, thrilling, frustrating, educational, protracted, full of possibilities and impossibilities. It has also been a privilege. Many hundreds of emails later, there is a stirring variety of contributors here. Quite a few I knew already – but others I approached more indirectly. I am extremely grateful to all those who out of a shared love of good writing have pulled together to make this book happen, and want to thank too those who gave help and good wishes but for all sorts of reasons couldn't contribute. It was a pleasure to approach some very distinguished writers, partly because some of them said yes, partly because even when they said no (as I knew many would) their replies were gracious and richly characteristic and suggestive.

In some cases the timing was simply wrong: 'I have just spent three years locked in a room in my house writing a long, long novel . . . I am so exhausted, the wires in my head are so frayed, the muscles throughout my body are so sore, that it would be physically and mentally impossible for me to write a single word of fiction just now and perhaps for the rest of time.' For some the very thought of compromising with someone else's imagination ruled out participation, in a way I had to respect. 'I am engaged in a project of my own – fully engaged – and can't afford to entertain a Jamesian takeover,' one told me; another, that 'this sort of thing isn't for me – it just doesn't go with the way I work'; another, that 'I'm busy mining my own imagination. I think Henry James would get in the way!' For others, the ideas were too Jamesian, too stamped with his artistic personality: 'They all seem such ideas for HJ, rather than for [me]'; 'Some of the ideas are off-putting in their length, and my reaction is Jamesian – too much detail, don't tell me so much, I need to invent!' For others still the process of choosing a subject had a complexity, and unpredictability, approaching what we find in James's own 'long figuring out' of subjects in what he calls 'the patient, passionate little *cahier* [notebook]': they had to attend to their own sometimes inscrutable inner workings through a not wholly voluntary or conscious programme of brooding. The role of instinct in finding and feeling out a subject made it agonising for some, sometimes with happy results, sometimes not: 'I've gone back and forth, back and forth, hunting and sniffing,' one told me; another finally didn't feel the stir of life in the chosen subject: 'I confess there are no wiggles'. I was anxious not to disturb this serious process; for as one said, bowing out, 'Good writing should always feel necessary.' The stories that have emerged from this hard process have, it seems to me, all taken on a life, a necessity, of their own.

I gave the writers a free choice: drew up a document containing over sixty subjects and simply tried to make sure no two writers picked the same subject – unknowingly, anyway. In fact, there were no conflicts. I'm almost sorry, as the comparison of two divergent tales stemming from a common subject would have been fascinating. I explicitly told everyone not to feel bound to stick strictly to James's plan – partly because James's plan might not have worked anyway (why, after all, *didn't* he write it?), partly because their value lies in their own unique perspective. There was carte blanche for invention. It was entirely up to the writers to choose the period and setting for their tales – James himself would freely transpose an anecdote from its original Italian setting to France (as for *The Reverberator*, 1888), or, crossing the border the other way, make an errant husband who was originally English, then French, into an Italian Prince (*The Golden Bowl*, 1904). He debated, and occasionally changed, the gender of characters (the protagonist of *The Wings of the Dove* 'seems to me preferably a woman, but of this I'm not sure'). He was a highly international writer – one of his least-known novels, for instance, *Confidence* (1879), takes characters to Siena, London, Paris, Le Havre and Étretat (renamed 'Blanquais-les-Galets'), California, Mexico, India, the Orient, Athens and New York. James was not just cosmopolitan, that is, he was global, engaged with an interconnected, permeable world that was just coming into being.

Some of the writers here, intrepid travellers, have made that territory – the world, now so much more *accessible* – especially their own: Paul Theroux, Joseph O'Neill, Amit Chaudhuri, Giles Foden. Part of the variety of this collection, then, is the variety of settings. But equally on display is a great range of modes and styles, and kinds of experience. As in James's own *oeuvre*, there are comic stories of great houses and their vicissitudes, as in Lynne Truss's satirical 'Testaments'; ghost stories about wasted lives and the traces they leave, as in Rose Tremain's haunting 'Is Anybody There?'; ironic stories of the literary life, as in Jonathan Coe's wry fable 'Canadians Can't Flirt'. Susie Boyt's 'People Were So Funny', a delicate account of a young life devoted to the cares of age, is in its own way as poised in its evocation of the plight of the carer as James's '"Europe"' or 'The Aspern Papers'. Sex, which usually simmers just below the surface in James, because of the manners of his age, has in places surged into view. Only one story, Colm Tóibín's, is set in James's own era – and there the surging is at its most turbulent. The other stories take place at a time close to our present; and it's observable that the finding of 'equivalents' to Victorian or Edwardian conditions in our own time nearly always brings stimulating differences. Paul Theroux's surprising mystery 'Father X' is animated by a rousing, and quite Jamesian, moral passion in its treatment of the Catholic Church in modern Boston. In 'The Poltroon Husband', Joseph O'Neill gives us a highly contemporary version of an American life in the woods, in which a nocturnal incident seems to crystallise some creeping anxieties.

Giles Foden's African adventure, 'The Road to Gabon', carries his compromised hero dauntingly far from the teacups of the homeland to a far-flung proving-ground. And Amit Chaudhuri's 'Wensleydale' takes an Anglo-American Jamesian subject and relocates it to a pungently evoked melancholic Calcuttan, or Kolkatan, milieu. Some germs seem conceived in such a way as to carry a certain set of values, and some authors have – with a thoroughly Jamesian freedom – chosen to unsettle or ironise those values, particularly where sex is involved, notably Tessa Hadley in her 'Old Friends', which approaches James's scenario from an invigoratingly different point of view. The valencies, then, are never equal; each chemical combination tends to produce some intriguingly new compound.

To read these stories as they came in has been a real honour: I've sensed in them both the unbroken currency of James's creative imagination, and the brilliance and originality of these authors of our own times, creating stories that are wholly their own. It has above all been *fun*, a term James himself used.

For one tale, when the deadline was looming, I approached myself – as an experiment, and with considerable reluctance. It had been fascinating, and inspiring, to watch so many fine writers tease out James's suggestions. And I felt the pressure of the idea that it was wrong to ask others to do something I wouldn't or couldn't at least attempt myself. There was a subject in the notebooks I felt drawn to, one that otherwise nobody was going to take on. The resulting story, however, wouldn't figure here at all if a few sympathetic readers whose judgement I respect had passed an adverse verdict. It is offered with modesty, not as an equal to the others, but as testimony to the fascination of the creative process in James's notebooks, in which I hope this collection will stir fresh interest.

*

Late in life James (for the money, but also it seems for the sociability of it) took part in a collaborative novel, called *The Whole Family* (1908), in which a succession of US writers, each contributing a chapter from the point of view of one family member, wrestled for control of plot and meaning. Fascinating as it is – and James's contribution above all – that book is a multi-vehicle car crash; and the only collaboration I have asked of the writers in these pages is whatever loose arrangement they wished to make, quite privately, with the spirit of James.

This book, then, is not a glorified party game like that: these are real stories in their own right. No doubt this book will be of interest to academics. But it is aimed at interested readers of all kinds. There is, I am delighted to say, plenty of playfulness here, and some allusiveness, but the origin of these stories in another writer's imagination – or one should say, perhaps, the fact that they have passed through and been honed by another's imagination, for who can say where they originated? – is, ultimately, only part of their appeal. This book constitutes a 'case', as James himself might have said – a demonstration of the continuing vitality of fiction as a form, and of continuities between the practitioners of our own time and the great writers of the past. But the test that matters most, as always, is the emotion, engagement, excitement and pleasure of readers.

Philip Horne, 2018

PAUL THEROUX

FATHER X

On the last of my monthly visits to him, my widowed father made a casual remark about his poor hearing. 'The worst of deafness is not silence,' he said. 'I could bear that. It's that I can actually hear voices, noises that sound like words spoken in the next room. But I'll be damned if I can understand them.' And he stared helplessly at me in bewilderment. He was in his late sixties but had a cherubic face, pink cheeks, blue eyes and tousled hair, like an elderly child. 'Indistinct voices.' And he smiled. 'What is being said to us?'

I drove five hundred miles to where I was living with my fiancée and got the news the next day that my father had died soon after I left – without warning; he was not ill, and not very old, but his heart failed; and I was too far away to be of any use. I hated that he had died alone – he had buried my mother, to whom he was devoted, three years before – and in my grief I clung to that casual remark he'd once made to me about being deaf. Hearing words but not understanding them.

The statement, characteristic of his honesty, helped me through the funeral arrangements, and I repeated the words to myself like a mantra. In the end it did not seem casual at all, but rather like an eternal truth, at least of my life, of being in the presence of a drama, aware of all its spoken details and taking it for meaningless mumbling, not realising that a revelation was being offered that might change my view of myself, my family, the world – everything, including what I am about to reveal about my father here.

'But I have faith,' he said. 'With faith all things are possible. Maybe one day I'll get it.'

He wanted so little; for as long as I knew him he was a housebound and unambitious man, content with his loving wife and his unusual writing career that was like a cottage industry, but of a spiritual kind.

I was alone at the wake, except for the few people who'd known him, the plumber and the electrician and the man who mowed the lawn after I left for college. Father had no close friends – he resisted intimacy with everyone except his wife, my mother, who was his whole world. When she died, my father helped me through that sadness, did all the paperwork, prepared the documents, and was resolute while I sobbed, bereft at the thought of losing my mother.

Father's patience gave him strength – goodness was his business, as I will explain in a moment; but goodness was his mode of being. My mother was such a part of him that I felt that when she died he was inconsolable and yearned to join her. I sometimes reflected that, though kindly towards me, my parents were so devoted to each other that in many respects they ignored me. Maybe this is a pattern with passionate couples who have kids? My folks were reserved towards everyone else, they had no room for friends, and they were disinclined to spend much time with me. I grew up in awe of them, intimidated by their closeness, while at the same time somewhat resenting the fact that for much of my early life I seemed to be in their way. The memory of this conflict made my grieving harder.

And then at the wake, alone with the funeral director, at the last hour, I got the shocking news.

'I thought the death certificate was in order, but it seems there's a problem,' he said, speaking much too slowly, because I wanted to know it all at once. His name was Ken Mortimer, of Mortimer Mortuary. 'And it's not a misfiling,' he added, as though to keep me in suspense.

We were standing so near the open casket I got a whiff of my father's body, the faint tang of chemicals, the perfumed hum of talcum and make-up that made his face puffy and doll-like.

'What is it?' I whispered, as though Father might hear. Proximity to a corpse awakens superstitions and provokes odd behaviour. I was keenly aware of being within the orbit of his aura. The inert body of the man seemed to have powers, and it was no consolation to me that he was not wearing his bulky hearing aid.

Mortimer the funeral director wasn't fussed; he was soft-spoken and correct, which made what he was telling me much harder to take, because his tone gave it a certainty that was almost unbearable.

'The death certificate can't be authenticated,' he said. 'There is no record of your father anywhere.'

'I don't understand. He has a birth certificate.'

'Not a true one. It doesn't check out. There is no record of your father's birth that we can find.'

'He was born here in Boston,' I said.

By shaking his head slowly, as though in sorrow, the man made a tactful effort to refute this. 'Willard Hope does not exist – at least on paper.'

Hearing his name spoken, with this denial, so near to his lifeless body, cushioned in the silk-lined casket, I whinnied and became breathless and put my hands to my face.

'Date and place of birth,' I said, protesting. 'It's on record.'

'No matches,' Mortimer said. I began to resent his dark suit, his somber necktie, his highly polished shoes, his pinky ring, the small gold lapel pin – all of it, for the authority it gave him; because I was rumpled and fatigued with grief and unsure of how to handle what he was telling me.

'What about my mother – her birth certificate? Her wake was held right here three years ago.'

Mortimer was trying to be kind, to let me down gently. His considerate way of dealing with grief was a key element in his work. He was in a sense a professional mourner, the soul of sympathy, grieving with his customers, role-playing perhaps, because high emotion was the day-to-day with him. He remained compassionate yet unfazed, like a doctor delivering bad news.

'Your father supplied the documents then, which we didn't question,' he said.

Each time he spoke I glanced at my father's powdered nose and rouged cheeks, his hair neatly combed, the trace of a smile on his lips, as though listening.

The man straightened and faced me. 'Forgeries.'

'Their marriage certificate.'

'No record of it.'

'He was a pious Catholic. It would have been in a church somewhere in Boston.'

Mortimer's saying nothing, his facing me without any expression, seemed the most severe way of refuting me.

'My father was an honest man. He would never involve himself in forgery.'

'I'm not saying he did it.' Then Mortimer sighed with regret. 'But the papers were certainly forged. The seal, the notary, the dates, the signatures – all of it was false. None of it checked out. He is not Willard Hope. Your mother was not Frances Hope.'

Dad always called her Frankie. He loved her, adored her,

made her happy, while I watched from a little distance, admiring their love but feeling rejected.

'Who is he, then?'

'I have no idea.'

He was lying in the casket before me, within earshot of all this, and I was reminded again of how he spoke of hearing words without understanding them.

'What will you do?'

'What we usually do. Keep some of his DNA. Maybe find a match. We took a sample, a swab from inside his mouth. And some hair.'

'What about fingerprints?'

'The service is being held in half an hour. We'll have to load the casket onto the hearse. It's a good twenty minutes to the church. There isn't time.'

But even as Mortimer was speaking I was calling the police on my cell phone, explaining the urgency; that fingerprints needed to be taken from a body immediately. 'A set of remains?' the dispatcher said: a melancholy description of my father. And I had the sad duty of standing before the casket, keeping the fretting Mortimer at bay, while a police woman (nametag *Cruz*) held Father's limp arm and rolled one finger after another onto the ink pad and then in the same motion onto the appropriate square of the document, taking his prints. Closing the lid of the casket Mortimer frowned at the sight of my father's inky fingers, as though we'd spoiled his work.

The service was held an hour late. The priest was annoyed, though the few mourners didn't seem to notice. But a large grieving family awaiting their own service, delayed by ours, stood in the parking lot, looking wounded, in sulky postures. I was struck by how many of them there were, their tears, their convoy of cars, each with a flag magnetized to the roof; they were a reproach to me, as I entered the church for our small huddled service.

The ritual was familiar; still, I sat baffled, wondering who it was that lay in the casket. That puzzlement made me sadder, and for the first time since hearing the news of my father's death, I wept – sobbing until my throat ached. But I was sure I was weeping for myself, feeling abandoned, tricked by the man in the casket on wheels, watching the priest shaking holy water on the lid.

Who was he? Who, for that matter, was I?

He was a recluse. You might have suspected agoraphobia except that when my mother was alive they often went out in the evening for a drive. They brought sandwiches. They parked near the harbor, facing the sea, and ate them. They left me at home, saying, 'You must have schoolwork to do,' and I said yes, because I knew from experience that they did not want me along. I seem to be suggesting that they were cold to me, but they were so loving towards each other I could not but admire them. They sometimes appeared to me like two people who shared an amazing secret that only they knew, that would never be revealed, that they marveled over in whispers in their parked car.

Their love radiated calm in the household. My mother glowed in his adoration. My father was humble, God-fearing, engaged in one of the more unusual professions – rewarding spiritually but not monetarily. He said he didn't mind. My parents lived frugally. They often spoke of the virtue of the Economy of Enough.

Pious, yet he seldom went to church, and when he did go to a holy mass he chose a service in a distant town, sneaked in by a side door, sat in a rear pew, his head down, more of his humility, reminding me of Christ's parable of the Pharisee and the Publican – my father the Publican who beat his breast because he felt unworthy, and did not raise his eyes to heaven, as the boastful Pharisee did in the Gospel of Luke. Then he sneaked out, by a different door.

His unusual profession? He wrote sermons for a living. He did not advertise but his business was well enough known so that after a while priests found him and solicited his help in composing the Sunday sermon, or the specific homilies for weddings and funerals.

In the beginning it was done by mail order, letters addressed to Father X, from priests requesting a thousand words on a particular topic or biblical text, usually enclosing an envelope of dollar bills, never a check; the sort of limp, faded dollar bills you might see in the collection basket or being inserted in the poor box.

'A donation,' the priest's note would say.

Father wrote in longhand, my mother typed the sermons, and it was she who mailed the letters at the post office, while Father stayed home.

It had started as a column in a Boston newspaper, where my father worked selling classified ads, at that time a profitable section of the paper: 'small ads'. Father liked it because it was all done on the telephone, he had regular office hours, he did not need to leave his desk; in his modesty, he seemed to enjoy the obscurity of the job. A regular feature of the paper was 'Thought for the Day' by 'Father X' – the name used by two journalists who wanted to conceal their identity. They took turns writing the 'Thought', which appeared beside the editorials, as a way of dignifying the page.

Overhearing the journalists complaining that they were behind in their work and had to produce a 'Thought', my father offered to help.

'You, Willard?'

His full name was Willard Lawrence Hope, he was then about forty-five, and I would have been five. I was Larry.

'Think you can do it?'

My modest father said, 'I'm willing to try. If you don't like what I write, don't use it.'

He wrote a column based on the story in John about Jesus curing the blind man. He made much of the Pharisees mocking Jesus, accusing him of being a sinner, pretending to work a miracle on the Jewish Sabbath, the byplay with the despised parents of the blind man, and the doubting Pharisees.

'I like the dialogue in this story,' he told me. 'It has the ring of human speech. "How can a sinner work miracles?" "He is a prophet." The parents protesting, "He was born blind." And, "I don't know if he's a sinner, but I was blind and now I see." And "I've told you already and you didn't hear." You can see them all standing in a little group, with the confused parents, near the mud puddle that the blind man rubbed on his eyes.'

And his favorite line in it from Jesus, when challenged, the odd ungrammatical protestation, 'Before Abraham was, I am.'

That column, on yellowed newsprint, was tacked to the wall of his study as his first effort, the one that earned him his job as Father X.

The two journalists were delighted, they ran the piece and asked for more, and soon my father had a new job at the paper. He still sold classified ads, but his 'Thought for the Day' was so popular it was syndicated in the other newspapers owned by the company. To his relief, after his success he worked from home – the classifieds, the daily 'Thought'. He liked working in his pajamas.

It had all happened quickly. He said he was not surprised. He was modest about his column, but he insisted there was another factor.

'No one likes to write,' he said to me more than once. 'Writing is a chore for even an experienced journalist. For the average person it is awful to contemplate – the blank page, how do I fill it, what do I say? Even a letter. Ask someone to put something in writing – "write me a letter" and you'll probably never receive it. Most people would rather do anything than write. Especially sermons.'

Another day he told me why.

'They're happy to condemn sinners – just talking. But a reasoned sermon, with biblical authority, is another story. It's much easier to condemn someone out of hand than denounce him in a well-written sermon. And anyway, Jesus taught love and forgiveness.'

'So you like to write?'

'I usually have something to say, which makes it easier. I believe in what I write. And I am inspired by the Word of God.'

The other journalists were writing the 'Thought' as a job. My father was doing it for pleasure and as a spiritual exercise.

'Maybe it's a form of prayer,' he said.

Yet he still sold small ads and made a reasonable living, while my mother busied herself looking after wayward souls – unwed mothers, battered wives, counseling them and helping them find their way.

Father X's columns, which he structured like sermons, were quoted in churches, from the pulpit, and my father received many letters of thanks, as well as an additional income, writing sermons to order. *How does one console the parents of a dead child?* he was asked. He answered by writing a page of consolation, and he received some money in return. *This is the money the parents gave me, in gratitude. Please accept it as a donation.* That happened so many times he had a regular correspondence with priests, stuck for ideas for sermons, who implored Father X to help them out.

He gladly did so. He felt in this way that he was speaking to a congregation through this priest. He said that when he felt the fervor of devotion he could write a sermon in ten minutes. 'And that small effort might change lives.' He had a thorough knowledge of scripture. 'The human parts – people speaking. Those are real voices. "I don't know if he's a sinner, but I was blind and now I see" – that's nice, that's real.'

Most people who tried to write had nothing to say. 'But this is the living word.'

He did not regard this writing as a business. It was a mission, these were donations, not fees; but he realized that towards the end of the week most priests were agonizing over the Sunday sermon.

One wrote to him, 'I'd planned to play golf today. I thought I'd miss the tee-time. Your help has allowed me to do this.'

Golf! he exclaimed. Priests had boats, parties to attend, friends and families to visit. My father writing their sermons freed them to do as they wished and gave meaning to their work.

'And you have the last word,' I said.

'Not me,' he said. He tapped his head and then pointed to the heavens.

Towards the end of the Nineties, when the newspaper closed, Father X's 'Thought' appeared on a website. He posted sermons, he fielded questions, he accepted commissions to write for special occasions. Perhaps he realized how much power he had as a writer, that on any given Sunday many priests would be standing before a congregation, reciting his words, always, as he said, a message of forgiveness.

'Priests are like college professors,' he said. 'They give the same lessons every year. They repeat themselves. That's why, after a while, I seldom hear from them again. They have all they need from me.'

He was never more passionate or persuasive than when he was writing of the sanctity of marriage, the word made flesh, God is Love. And that was the man I knew, the salesman in Classifieds who became a columnist, who ended up writing sermons for desperate priests – who were desperate perhaps because they had faltered in the faith.

But he was not Father X. Nor, as I learned, was he Willard Hope. And if he was not Willard Hope, I was not Larry Hope.

When the funeral rituals ended I did not go back to Maryland, where I had been living with my fiancée, Beth. I simply told her, 'I need to stay a while, to sort out my father's papers.' She accepted that explanation.

How could I tell her that I was not the man she thought I was? My identity was in doubt, my pious father had lied about his name, and so had my mother. Beth and I had talked about marrying soon. That had cheered my father. Once I had told him that his piety had inspired me to think of the priesthood – that I might have a vocation. 'Think hard,' he said. 'It's a torment for many priests. Look how desperate they are,' and he showed me their letters, begging him to write for them.

My birth certificate was clearly as false as my father's. How could I get married if I did not know who I was? I looked again at my birth certificate, though I knew all the details, my name Lawrence Hope, my father Willard Hope, his profession given as *Journalist*, a modest way of describing someone writing spiritual texts for uplifting congregations; his date of birth; my mother was Frances, profession *Housewife* – more modesty, for as a social worker she eased the lives of many single mothers.

I looked for more paper, for any documents in my father's desk or around the house that might help explain who he was. There was nothing. He had not been in the army, he had not applied for a passport, he had never been in trouble with the law: more and more he seemed like a shadow.

'No hits,' Mortimer, the funeral director said, when I called to ask about the DNA samples.

This call reminded me that I had fingerprints. I took them to police headquarters and explained my problem, saying that I needed to establish my father's true identity in order to find out who I was.

'But I don't have much hope,' I said. 'I can't think of any occasion when my father would have been fingerprinted.'

'You'd be surprised,' the desk sergeant said, taking the envelope of prints.

That same week I got a call saying that they had a match, his fingerprints were on file in the federal database. I made an appointment to examine the relevant documents.

'These are the prints of Jeremiah Fagan,' the officer said at my interview, pushing a piece of paper across the counter. 'Here's his address and his details. They might be out of date – this was filed twenty-odd years ago.'

'It's a firearms application,' I said, with disbelief, and I saw that the date on it was the year I was born.

'And you can see it was approved. He had a license to carry a Class A firearm.'

'My father carried a gun?'

'This is your father?'

To identify myself I had shown him my driver's license, where I was Lawrence Hope.

'I think my father changed his name.'

'No, he didn't. That would have come up in the search. A name change would have invalidated the gun license.'

'Why would he want to carry a gun?'

'There's his reason on the application,' the sergeant said. 'Line five. "Personal protection". If you want a copy it's two dollars.'

I sat in a coffee shop studying the application, trying to fit the new name to my father's face, reflecting on the date of the document, which was so near to my birthday; and at last I examined my father's home address, 600 Harrison Avenue.

Harrison Avenue is one of Boston's major thoroughfares – long and lined with important buildings, running south from Chinatown almost to Malcolm X Boulevard, which suggests the racial diversity of its residents. But where my father's house should have stood there was an imposing brick building that looked more like a school than an apartment house. Walking around it I saw, looming behind it, the granite steeples of the Cathedral of the Holy Cross.

The address I had was not a school at all, but the cathedral rectory. I knocked. A woman in an apron answered and said that the priests were either busy or away, and that if I wanted to talk to one I would need to make an appointment.

I said, 'Tell me, who is the oldest priest here?'

'That would be Monsignor Bracken.'

'Is he about sixty-five or seventy?'

'Could be.'

'May I leave him a note?'

The woman agreed, and helped by offering me a piece of paper. I wrote that I hoped that I might meet Monsignor Bracken at his convenience the following Sunday, before he said Mass (as the schedule indicated) at one of the side altars of the Cathedral.

Although I wrote my name and telephone number on the note I did not receive a reply. After some days of speculation, I was eager to find out the truth. On the Sunday, I stopped at the rectory at nine and was met by a young priest. I said that I was there to see Monsignor Bracken.

'Do you have an appointment?'

'I left a message for him.'

'Just a moment.'

He left me standing in the foyer, in the odor of candlewax and incense and starched linen and furniture polish. I heard what sounded like a complaint from a few rooms away, and then the young priest returned.

'You can go through,' he said. 'Second door on your left.'

The old priest, Monsignor Bracken, was seated in an armchair and looking like a plump pink granny with tangled hair, a frilly blouse over his sloping stomach, and a shawl around his neck – vestments, of course, and his cassock like a gown.

He welcomed me – 'Take a seat' – but was so abrupt I felt I had intruded upon him. And perhaps I had. In his lap, there was a sheet of paper, obviously something he was studying, with words in large letters, the sort of typeface that aids a public speaker.

'I'm sorry to bother you, monsignor.'

He looked troubled, as though I'd ambushed him and might have a serious problem to raise. But he cautioned me in a kindly way, 'I don't have a great deal of time. I'm saying Mass at ten. Might we meet afterwards in the sacristy?'

'Just a simple question.'

'What is it, my son?'

'I am inquiring about a man named Jeremiah Fagan.'

He made a disgusted face and at the same time gripped the arms of his chair with his plump hands, his fingers growing pale with the pressure of his grip, and for a moment from the sour way he twisted his lips I thought he was going to spit.

'What of him?'

'Am I right in thinking he once lived here?'

'Father Fagan was a disgrace, an immoral man, one of the priests that did violence to the reputation of the Church. I don't want to hear about him. Now please leave me in peace.'

'May I ask in what way immoral?'

Monsignor Bracken rose from his chair as a way of urging me

to get up, and he directed me to the door using his big bumping belly, the skirts of his cassock whirling as he hurried forward, all this motion like an elaborate gesture of rejection.

'Yes, he was a priest here, but he sinned – grievously. And he tainted others with his immorality. It was a great scandal. But he will have to explain that to Almighty God.'

'He died recently.'

'Then he is in hell,' the monsignor said, and outstretched his arms to shoo me away, as you would a pestering hound. 'That's all you need to know. We will never forgive him for the damage he did. Now go.'

The young priest who had let me in must have heard some of this, because he looked fussed but said nothing, only snatched open the rectory door and shut it as soon as I stepped over the threshold, ejecting me.

Father Fagan: I wanted to know more. I lingered, trying to make connections, and to calm myself I walked around the corner to the Cathedral, and entered, glad for a place to sit. It was so easy to see my father as a priest – he had the temperament, the piety, the humility – but what was the scandal? I hated to think that he had trifled with small boys, as many of the priests in Boston had done. But Monsignor Bracken had been so angry, damning him as immoral, it was possible that he'd been one of those predatory priests.

The tinkle of bells from a side altar distracted me from these confused thoughts, and I saw emerging from an adjacent door Monsignor Bracken, in a little procession, two women by his side, their eyes downcast. I crept towards them and took a seat at the back, near a pillar, where I could not easily be seen – nor could I see the action at the altar. Though my father seldom went to church, he had always encouraged me to attend Mass, but I had not been good about it. I was so out of touch, I was surprised to see women serving the water and wine, helping with the communion hosts, where I had been used to seeing altar boys.

I heard the Mass being said, Monsignor Bracken speaking in his liturgical singsong, and the serving women's responses, echoed by the muttering people in the pews.

And after a while the monsignor ascended the pulpit, he cleared his throat, and when he began to speak, at first slowly, glowing with confidence, as though inspired, I heard my father's voice, my father's wisdom, one of his sermons, with the dialogue he loved, Peter asking Jesus, 'What if my brother sins against me seven times?' and Jesus saying, 'I do not say to you seven times, but seventy times seven.' And Monsignor Bracken was emphatic in uttering the numbers, making it plain that there was no limit in forgiving someone.

It was as though my father was at that altar, in that pulpit, offering a message of compassion, speaking through that priest.

With his name I was able to find his story in the Boston newspapers, how Father Fagan had been surprised in a motel with a nun, a Sister of Charity, named Sister Constance; the investigation into their behavior, the violent threats against them, how they'd vanished together, and been denounced; how they had stayed in hiding, undetected, and ultimately their scandal was overtaken by the greater one of the pedophile priests.

But they had remained in the Boston area. I found their marriage certificate, on file in Boston City Hall, with their proper names on it – the marriage had taken place six months before I was born – and at last more papers, a house full of them, the sermons, the homilies, the gentle words of love and forgiveness my father had written under a pen name for the priests who had condemned him.

COLM TÓIBÍN

SILENCE

34 DVG, January 23d, 1894
Another incident – 'subject' – related to me by Lady G. was that of the eminent London clergyman who on the Dover-to-Calais steamer, starting on his wedding tour, picked up on the deck a letter addressed to his wife, while she was below, and finding it to be from an old lover, and very ardent (an engagement – a rupture, a relation, in short), of which he never had been told, took the line of sending her, from Paris, straight back to her parents – without having touched her – on the ground that he had been deceived. He ended, subsequently, by taking her back into his house to live, but never lived with her as his wife. There is a drama in the various things, for her, to which that situation – that night in Paris – might have led. Her immediate surrender to some one else, etc. etc. etc.

From *The Notebooks of Henry James*

Sometimes when the evening had almost ended, Lady Gregory would catch someone's eye for a moment and that would be enough to make her remember. At those tables in the great city she knew not ever to talk about herself, or complain about anything such as the heat, or the dullness of the season, or the antics of an actress; she knew not to babble about banalities, or laugh at things that were not very funny. She focused instead with as much force and care as she could on the gentleman beside her and asked him questions and then listened with attention to the answers. Listening took more work than talking; she made sure that her companion knew, from the sympathy and sharp light in her eyes, how intelligent she was, and how quietly powerful and deep.

She would suffer only when she left the company. In the carriage on the way home she would stare into the dark, knowing that what had happened in those years would not come back, that memories were no use, that there was nothing ahead except darkness. And on the bad nights, after evenings when there had been too much gaiety and brightness, she often wondered if there was a difference between her life now and the years stretching to eternity that she would spend in the grave.

She would write out a list and the writing itself would make her smile. Things to live for. Her son Robert would always come first, and then some of her sisters. She often thought of erasing one or two of them, and maybe one brother, but no more than one. And then Coole Park, the house in Ireland her husband had left her, or at least left their son, and to which she could return when she wished. She thought of the trees she had planted at Coole, she often dreamed of going back there to study the slow progress of things as the winter gave way to spring, or autumn came. And there were books and paintings and how light came into a high room as she pulled the shutters back in the morning. She would add these also to the list.

Below the list each time was blank paper. It was easy to fill the blank spaces with another list. A list of grim facts led by a single inescapable thought – that love had eluded her, that love would not come back, that she was alone and she would have to make the best of being alone.

On this particular evening, she crumpled the piece of paper in her hand before she stood up and made her way to the bedroom and prepared for the night. She was glad, or almost glad, that there would be no more outings that week, that no London hostess had the need for a dowager from Ireland at her table for the moment. A woman known for her listening skills and her keen intelligence had her uses, she thought, but not every night of the week.

She had liked being married; she had enjoyed being noticed as the young wife of an old man, had known the effect her quiet gaze could have on friends of her husband's who thought she might be dull because she was not pretty. She had let them know, carefully, tactfully, keeping her voice low, that she was someone on whom nothing was lost. She had read all the latest books and she chose her words slowly when she came to discuss them. She did not want to appear clever. She made sure that she was silent without seeming shy, polite and reserved without seeming intimidated. She had no natural grace and she made up for this by having no empty opinions. She took the view that it was a mistake for a woman with her looks ever to show her teeth. In any case, she disliked laughter and preferred to smile using her eyes.

She disliked her husband only when he came to her at night in those first months; his fumbling and panting, his eager hands and his sour breath, gave her a sense that daylight and many layers of clothing and servants and large furnished rooms and chatter about politics or paintings were ways to distract people from feeling a revulsion towards each other.

There were times when she saw him in the distance or had occasion to glance at his face in repose when she viewed him as someone who had merely on a whim or a sudden need rescued her or captured her. He was too old to know her, he had seen too much and lived too long to allow anything new, such as a wife thirty-five years his junior, to enter his orbit. In the night, in those early months, as she tried to move towards him to embrace him fully, to offer herself to his dried-up spirit, she found that he was happier obsessively fondling certain parts of her body in the dark as though he were trying to find something he had mislaid. And thus as she attempted to please him, she also tried to make sure that, when he was finished, she would be able gently to turn away from him and face the dark alone as he slept and snored. She longed to wake in the morning and not have to look at his face too closely, his half-opened mouth, his stubbled cheeks, his grey whiskers, his wrinkled skin.

All over London, she thought, in the hours after midnight in rooms with curtains drawn, silence was broken by grunts and groans and sighs. It was lucky, she knew, that it was all done in secret, lucky also that no matter how much they talked of love or faithfulness or the unity of man and wife, no one would ever realise how apart people were in these hours, how deeply and singly themselves, how thoughts came that could never be shared or whispered or made known in any way. This was marriage, she thought, and it was her job to be calm about it. There were times when the grim, dull truth of it made her smile.

Nonetheless, there was in the day almost an excitement about being the wife of Sir William Gregory, of having a role to play in the world. He had been lonely, that much was clear. He had married her because he had been lonely. He longed to travel and he enjoyed the idea now that she would arrange his clothes and listen to him talk. They could enter dining rooms together as others did, rooms in which an elderly man alone would have appeared out of place, too sad somehow.

And because he knew his way around the world – he had been governor of Ceylon, among other things – he had many old friends and associates, was oddly popular and dependable and cultured and well informed and almost amusing in company. Once they arrived in Cairo therefore, it was natural that they would stay in the same hotel as the young poet Wilfrid Scawen Blunt and his grand wife, that the two couples would dine together and find each other interesting as they discussed poetry lightly and then, as things began to change, argued politics with growing intensity and seriousness.

Wilfrid Scawen Blunt. As she lay in the bed with the light out, Lady Gregory smiled at the thought that she would not need ever to write his name down on any list. His name belonged elsewhere; it was a name she might breathe on glass or whisper to herself when things were harder than she had ever imagined that anything could become. It was a name that might have been etched on her heart if she believed in such things.

His fingers were long and beautiful; even his fingernails had a glow of health; his hair was shiny, his teeth white. And his eyes brightened as he spoke; thinking made him smile and when he smiled he exuded a sleek perfection. He was as far from her as a palace was from her house in Coole or as the heavens were from the earth. She liked looking at him as she liked looking at a Bronzino or a Titian and she was careful always to pretend that she also liked looking at his wife, Byron's granddaughter, although she did not.

She thought of them like food, Lady Anne all watery vegetables, or sour, small potatoes, or salted fish, and the poet her husband like lamb cooked slowly for hours with garlic and thyme, or goose stuffed at Christmas. And she remembered in her childhood the watchful eye of her mother, her mother making her eat each morsel of bad winter food, leave her plate clean. Thus she forced herself to pay attention to every word Lady Anne said; she gazed at her with soft and sympathetic interest, she spoke to her with warmth and the dull intimacy that one man's wife might have with another, hoping that soon Lady Anne would be calmed and suitably assuaged by this so she would not notice when Lady Gregory turned to the poet and ate him up with her eyes.

Blunt was on fire with passion during these evenings, composing a letter to *The Times* at the very dining table in support of Arabi Bey, arguing in favour of loosening the control that France and England had over Egyptian affairs, cajoling Sir William, who was of course a friend of the editor of *The Times*, to put pressure on the paper to publish his letter and support the cause. Sir William was quiet, watchful, gruff. It was easy for Blunt to feel that he agreed with every point Blunt was making mainly because Blunt did not notice dissent. They arranged for Lady Gregory to visit Arabi Bey's wife and family so that she could describe to the English how refined they were, how sweet and deserving of support.

The afternoon when she returned was unusually hot. Her husband, she found, was in a deep sleep so she did not disturb him. When she went in search of Blunt, she was told by the maid that Lady Anne had a severe headache brought on by the heat and would not be appearing for the rest of the day. Her husband the poet could be found in the garden or in the room he kept for work, where he often spent the afternoons. Lady Gregory found him in the garden; Blunt was excited to hear about her visit to Bey's family and ready to show her a draft of a poem he had composed that morning on the matter of Egyptian freedom. She went to his study with him, not realizing until she was in the room and the door was closed that the study was in fact an extra bedroom the Blunts had taken, no different from the Gregorys' own room except for a large desk and books and papers strewn on the floor and on the bed.

As Blunt read her the poem, he crossed the room and turned the key in the lock as though it were a normal act, what he always did as he read a new poem. He read it a second time and then left the piece of paper down on the desk and moved towards her and held her. He began to kiss her. Her only thought was that this might be the single chance she would get in her life to associate with beauty. Like a tourist in the vicinity of a great temple, she thought it would be a mistake to pass it by; it would be something she would only regret. She did not think it would last long or mean much. She also was sure that no one had seen them come down this corridor; she presumed that her husband was still sleeping; she believed that no one would find them and it would never be mentioned again between them.

Later, when she was alone and checking that there were no traces of what she had done on her skin or on her clothes, the idea that she had lain naked with the poet Blunt in a locked room on a hot afternoon and that he had, in a way that was new to her, made her cry out in ecstasy, frightened her. She had been married less than two years, time enough to know how deep her husband's pride ran, how cold he was to those who had crossed him and how sharp and decisive he could be. They had left their child in England so they could travel to Egypt even though Sir William knew how much it pained her to be separated in this way from Robert. Were Sir William to be told that she had been visiting the poet in his private quarters, she believed he could ensure that she never saw her child again. Or he could live with her in pained silence and barely managed contempt. Or he could send her home. The corridors were full of servants, figures watching. She thought it a miracle that she had managed once to be unnoticed. She believed that she might not be so lucky a second time.

Over the weeks that followed and in London when she returned home, she discovered that Wilfrid Scawen Blunt's talents as a poet were minor compared to his skills as an adulterer. Not only could he please her in ways that were daring and astonishing but he could ensure that they would not be discovered. The sanctity of his calling required him to have silence, solitude and quarters that his wife had no automatic right to enter. Blunt composed his poems in a locked room. He rented this room away from his main residence, choosing the place, Lady Gregory saw, not because of the ease with which it could be visited by the muses but rather for its position in a shadowy side-street close to streets where women of circumstance shopped. Thus no one would notice a respectable woman who was not his wife arriving or leaving in the mornings or the afternoons; no one would hear her cry out as she lay in bed with him; no one would ever know that each time in the hour or so she spent with him she realised that nothing would be enough for her, that she had not merely visited the temple as a tourist might, but had come to believe in and deeply need the sweet doctrine preached in its warm and towering confines.

She never once dreamed of being caught. Sir William was often busy in the day; he enjoyed having a long lunch with old associates, or a meeting of some sort about the National Gallery or some political or financial matter. It seemed to make him content that his wife went to the shops or to visit her friends as long as she was free in the evenings to accompany him to dinners. He was usually distant, quite distracted. It was, she thought, like being a member of the cabinet with her own tasks and responsibilities with her husband as Prime Minister, her husband happy that he had appointed her, and pleased, it appeared, that she carried out her tasks with the minimum of fuss.

Soon, however, when they were back in England a few months, she began to worry about exposure and to imagine with dread not his accusing her, or finding her in the act, but what would happen later. She dreamed, for example, that she had been sent home to her parents' house in Roxborough and she was destined to spend her days wandering the corridors of the upper floor, a ghostly presence. Her mother passed her and did not speak to her. Her sisters came and went but did not seem even to see her. The servants brushed by her. Sometimes, she went downstairs, but there was no chair for her at the dining table and no place for her to sit in the drawing room. Every place had been filled by her sisters and her brothers and their guests and they were all chattering loudly and laughing and being served tea and, no matter how close she came to them, they paid her no attention.

The dream changed sometimes. She was in her own house in London or in Coole with her husband and with Robert and their servants but no one saw her, they let her come in and out of rooms, forlorn, silent, desperate. Her son appeared blind to her as he came towards her. Her husband undressed in their room at night as though she were not there and turned out the lamp in their room while she was still standing at the foot of the bed fully dressed. No one seemed to mind that she haunted the spaces they inhabited because no one noticed her. She had become, in these dreams, invisible to the world.

Despite Sir William's absence from the house during the day and his indifference to how she spent her time as long as she did not cost him too much money, she knew that she could be unlucky. Being found out could happen because a friend or an acquaintance or, indeed, an enemy could suspect her and follow her, or Lady Anne could find a key to the room and come with urgent news for her husband or visit suddenly out of sheer curiosity. Blunt was careful and dependable, she knew, but he was also passionate and excitable. In some fit of rage, or moment where he lost his composure, he could easily, she thought, say enough to someone that they would understand he was having an affair with the young wife of Sir William Gregory. Her husband had many old friends in London. A note left at his club would be enough to cause him to have her watched and followed. The affair with Blunt, she realised, could not last. As months went by, she left it to Blunt to decide when it should end. It would be best, she thought, if he tired of her and found another. It would be less painful to be jealous of someone else than to feel that she had denied herself this deep fulfilling pleasure for no reason other than fear or caution.

Up to this she had put no real thought into what marriage meant. It was, she had vaguely thought, a contract, or even a sacrament. It was what happened. It was part of the way things were ordered. Sometimes now, however, when she saw the Blunts socially, or when she read a poem by him or heard someone mention his name, the fact that it was not known and publicly understood that she was with him hurt her profoundly, made her experience what existed between them as a kind of emptiness or absence. She knew that if her secret were known or told, it would destroy her life. But as time went by, its not being known by anyone at all made her imagine with relish and energy what it would be like to be married to Wilfrid Scawen Blunt, to enter a room with him, to leave in a carriage with him, to have her name openly linked with his. It would mean everything. Instead, the time she spent alone with him often came to seem like nothing when it was over. Memory, which was once so sharp and precious for her, was now a dark room in which she wandered longing for the light to be switched on or the curtains pulled back. She longed for the light of publicity, for her secret life to become common knowledge. It was something, she was well aware, that would not happen as long as she lived if she could help it. She would take her pleasure in darkness.

When the affair ended, she felt at times as if it had not happened. There was nothing solid or sure about it. Most women, she thought, had a close, discreet friend to whom such things could be whispered. She did not. In France, she understood, they had a way of making such things subtly known. Now she understood why. She was lonely without Blunt, but she was lonelier at the idea that the world went on as though she had not loved him. Time would pass and their actions and feelings would seem like a shadow of actions and feelings, but less than a shadow in fact, because cast by something that now had no real substance.

Thus she wrote the sonnets, using the time she now had to work on rhyme schemes and poetic forms. She wrote in secret about her secret love for him and then kept the paper on which she had written it down:

> Bowing my head to kiss the very ground
> On which the feet of him I love have trod,
> Controlled and guided by that voice whose sound
> Is dearer to me than the voice of God.

She put on paper her fear of disclosure and the shame that might come with it; she hid the pages away and found them when the house was quiet and she could read of what she had done and what it meant:

> Should e'er that drear day come in which the world
> Shall know the secret which so close I hold,
> Should taunts and jeers at my bowed head be hurled,
> And all my love and all my shame be told,
> I could not, as some women used to do,
> Fling jests and gold and live the scandal down.

When she asked, some months after their separation, to meet him one more time, his tone in reply was brusque, almost cold. She wondered if he thought that she was going to appeal to him to resume their affair, or remonstrate with him in some way. She enjoyed how surprised he seemed that she was merely handing him a sheaf of sonnets, making clear as soon as she gave him the pages that she had written them herself. She watched him reading them.

'What shall we do with them?' he asked when he had finished.

'You shall publish them in your next book as though they were written by you,' she said.

'But it is clear from the style that they are not.'

'Let the world believe that you changed your style for the purposes of writing them. Let your readers believe that you were writing in another voice. That will explain the awkwardness.'

'There is no awkwardness. They are very good.'

'Then publish them. They are yours.'

He agreed then to publish them under his own name in his next book, having made some minor alterations to them. They came out six weeks before Sir William died. Lady Gregory did her husband the favour in those weeks of not keeping the book by her bed but in her study; she managed also to keep these poems out of her mind as she watched over him.

As his widow, she knew who she was and what she had inherited. She had loved him in her way and sometimes missed him. She knew what words like 'loved' and 'missed' meant when she thought of her husband. When she thought of Blunt, on the other hand, she was unsure what anything meant except the sonnets she had written about their love affair. She read them sparingly, often needing them if she woke in the night, but keeping them away from her much of the time. It was enough for her that all over London, in the houses of people who acquired new books of poetry, these poems rested silently and mysteriously between the pages. She found solace in the idea that people would read them without knowing their source.

She rebuilt her life as a widow and took care of her son and began, after a suitable period of mourning, to go out in London again and meet people and take part in things. She often asked herself if there was someone in the room, or in the street, who had read her sonnets and been puzzled or pained by them, even for a second.

She had read Henry James as his books appeared. In fact, it was a discussion about *Roderick Hudson* that caused Sir William to pay attention to her first. She had read an extract from it but did not have the book. He arranged for it to be sent to her. Some time after her marriage, when she was visiting Rome with Sir William, she met James and she remembered him fondly as a man who would talk seriously to a woman, even someone as young and provincial as she was. She remembered asking him at that first meeting in Rome how he could possibly have allowed Isabel Archer to marry the odious Osmond. He told her that Isabel was bound to do something foolish and, if she had not, there would have been no story. And he had enjoyed, he had said, as a poor man himself, bestowing so much money on his heroine. Henry James was kind and witty, she had felt then, and somehow managed not to be glib or patronizing.

Since her husband died she had seen Henry James a number of times, noticing always how much of himself he held back, how the expression on his face appeared to disguise as much as it disclosed. He had always been very polite to her, and they had often discussed the fate of the orphan Paul Harvey, with whose mother they had both been friends. She was surprised one evening to see the novelist at a supper that Lady Layard had invited her to; there were diplomats present and some foreigners, and a few military men and some minor politicians. It was not Henry James's world, and it was Lady Gregory's world only in that an extra woman was needed, as people might need an extra carriage or an extra towel in the bathroom. It did not matter who she was as long as she arrived on time and left at an appropriate moment and did not talk too loudly or compete in any way with the hostess.

It made sense to place her beside Henry James. In the company on a night where politics would be discussed between the men and silliness between the women, neither of them mattered. She looked forward to having the novelist on her right. Once she disposed of a young Spanish diplomat on her left, she would attend to James and ask him about his work. When they were all dead, she thought, he would be the one whose name would live on, but it was perhaps important for those who were rich or powerful to spend their evenings keeping this poor thought at bay.

It was the Spaniard's fingers she noticed, they were long and slender with beautiful rounded nails. She found herself glancing down at them as often as she could, hoping that the diplomat, whose accent was beyond her, would not spot what she was doing. She looked at his eyes and nodded as he spoke, all the time wondering if it would be rude for her to glance down again, this time for longer. Somewhere near London, Wilfrid Scawen Blunt was dining too, she thought, perhaps with his wife and some friends. She pictured him reaching for something at the table, a jug of water perhaps, and pouring it. She pictured his long slender fingers, the rounded nails, and then began to imagine his hair, how silky it was to the touch, and the fine bones on his face and his teeth and his breath.

She stopped herself now and began to concentrate hard on what the Spaniard was saying. She asked him a question that he failed to understand so she repeated it, making it simpler. When she had asked a number of other questions and listened attentively to the replies, she was relieved when she knew that her time with him was up and she could turn now to Henry James, who seemed heavier than before as though his large head were filled with oak or ivory. As they began to talk, he took her in with his grey eyes, which had a level of pure understanding in them that was almost affecting. For a split second she was tempted to tell him what had happened with Blunt, suggest that it occurred to a friend of hers while visiting Egypt, a friend married to an older man who was seduced by a friend of his, a poet. But she knew it was ridiculous, James would see through her immediately.

Yet something had stirred in her, a need that she had ruminated on in the past but kept out of her mind for some time now. She wanted to say Blunt's name and wondered if she could find a way to ask James if he read his work or admired it. But James was busy describing the best way to see old Rome now that Rome had changed so much and the best way to avoid Americans in Rome, Americans one did not want to see or be associated with. How odd he would think her were she to interrupt him or wait for a break in the conversation and ask him what he thought of the work of Wilfrid Scawen Blunt! It was possible he did not even read modern poetry. It would be hard, she thought, to turn the conversation around to Blunt or even find a way to mention him in passing. In any case, James had moved his arena of concern to Venice and was discussing whether it was best to lodge with friends there or find one's own lodging and thus win greater independence.

As he pondered the relative merits of various American hostesses in Venice, going over the quality of their table, the size of their guest rooms, what they put at one's disposal, she thought of love. James sighed and mentioned how a warm personality, especially of the American sort, had a way of cooling one's appreciation of ancient beauty, irrespective of how grand the palazzo of which this personality was in possession, indeed irrespective of how fine or fast-moving her gondola.

When he had finished, Lady Gregory turned towards him quietly and asked him if he was tired of people telling him stories he might use in his fiction, or if he viewed such offerings as an essential element in his art. He told her in reply that he often, later when he arrived home, noted down something interesting that had been said to him, and on occasion the germ of a story had come to him from a most unlikely source, and other times, of course, from a most obvious and welcome one. He liked to imagine his characters, he said, but he also liked that they might have lived already, to some small extent perhaps, before he painted a new background for them and created a new scenario. Life, he said, life, that was the material that he used and needed. There could never be enough life. But it was only the beginning, of course, because life was thin.

There was an eminent London man, she began, a clergyman known to dine at the best tables, a man of great experience who had many friends, friends who were both surprised and delighted when this man finally married. The lady in question was known to be highly respectable. But on the day of their wedding as they crossed to France from Dover to Calais, he found a note addressed to her from a man who had clearly been her lover and now felt free, despite her new circumstances, to address her ardently and intimately.

James listened, noting every word. Lady Gregory found that she was trembling and had to control herself; she realised that she would have to speak softly and slowly. She stopped and took a sip of water, knowing that if she did not continue in a tone that was easy and nonchalant she would end by giving more away than she wished to give. The clergyman, she went on, was deeply shocked, and, since he had been married just a few hours to this woman, he decided that, when they had arrived in Paris, he would send her back home to her family, make her an outcast; she would be his wife merely in name. He would not see her again.

Instead, however, Lady Gregory went on, when they had arrived at their hotel in Paris the clergyman decided against this action. He informed his errant wife, his piece of damaged goods, that he would keep her, but he would not touch her. He would take her into his house to live, but not as his wife.

Lady Gregory tried to smile casually as she came to the end of the story. She was pleased that her listener had guessed nothing. It was a story that had elements both French and English, something that James would understand as being rather particularly part of his realm. He thanked her and said that he would note the story once he reached his study that evening and he would perhaps, he hoped, do justice to it in the future. It was always impossible to know, he added, why one small spark caused a large fire and why another was destined to extinguish itself before it had even flared.

She realised as the guests around her stood up from the table that she had said as much as she could say, which was, on reflection, hardly anything at all. She almost wished she had added more detail, had told James that the letter came from a poet perhaps, or that it contained a set of sonnets whose subject was unmistakable, or that the wife of the clergyman was more than thirty years his junior, or that he was not a clergyman at all, but a former member of parliament and someone who had once held high office. Or that the events in question had happened in Egypt and not on the way to Paris. Or that the woman had never, in fact, been caught, she had been careful and had outlived the husband to whom she had been unfaithful. That she had merely dreamed of and feared being sent home by him or kept apart, never touched.

The next time, she thought, if she found herself seated beside the novelist she would slip in one of these details. She understood perfectly why the idea excited her so much. As Henry James stood up from the table, it gave her a strange sense of satisfaction that she had lodged her secret with him, a secret over-wrapped perhaps, but at least the rudiments of its shape apparent, if not to him then to her, for whom these matters were pressing, urgent and gave meaning to her life. That she had kept the secret and told a small bit of it all at the same time made her feel light as she went to join the ladies for some conversation. It had been, on the whole, she thought, an unexpectedly interesting evening.

ROSE TREMAIN

IS ANYBODY THERE?

I

She was a widow, like me. Or so she wanted me to believe. She once showed me a faded photograph of a soldier in the uniform of the Irish Guards. 'That was him,' she said, 'my man.'

I asked her a few questions about him, but she didn't care to answer them. All she said was, 'Well he was Irish, like yours truly. You can tell, can't yer? Something in the set of the eyes. And see how pale he was. Pale as water. But that's all I can say.'

Her name was Nell Greenwood. She was ten years older than me. She and I were neighbours on a lonely stretch of Norfolk road. Our two cottages were joined to each other, like they should have been one house, but she said, 'No, no, they were never one house; they were always two. Farm workers' cottages. Two for the price of one, see? Meant for families. Babies and toddlers crying both sides of the wall. No insulation. Everybody awake till dawn.'

Now, just two elderly women, with our lives trailing behind us, like half-remembered dreams we kept tugging along. We each had a garden at the back, with an old picket fence between the two. On my plot, I grew beans in summer and potatoes and rhubarb. I had a bed of bright flowers, hollyhocks, gladioli and marigolds. I kept a few chickens in a wire pen. And a man from

East Dereham had come and laid a brick patio for me, where I sometimes sat in a folding canvas chair and listened to the hens and the pigeons calling from the woods.

On Nell's plot, there were nettles and tall grasses and wild weeds which she said had been 'sown by God'. I privately thought of Nell's garden as a bit of an Irish kind of disgrace, but she didn't see it like that. She liked it. She said it was 'Nature obeying itself, not being pushed and pulled about'. I would sometimes see her walking there, not minding the nettles, stroking the feathery grasses with her fingers, clearly pleased with it all, gathering stems of Ragged Robin to put in a jar for her kitchen table. At the end of her garden, there was a child's swing hanging from a metal frame once painted red but now rusted to the colour of the earth. I noticed that Nell would never go right up to the swing, but stand a little way off – stand very still, seemingly held by the sight of it.

One day, I said to her, 'Was the swing there when you came to live in your cottage?'

'Oh,' she said, looking sideways, away from me. 'I can't remember, but I think it was. I have the feeling it was there of its own accord.'

We were standing each on our own side of the picket fence. It was a hot August morning and by the bright light falling on us I could see that Nell appeared sickly, with tired eyes and a greyish colour to her skin. I was about to ask her something more about the swing, but instead I said, 'Are you all right, Nell?'

She stared at me angrily, as though I'd said something unkind. 'All right?' she said. 'At my time of life? At the age of almost ninety? *All right*, are you askin'? At the age of eighty-nine and three quarters? For Jesus' sake. You should save your breath, Mrs.'

*

She'd been like that a few times before: suddenly rude, suddenly agitated. I thought that perhaps if you lived in solitude, as we both did, you stopped censoring your thoughts and feelings when you were with other people and just blurted out whatever words came first to your mind. I knew that I could sometimes act like a person in need of the Social Services; I talked back to people on the TV, or threw cushions at them. I treated my chickens as though they were my children. 'Lovebirds, you are,' I'd say. 'You're my lovely poppets.' All old people are at least thirty or forty per cent crazy, in their own particular way. Life does this to you: it drives everybody insane. But that August night, the night after the moment by the picket fence, something particularly crazy happened.

I was woken at three o'clock by a ringing of my doorbell.

It was still dark. I went to my wardrobe and got out the shotgun that I always keep cleaned and ready in case a fox threatens my precious birds. I crept down my stairs, holding the gun. When I got to the door, I called out, 'Who's there? Who is it?'

For a pace, there was silence. The night was hot and I could feel sweat creeping down between my shoulder blades. Then Nell's voice called out: 'Let me in, Mrs. I've come to help you.'

I put the safety catch on the gun and propped it up by the umbrella stand and opened the door. There was Nell, with her grey hair in a tangle and wearing a nightdress that was half in rags. She stared at me. 'I thought I might have to break in,' she said.

'Break in?'

'I thought you might be trapped in your room.'

'Why trapped in my room?'

'That knocking you were doing. It woke me with such a start.

I couldn't think what it was at first. Then I thought, oh Jesus-Mary-Joseph, that's herself next door and she must be callin' for help, so let me come in and make sure you're not bleedin' from the brain.'

I put on a light. Nell pushed my door open wide and came and stood in my little hallway, which is identical to hers and neither is really a hallway at all, but just a small rectangle of space, leading directly to the stairs. She reached out to me and put her arm round my shoulder and said, 'Now then, Mrs. You tell me what.'

I gaped at Nell.

'What?' I said.

'You mean, you don't know? You woke me all for nothing? All that knocking and knocking for a pinch of snuff?'

I moved away from Nell and sat down on the stairs.

'I was asleep when you rang the bell,' I said. 'I didn't do any knocking.'

'Eh?' said Nell.

'I didn't knock on your wall, Nell.'

'Well now,' she said. 'I know exactly how these houses are arranged and your bedroom is to the right of the stairs and mine is to the left of mine, so all that separates our rooms is that bit of lath and plaster they call a wall. I can hear you snoring sometimes. I'm not fibbin'. So when the knocking came, I knew it was you. Don't you pretend otherwise. And I'm here now, see: the Good Samaritan.'

I rubbed my eyes. The sweat on my back was drying and making me shiver.

'It was kind of you to come round,' I said. 'But I promise you I never knocked on your wall.'

'Then you did it in yer sleep, then. Knock-knock-knock, three times. Then a pause and then another three. And so loud, my head bounced clean off the feckin' pillow.'

I didn't know what more to say.

*

That was how it began.

There were calm nights, when my sleep was undisturbed, but time after time I was woken, sometimes at three, sometimes nearer dawn, with Nell either ringing my bell or just beating on my bedroom wall with some instrument that sounded as though it was a hammer, and Nell shouting 'Stop! Stop it, Mrs! You stop this or I'll have you done for Public Nuisance!'

It was still summer. The grasses and nettles in Nell's garden grew so high, they almost obscured the swing. And after she accused me of knocking on her bedroom wall she never walked there any more. When I was in the garden, I always looked over to Nell's patch, which was now seeding itself with thistles, hoping that she'd be there, so that we could talk sanely, rationally, in the sunshine, but she stayed locked up in her house.

I decided to take her the gift of some eggs. Alone as we both were, we'd always been thoughtful neighbours to each other. For why not?

For some reason, people who don't know hens prefer brown eggs to white, as though they imagine (wrongly) there may be more flavour to them, so I selected six brown eggs and put them in a blue china bowl. I thought they looked beautiful, arranged like that: the pale brown colour and the blue.

Nell had no doorbell, so I had to knock on her front door. When she opened it, she said, 'I knew it was you. You, with your knocking! What is it this time?'

I held out the bowl of eggs. 'These,' I said. 'Laid yesterday.'

Nell was wearing a threadbare cotton scarf round her neck, and she pulled this up over her mouth. 'I can't eat much at the moment,' she said. 'I might not get round to cooking them.'

She looked thin and very tired. Behind her, I could see that her stairs were now strewn with her possessions – clothes, shoes, magazines, medicine bottles, bundles of letters – as though she'd decided to empty out all her chests of drawers and hurl everything away down the waterfall of her green stair carpet. She saw me staring at these things and she turned to face them. 'I've been searching,' she said. 'Searching everywhere for something. But I can't find it.'

'What are you searching for?' I said. 'Perhaps I can help you?'

'Well now,' she said, 'that's a daft thing to say, Mrs. If I knew what I was searching for, I'd find it, wouldn't I?'

She smiled a wan smile. 'Let me come in and boil you one of these eggs,' I said. 'You can tell me how long you'd like it done.'

'Four and a half minutes!' she snapped. 'I can't abide anything but the exact four and a half minutes.'

We walked through into her small kitchen, a mirror replica of mine, except that here, every surface was crammed with utensils and pans Nell had taken out of the cupboards.

'So you were searching in here, too?' I said.

'Of course I was,' said Nell. 'I've searched every room in the house.'

I made a pot of tea and boiled two eggs. I thought if I ate one of them, this might encourage Nell to eat hers.

She cleared a space at the little Formica table and we sat opposite each other, drinking the tea. Nell took the top off her egg and stared at it. 'In Ireland, we kept birds,' she said, 'when I was a girl. And we had a cockerel with blue-black tail feathers strutting about in the yard. He thought he was King of County Cork, he did, and I used to think, I'd like to be that – King of

Somewhere, or even Queen of Something-or-Other, I wasn't fussy about the gender. But it didn't turn out like that.'

'It never does,' I said.

'Well that's right enough. It never does.'

She took a tiny mouthful of egg, sucking on it like a baby. I sipped my tea. And it was then that Nell went very still, her head tilted on one side, listening.

'There it is!' she said. 'There it is again! Can you hear it?'

'Hear what?'

'The knocking.'

My hearing, in recent years, had diminished. If I sat silent on my patio, I could hear the hens and the pigeons and the wind in the trees. But I had to turn the TV volume high sometimes, to catch the words. I held my breath now, and then I heard it, a tap-tap-tap on Nell's door.

'It's your front door, Nell,' I said. 'It could be the postman.'

'Oh,' she said, 'Oh . . . '

She got up, dabbing at her mouth with a napkin. She went to the front door and opened it a crack. I followed her into the little hall. I waited to hear the cheerful voice of our postman whose name was Reg – a person who seemed to take the greatest care with his work, so that nothing would ever be forgotten or lost. But there was nobody at the door. Nell opened it wide and we both went out into the tiny front garden and looked left and right down the road.

'No one,' said Nell. 'But you heard the knocking.'

'I did.'

'I wasn't making that up.'

'No.'

'But this time it was on the door and not on the wall. What does that mean?'

I took Nell's bony arm in my hand. 'I don't know,' I said. 'But one thing is certain, Nell. It wasn't *me* knocking at your door. Was it? I was eating my egg.'

Nell stared at me. 'So you were,' she said. 'So you were.'

'And I tell you now, I swear on what's left of my life, it isn't me knocking on your bedroom wall in the night.'

It was now the end of September and sudden cold winds visited our lonely road and set the Norfolk pines sighing on their tortured stems. One such gust of wind arrived and tugged at our clothes and we could hear the chain of the rusted swing squeaking on its hooks.

'Oh,' said Nell. 'There's the swing, talking to me now. The swing, Mrs! And I never thought about that in all my searches. It was the one place I never went to look.'

'Right,' I said. 'Shall we finish our eggs, and then go out to the swing?'

'No, no, we must go now. Not a minute to lose.'

We walked round the outside of Nell's house to the back garden where God had sown all His fragrant weeds. Behind us, I heard Nell's front door slam, and I imagined us locked out now, with the boiled eggs going cold in their cups, but Nell gave this no mind.

We pushed our way through the tall grasses and the stems of dock. The sky seemed to darken above us. The swing was hurtling back and forth, as though some invisible, fearless child were pushing it higher and higher.

'Will yer look at that, now?' said Nell. 'It's going manic-berserk, like I've never seen.'

Nell reached the swing and she put out an arm to steady it, but it came at her with the full rush of the wind and knocked her smack on the temple and she fell backwards into the tangled grass. I heard myself cry out. The swing screeched on its chain. Nell lay on the ground and stared up at the sky, like a dead woman. I steadied the flying swing, then went behind her and bent down to ease her body backwards. Then I kneeled over her and took her hand, which was icy in mine, like a stone from a winter field.

'Nell,' I said, 'can you hear me?'

Her mouth moved a bit, trying to make words.

'Nell,' I said again, 'can you say something to me?'

She was still staring up at the sky and now fat drops of rain began to splash down on us. I lifted her shoulders and rested her head on my lap. I watched the rain slathering Nell's wounded forehead, as if with baptismal oil. I stroked her face, to get the oil away.

'Who is it?' she said.

So thin, she was, she weighed less than a child. I carried her through the weeds and over the low picket fence and in through my back door. I heard the hens come rushing to their wire when they saw me, like the woman in my arms was a bag of grain. 'Not now, pets,' I said.

I rested awhile in my kitchen, laying Nell on the floor and fetching a cushion for her head and a blanket to cover her. I put iodine on her wound and bandaged her head. Her eyes kept moving, wondering and wondering what had happened to her.

I was about to dial 999, to get an ambulance to come, but something stopped me doing this. The 'something' was that I had never dialled the emergency number in my whole life, so it was as if I feared it was just a mythical number, a construct of the human mind, with nobody on the end of it. It would ring and ring, but no voice would answer.

Instead, I went up to my room and turned on the gas fire and straightened up the bed. Then I went back to Nell, who now looked as though she was sleeping, and when I lifted her, this was how she felt – heavy with sleep, or else with death.

I struggled up the stairs. My heart began aching and my legs felt weak, but I kept on, for this is the kind of person I have attempted to be, like Reg the postman, trying always to keep going, however arduous the task or whatever the weather.

I put Nell into my bed. The ceiling above it is low – as it would be in her cottage – and after a moment, Nell reached up, as if to try to touch it.

'At least, now, I know you're not dead,' I said with a relieved smile on my face.

Nell stared at me. Her hand moved down and touched the wall and pressed very hard against it.

I sat on the end of the bed. I looked at Nell and thought, I've taken her into my house now. Her door slammed and the eggs are cold in their cups. She is my burden.

2

There was a secret in Nell's life, a thing so buried by time that she could only unearth it piece by piece, struggling with memories like an archaeologist struggles to make sense of found bones.

She occupied my bed and I sat by her side, listening. Sometimes, I asked her a question – if I thought she was capable of answering it. Mostly, I kept silent. In these silences, she sometimes went to sleep and I would tiptoe to the kitchen and make soup for her, or now and then an Irish stew with lamb neck and vegetables and pearl barley. In Cork, she said, they had eaten Irish stew every Sunday. 'That one cheap meal kept us alive,' she said. 'My heart was confected from scrag end and carrots.'

She passed from telling me about the stew to telling me about her husband in the Irish Guards, 'for the reason,' she said, 'that he never was a proper husband, because he had a wife already in England. Would you believe that?'

'I'd believe anything,' I said.

'So he left me in due time and came back here to his wife. And I was stuck in Ireland, alone with my Mam, eating stew and workin' in a factory that made loft insulation out of sheep's wool. But you know how yer heart cramps up for a departed lover? I just couldn't stand those cramps any more, so I left my job and took the boat and came to England. I wanted my man back. I knew his regiment was stationed somewhere here in Norfolk, so I looked about for a cheap place to live, and I rented this place from an old beet farmer named Ernie-something. He had hands that shook and he was dumber than any of my neighbours in County Cork, but he was kind.

'Your side of the cottage was empty and had been empty since before the war. There wasn't a stick of anything in it, except a bed, in this room we're in: your room. It reminded me of those places in Ireland which people had abandoned in the Famine, and they just fell to pieces as the years passed and looters took everything out of them, but no one ever came back to live there.'

'And,' I said, 'what about your man? Did you find him?'

Nell hit the un-wounded side of her temple with the flat of her hand. 'Men!' she said. 'I found him all right, but it never worked out. So I didn't bother again, after that. After he was gone for good, I never took up with another man. For what do they do except break you down, bit by bit, until you feel you're no one at all?'

After a few days Nell suggested that she should go back to her side of the cottage and not trouble me any more, but she was still weak and giddy from her head wound, and anyway, the truth was I didn't want her to go back. I liked caring for her. It gave purpose to my life, beyond the flowers and the chickens.

I didn't mind her having stolen my bed. I made up the narrow cot in the room next door and slept there.

She hardly moved from my room, except to go to the lavatory, or to take a bath. She asked me to wash her hair one day and so I removed her bandage and took great care with the shampooing, drying her brittle hair and setting it into soft pin curls. When these came out of their pins and were brushed through, Nell smiled like a girl at this new reflection of herself. And then she said, 'I just realised a wonderful thing, Mrs. Since I came into your house, that infernal knocking has gone quiet. But I don't know why. What d'you make of that now?'

'I don't know, Nell,' I said. 'Was it all in your mind, d'you think?'

'But you heard the knocking on my door, that day I fell.'

'I did. But perhaps it was those lads from the bungalow down Hare Lane, rapping on your door and then running and hiding?'

'Could've been. Might've been, I suppose. So that bit was real and the knocking on the wall was in my mind?'

'I'm not saying it was, but all I know is, you thought it was me knocking on the wall, but it wasn't.'

'Unless you did it in your sleep.'

'Yes. But then I would have woken myself up, wouldn't I?'

'Well now, you can't be certain of that. Not at all. For haven't you heard of people getting out of their beds, still in the Land of Nod, and walking to the window and throwing themselves out and never waking until they were dead?'

Most days, she reminded me that there was something she was searching for. She dreamed about her search, she said, and in the dream she heard herself refer to this unfound thing as The Sorrow. 'But what in the world is it?' she said. 'Why do I call it that? And will I ever find it?'

'I don't know, Nell. I wonder if it was companionship you were searching for and now you *have* found it: you've found me.'

She went silent and looked at me, critically, as though I had suddenly become a stranger to her again. Then, she said: 'I've always call you "Mrs", haven't I? For years I've called you that. Is it that you don't have a name?'

'I have a name,' I said, 'but you may not want to bother remembering it.'

'That's true,' she said. 'I might not. Or worse, I might keep getting it wrong. And then we'd be in a terrible muddle.'

A few nights after this conversation, she called for me at one in the morning and I went into her room and saw her kneeling up in my bed and stroking the wall and laying her face against it. The wall was covered with a girlish paper, depicting meadow flowers in tiny garlands.

'It was here,' she said. 'I remembered it! When I saw the moonlight glancing on these weeds, it came tumbling back to me.'

'The Sorrow?'

'Yes. All of it. Because this is where she was. Right here.'

I sat down on the end of the bed. It was cold in the room.

'Who was right here?' I said.

'Katie,' she said. 'Later, they said that was never her name, but that's what I called her and that's what she answered to. She was always "Katie" to me. And this was how she found me – by knocking on this wall.'

I left her as she was, unmoving, with her cheek and her hands pressed to the wall and went and tugged on my dressing gown. I told her I would be back with a hot drink and I went down and boiled milk for chocolate.

I set the warm drinks down on her bedside table and put on the bedside light, with its dim little parchment shade. 'Now,' I said, 'tell me about Katie.'

It was difficult for her to begin. She said she thought she had to start at the end, where The Sorrow resided.

'I was in prison,' she said. 'No idea how long for. Months or years. The charge was kidnap. And there is no silence in prison, did you know that? There is literally none. Even in the night, there are people screaming.'

'Do you want to have a sip of the hot chocolate, Nell?' I asked.

'No. I'll take a sip when I'm over this bit, the prison bit. When I'm back again in my cottage. On second thoughts, I'll go there right away. For I can't talk about prison. I never could.

'But I remember walking back into my house and everything was filthy, for no one had been near the poor place. Filthy! And I was, too. I stank of the jail. I lit the Baxi, to get some hot water, and when it came hot I soaked myself for hours on end in the tub, to get that stench away. And what did I hold in my hands all that time but a little yellow plastic duck I found on the rim of the tub, and which had belonged to Katie. The eejit thing could never could stay upright in the water and we used to laugh, so we did, every time it fell over – laugh and laugh. And that sound of Katie's sweet laughter, I thought that would stay with me, in my mind and never go away, but it did, see? It did. It all went away and left me searching.'

'Now,' I said. 'Take a little gulp of the chocolate.'

She did this. She said sweet things had always tortured her with desire, she'd had so few of them as a child in Ireland. 'Sometimes,' she said, 'once in a hundred blue moons, my Mam would buy me an ice cream and I used to see how long I could make it last. Then I'd wait *too long* and what I got was the dribble of the cream running all down my arms, and my Mam would say, "See, you didn't really want it, did you? So now you've mucked your pullover and wasted sixpence".'

'What about Katie?' I said after a little while. 'Did she like ice cream?'

'Oh yes,' said Nell. 'She'd never tasted it in the Children's House – that place she'd been sent when she was five. Nor had they fed her right at all. She was so thin. I called her my Thistledown Girl. She was eight when she came to me, but she looked younger, she was so small. From the day I took her in, I did my best to get good food for her. Potatoes and pies. Ham. Baked beans. Fresh milk. Crab paste. Chocolate flakes. And sometimes, we'd have a picnic lunch in the long grass out there: hard boiled eggs and ham sandwiches. Triangles of cheese in silver wrappers. Cider in an old brown jar. And didn't she just love that! She'd say "Nanny Nell" – that's what she called me, Nanny Nell – "I think I'm in heaven now".'

'So Katie was an orphan, was she?'

'No. She wasn't. That was the foolish pity of it all. She was one of those children who get put into care because the Mam is crazy and on the cider and can't look after them. But it was bad in that place, the place they called the Children's House. Out beyond Dereham. You might have heard of it? They starved the kids to save money and the children were locked in their rooms for half the time, never breathing the fresh air, nor the scent of horses in a field, nor hear the robin singing . . .

'Katie was there three years. They never taught her reading or writing, or anything at all in the way of learning. Then she crept away one night, with just a scarlet coat on her back. Imagine that? Little Katie walking through the dark ten miles in her red coat. Walking and walking and then getting so tired and cold she had to lay herself down. And so she went into your cottage – this cottage, which was all derelict, with its door swinging off – and climbed the stairs and lay on this bed. And then, near to morning, when I could just see light at the window, she knocked on my wall.'

Nell warmed her hands on her mug of chocolate. She held herself very still, as though she needed to be motionless to remember the things she'd forgotten for so long. I stayed silent and waited for her to go on. Outside, I heard an owl calling.

'I took her in. What would you have done, Mrs? I told her she was safe with me and need never go back to the Children's House. I ran a bath for her, to warm her, and that's when she showed me the little yellow duck she'd brought with her. She said it was the only toy that was hers and hers alone, that no one had stolen or confiscated. And we set the duck bobbing on the bathwater and watched it keep on falling over and that's when I heard her laughter.

'I had food in the house. I always kept hams hanging above the fireplace, liked we'd hung them in Ireland, so the smoke would preserve them. I think I probably kept them there, in truth, in case my man came back. There's a woman's folly, if ever there is one! Thinking all the while about what a man would like to eat and trying to lure him back with that! A man who's gone back to a wife he never really left. And I'm buying and smoking hams for months on end. What kind of eejit does a thing like that?'

'A smoked ham is a lovely piece of food.'

'You're right, Mrs. It is. And now it was there to give to Katie. She sat in my kitchen, drinking milk and eating the good ham with bread and butter and I said to her, "Is there anybody I should contact for you, or would you like to stay with me for a while?" She didn't say anything at first, but when she'd eaten her ham she said she'd like to sleep. So I took her upstairs and put her in my bed and she held the little yellow duck to her face and slept, and when the morning came she said she wanted to stay with me and never go back into the world, for there was no one there who wanted her.'

Nell put down her empty mug. She lay back on the pillow and said she had to sleep now. She told me her brain was brimming with remembered things and remembered things could explode in your skull like brimstone, so strong and insistent you half imagined lava seeping out of your eyes.

She wasn't able to tell me how long Katie had stayed with her. She said she thought it was more than a year, because Katie played on the swing all summer long and then the late summer came and the oaks along our road began dropping acorns, which the little girl liked to collect and polish with shoeshine and line up on her windowsill. And then the winter arrived once more, but Nell banked up the fire in the cottage parlour and bought books and pens, to teach Katie how to read and write. 'She found this hard,' said Nell, 'because they'd never taught her the rudiments. But she was terrible good at pictures! She was a real little artist. She could make a colouring of an acorn look true to itself and a three-masted ship float on a turquoise ocean. And she made a drawing of me, once. She put a golden halo round my head and wings on my shoulders.'

I had to ask whether anybody had come looking for Katie. I saw her go pale when I said this. 'They did,' she said. 'And it was all in the papers, how a girl from the Children's House had gone missing. But you see, Mrs, they were looking for the wrong thing: they were looking for a corpse. They thought Katie had been abducted and murdered. I wanted to say to them, "Don't be behaving like you were in some stupid police soap on the TV. Nobody's dead. Katie was searching for someone to care for her, that's all, and she found her Nanny-Nell."

'But of course I said none of this. They sent a young policewoman, who looked like a schoolgirl herself. I wouldn't let her in. I told her to run along and not keep bothering strangers with her nonsense and I saw her colour up in shame. I knew Katie was safely out of sight, playing on the swing. I informed the police girl I'd lived alone for years and years and had never been a mother, and how in the world did she think I could abide to have a child messing up my parlour? I asked her if she wanted a good recipe for Irish stew, and she went away. She no doubt thought that somebody who could break off from a murder investigation to discuss cookery was a waste of her time. If she'd come round the back of my house, she'd have seen the swing, and Katie on it, but she never bothered looking there. I don't think she knew one lick of police procedure.'

Nell told me she had never had any money, bar a few state benefits, but she bought clothes for Katie from a charity shop in East Dereham. The two of them went for walks at dusk and heard pheasants squawking in the fields. She said everything was all right, everything was as happy as could be, until one day, Aunt Babbage turned up, unannounced.

'Who's Aunt Babbage?' I asked.

'Aunt Babbage,' she said, 'was my Mam's younger sister, Barbara. We always called her "Babbage" – I can't recall why. I guess we started out calling her "Babs" and then it got added to. Sometimes you take away from a name and sometimes you add to it, and who knows the meaning of this little human game?

'Babbage had looked out for me when I was a girl and sometimes bought me a stick of rock from the kiosk on the sea strand. But she'd stayed in Ireland when I went away. I thought I might never see her again. But she was a woman who loved surprises and her face, when she stood on my doorstep, had sheer joy all seepin' out of it.

'It was the middle of a winter afternoon and Katie and I had been by the fire, drawing pictures, so didn't my precious girl come running, to see who this was at my door and Aunt Babbage said, "Who in the world is this child, Nellie?"

'I was stuck for words. I loved Aunt Babbage. I wanted to tell her everything that had happened, but I knew I couldn't. I told her Katie belonged to a sick mother (which of course had been true, long ago) and that I was caring for her while the woman mended herself.

'Aunt Babbage came in. She had a suitcase with her, one of those old things made of card, but with proper locks on them that pop up like a jack-in-the-box when you slide a little bolt. She asked me if I'd got her letter and I said "There was no letter, Babs, perhaps because we have a new postman, name of Reg, who doesn't know his round yet." She said, "Well too bad, Nellie, but I'm staying two weeks here, if that's all right with you. England is a foreign place to me, so you'd better take care of your Aunty and explain the behaviour of the natives to me, or I might get lost in a British fog!" She was a one for jokes. Katie took to her right away and began showing her drawings of pirates and frogs and fishing boats and me with my halo, and the two of them were friends in no time.

'All that night, I stayed awake, wondering if I should confide in Aunt Babbage. The thing was, Mrs, what I'd done seemed right and normal to me, but I knew how anyone from the outside world would see it: they'd think I'd kidnapped Katie, stolen her away from her life. Yet the opposite was true. She'd had no "life" at the Children's House, just neglect and sadness. She'd arrived in my life, like a soft breeze arrives unannounced in summer, but nobody could be expected to understand that, could they now?'

Once Nell had begun on her memories of Katie, she wanted to keep on and on telling them to me. She said she had a film (she pronounced it 'fillem') spooling round inside her and she had to keep talking until the movie got to its end. But I could see that the talking tired her. Her appetite seemed to fail and she slept a deep sleep for long periods of the day. I asked her if she'd like to leave her story here, with Aunt Babbage's visit, but she said no, she had to come back to the next bit, when The Sorrow began.

She said: 'Aunt Babbage was smart, you see, Mrs? She knew that Katie had been living with me for a good while, and one night, when Babs and I had been drinking brandy and ginger wine, she persuaded me to tell her how it had all come about. And afterwards, Babbage, she says to me "There's criminality in our family, Nell, true Irish wickedness, and this is what you'll be accused of if you don't go to the Social Services and tell them everything. Because sooner or later, the police are going to track Katie down."

'I refused to do it, point blank. I said Katie was happy now. She had a swing and a garden of wild flowers. Why give her back her old unhappiness and blight her future? But Aunt

Babbage said, "There is no future for the two of you and you know it, Nell Greenwood. That child should be properly educated and leading a normal life, so you go along tomorrow and confess everything, or I'll have to do it for you."

'She understood how sorrowful I was at the thought of losing Katie. She suggested that when the Social people heard my story, when they understood that Katie was happy with me and that I cared for her, they might let her stay on, provided I put her into school.

'But she only said that to tempt me to go and come clean about what I'd done. Aunt Babbage knew that Katie would be taken away and of course she was. She wasn't wearing that little red coat she'd had. She'd long grown out of that. But that's how my mind thinks of her leaving: going away into the police car, in her red coat and turning and waving to me and her little face all blotchy with crying.

'And that was the end of me, Mrs. I won't bother tellin' you the next bit, where I was arrested and accused of all kinds of terrible things I'd never done. You can imagine it, can't you? And then that shrieking prison. I was banned from ever visiting Katie again for as long as I lived. And I thought, well, in that case, I hope I don't live long.

'But I have, see? It's that strange, isn't it? I suppose I could have put an end to myself with that shotgun you keep for the foxes, but I didn't. You've been good to me, Mrs, and I didn't want to spoil your kitchen linoleum. But I've never really seen, since that day when Katie left, what was the point of me. I think that's why I forgot everything for so long, until that knocking began again. I couldn't really get it into my head that I was still walking around on the earth. I've felt as though I wasn't really here any more.'

*

Nell died in due time.

There was nobody at the funeral, except me and the Vicar, so there was a breathless quiet in the church. But I told myself that Nell, who had been so disturbed by the noise in the jail, wouldn't have minded this. And outside, on the village green, I could hear the voices of children playing on the roundabouts and swings.

JONATHAN COE

CANADIANS CAN'T FLIRT

Having left Muswell Hill in good time, and arrived at Bank station with half an hour to spare, Martin begin to walk the streets at random and very soon he was lost. He rarely came to the City, and he had a poor sense of direction at the best of times. Tonight, as fog insinuated itself around the curves and corners of this enigmatic quarter – half ancient and half modern – coiling around columns and lamp posts, advancing snake-like into narrow side streets and lamplit passageways, he stood no chance at all. The night was cold and the sky had long since turned blue-black. The traffic had thinned, and consisted now only of rattling taxis and the occasional delivery truck. Martin remembered that the restaurant was tucked somewhere towards the end of a particularly occult and shadowy street but for the moment he couldn't find it. This whole district confused him. Every time he turned a corner he seemed to come upon a different branch of Eat or Pret A Manger, its lights dimming, the staff locking doors and sweeping up. Or was it the same branch? It was very hard to tell; they all looked identical. (This, presumably, being the point.) All he knew was that, having arrived ahead of schedule, he was now going to be late for the dinner, which was a disaster because it meant that he would be the last guest to be seated and would therefore have no choice about his place at the table. He would be lucky to sit anywhere near Lionel, and even luckier to sit next to Hermione.

Seeing the station's illuminated sign ahead of him at last, and realising that he had walked full circle, Martin swore under his breath and now paced hurriedly towards his destination, feeling his stomach twist itself into that familiar tight knot of anxiety. Social occasions always made him nervous, especially when they were bound up with his professional life. He already knew that he was lucky to be invited to this dinner at all. The invitation had come by email over the weekend, three days before the event itself: the publicist could hardly have made it clearer that he was a last-minute replacement. And yet he was in no position to complain. Ten years ago (in fact, why kid himself, it was nearer fifteen) he had been considered a rising star in the world of letters and his mantelpiece had been cluttered with invitations, one for every night of the week. But these days he couldn't afford to be choosy. It was almost a decade since his first – and only – novel had appeared, to cursory reviews and public indifference. His literary journalism, once considered required reading for its iconoclastic brio, had in recent years grown fatally polite and repetitive. His star was no longer rising, or even hanging in the firmament, at the summit of its arc. It was falling, plain and simple. Which made him think that even if tonight's dinner proved – as it would, in all probability – to be an awkward occasion, it was a dinner at least, and much better than another night spent home alone, scrolling wearily through his Twitter timeline in an attempt to ward off thoughts of what might have been.

Making his unseen entrance to the restaurant itself, Martin found that the management had rendered it cautiously festive. At any time of year it was a snug, whimsical, welcoming place, carved up into nooks and corners, its atmosphere so unabashedly Dickensian that it would have been a powerful magnet for tourists were it not so difficult to find. Tonight, fires crackled and popped in the various grates; candles flickered upon the tables, embedded in miniature wreaths of holly; the heavy gilded picture frames were draped in tinsel; and Christmas carols looped almost inaudibly on the miniature speaker system, only the occasional familiar phrase or cadence rising up during short intervals in the cheerful, laughter-punctuated conversation which babbled throughout the room, most of it emanating from a cramped table for ten in a well-hidden alcove – the very table for which Martin now realised he was headed.

There were nine people already seated. The pre-eminent object of Martin's interest, Hermione Dawes, was placed near the centre, flanked by guests on either side, wholly inaccessible. Her back was to him at the present moment, and his first impression was merely of her luscious, billowing golden hair, and her bare, equally golden arms and shoulders shining in the candlelight. She turned and smiled a brief 'Hello, Martin', as he approached, but there was no rising to her feet, no kiss. Really, why should he have expected anything else? Their paths hadn't crossed that often. Although Hermione had started out as a literary journalist, her column these days was mainly about politics, which meant that she was now moving in different, probably more interesting and influential circles. Also, in the last year or two, she had come to realise the advantage of taking up positions which set her apart from her predictably liberal colleagues. She was not only stridently pro-Brexit, but outspoken in her support for Donald Trump. Her career was now doing very nicely as she rode this populist wave. She was a talented writer, no doubt, and Martin was drawn to her for that reason, but he had another reason, too: the grudging respect Hermione inspired even amongst her enemies for her dextrous use of sarcasm, her ruthless irony and devastating litotes, was matched only by her reputation for wild promiscuity. Her nickname at Oxford, it was rumoured, had been 'Open Dawes'. Martin found this combination of abrasive politics and sexual loucheness to be incredibly titillating. He thought about it often, and shocked even himself with the grotesquerie and lurid specificity of the fantasies he sometimes entertained about Hermione at night.

After she had greeted him, the whole table fell silent. It was a silence that lasted a little too long – two or three seconds – just long enough to make it embarrassing, and to suggest the possibility that they had all been talking about him before he arrived. (Which was, in fact, true. The publicist who had invited Martin had raised the question of his perpetual bachelor status, leading to general speculation as to whether he was a repressed homosexual.) But then Lionel himself stood up, held out his hand, and said: 'Martin, old boy. Lovely that you could come.' And once again Martin found himself gripped by that strange combination of awe, nervousness and (though it always seemed presumptuous) affection that he had become used to feeling when in the presence of Lionel Hampshire.

Lionel Hampshire. One of the most famous writers in the country. Or at least one of the most famous 'serious' writers, which admittedly implied a significant lowering of the bar as far as fame was concerned. Whether or not he could be described as a household name depended very much on the kind of household you had in mind. His novels, let us say, were among the books you were most likely to discover on the shelves of Tuscan villas rented by the British during their summer holidays; and none was more likely to be found there than the book which had made his name, a quarter of a century earlier: *The Twilight of Otters*, his Booker-prizewinning *magnum opus*, although (again) whether the word *magnum* could really be applied to a book whose publishers had struggled to stretch it out to 200 pages is a matter for debate. Magnum or not, the novel had been a roaring success on its own terms. It had been helped on its way by a genteel controversy over whether it should be classified as memoir or fiction, since its tremulous narrative of sexual awakening was apparently based on the author's own adolescent memories. Now, in any case, twenty-three years after publication, and with more than one and a half million copies of the English-language edition sold, it had been officially designated a 'modern classic' (by its own publishers, no less) and reissued with a stylish but sober new cover illustration. It was to celebrate this auspicious event that tonight's dinner was being held.

Martin was still not sure why he had been invited, beyond the obvious fact that somebody else must have dropped out at short notice. He presumed that it was because, three years ago, he had profiled Hampshire for the arts pages of a national broadsheet. (The article appearing, as chance would have it, on the same page as one of Hermione's columns, right next to her delectable byline portrait.) In days gone by he would not have dreamed of accepting that commission, let alone writing the interview up as obsequiously as he had done, but times were hard and he could no longer afford to turn down such a prestigious piece of work, nor to alienate Hampshire's publishers by composing a piece that was combative in any way. He had approached the encounter with a good deal of trepidation, all the same, because he had not always been kind to the Hampshire *oeuvre*. On publication of his fifth novel, an odd excursion into feminist sci-fi entitled *Fallopia*, Martin had reviewed it for the *TLS* and shown not the slightest mercy. Despite this lapse of judgement, his first meeting with the great man of letters had been cordial enough, and

Martin had been relieved, in particular, by this section of their interview:

> *'I never read reviews,' Hampshire declares, stirring his macchiato with polished insouciance and smiling wryly, as if reflecting on the folly of those authors who don't follow his example. 'My wife reads them for me, and if it's a good one she gives me the gist. If it's a stinker she screws it up and throws it away.'*

This, then, would certainly have been the fate of Martin's ill-advised hatchet job. So no harm done, fortunately. And after their interview, they had remained on friendly terms: Hampshire had dropped him a short email to thank him for 'what I'm told was a far too generous write-up', had made a point of being nice to him at parties ever since, and had even requested his services as on-stage interviewer for his most recent appearance at the Hay Festival. It seemed, bizarrely enough, that the great writer actually *liked* him, and Martin, somewhat his junior in years and very much his inferior in literary status, could not quite get over the fact.

'You're looking in the pink,' Lionel said now, pumping his hand and patting him on the back.

'Really?' said Martin, who had been in bed with a cold for most of the week. 'You too. All that tennis, I suppose.'

'Three times a week now,' Lionel answered, 'and squash on Tuesdays.'

It was true that, for a man pushing sixty, he was in excellent shape. He looked both younger and older than Martin: younger because he exercised more, carried himself more confidently, had better skin, wore more stylish and expensive clothes and a more stylish and expensive haircut; older because of the unmistakable aura of success and eminence which gave him an air of seniority, not just over Martin but over everyone else at the table.

'When are you going to take me on at squash?' said Hermione, who was sitting at Lionel's left-hand side, and now turned to glance up at him with her most coquettish smile. 'You're always promising.'

'You couldn't handle me,' said Lionel. 'I'm sorry, but it would be an embarrassment for both of us. I couldn't do that to you. Look,' he continued, turning back to Martin, 'do take a seat. I'm sorry you have to be perched at the end but we'll all swap over in a bit and we can have a proper chat.'

Having banished Martin to the far reaches of the table in this genial manner, Lionel sat down again and leaned in towards Hermione, resuming a conversation which no doubt revolved exclusively around the finer points of squash. Martin, for his part, found that he had been placed to the right of Lionel's editor, an earnest man in his early forties who, having entered publishing many years ago because of his youthful love of literature, and now finding that his working life was entirely taken up with sales targets and marketing strategies, was always hungry for intellectual discussion on occasions like this, and was bound to keep him pretty busily occupied in that respect. Opposite Martin, meanwhile, was Lionel's wife, whose name he seemed to remember was June. She was younger than her husband – just the right side of fifty, he would guess – and her attractive features, although sometimes still capable of lighting up into something approaching animation, seemed more often to be settled into a look of resigned melancholy. They had met only once or twice before, so he was rather surprised that she made a point of leaning across the table to kiss him warmly – very warmly – on the cheek, and to say:

'Martin. This is the nicest surprise. How are you, my dear?'

'I'm very well.'

She picked up his menu from his place mat and thrust it at him. 'We all ordered, a few minutes ago. You'd better choose something quickly.'

The menu offered traditional English food. The mention of a whole roast partridge caught Martin's eye, and he communicated his wish to a waiter after attracting his attention with some small but humiliating difficulty.

'Excellent move, I'm sure,' said Oliver, the editor, sitting to his left. 'I plumped for the trout. Not sure it was the right choice.' He poured red wine into Martin's glass. 'Cheers. Good to see you again.'

Martin, Oliver and June clinked glasses and sipped.

'Did you read,' Oliver now said, by way of opening gambit, 'that the morning after Trump was elected, the Canadian immigration website crashed? There was a huge surge in applications for citizenship from terrified Americans.'

'Amazing,' said Martin. 'But personally I'd rather take my chance in Trump's America than go to Canada.'

'Why's that?' June asked.

'Well, I've only been there twice, but it struck me both times as being the most boring country in the world.'

His listeners took a moment to digest this sweeping statement.

'Incredibly beautiful, though,' Oliver said. 'That has to count for something.'

'It's the *people*, though.'

'What about them?' said June.

'No sense of humour.' And here it struck him, at once, that he had the opportunity to make a brilliant start to the evening's conversation by rehearsing a favourite theory, one of which he was secretly very proud. 'Have you ever met a funny Canadian? Or a funny New Zealander, for that matter? Of course not – and the reason's the same. We're talking about two of the most orderly, just and well-regulated countries in the world, with low crime rates and amazing natural beauty into the bargain. Two countries with a fantastic quality of life. So why would they need humour? Why would they want to tell jokes? Humour is the human race's way of coping with adversity. Build a fair society and you don't need it any more. For Canadians, a sense of humour is quite simply unnecessary. That's why they've never developed one.'

Sounding less impressed than Martin had expected him to be, Oliver thought for a moment or two before replying: 'Well, that's an interesting theory, certainly. And rather a bold one to put forward, in the present company.'

'Why the present company?' Martin asked.

'Why? Because Mrs Hampshire is Canadian, of course.'

June smiled at him in a reassuring way. 'Don't worry,' she said. 'Another thing about Canadians – we don't take offence very easily.'

A burst of laughter from the middle of the table distracted them briefly. Whatever Hermione had said, it must have been more provocative than usual; the laughter was coloured by delighted outrage as well as amusement. Lionel's laugh was the loudest and most complicit; he rocked back and forth in his chair, and came to rest, when it was over, against Hermione's glimmering shoulder, resting his tousled black hair there for longer than was strictly necessary.

'How old is that woman?' June asked, taking in this spectacle calmly and then turning back to Martin.

'Not sure – late twenties, I think.'

'Hmm . . . thirty years younger than my husband. And yet they seem to get on so well.' Something crossed her face – a spasm of what looked to Martin (though he couldn't be sure, and it was gone so quickly) like agony – before she adopted a musing tone and said: 'I look at her columns sometimes, do you? Such a strange way to make your living. A paid contrarian, I suppose you'd call her. A very modern way, that's for sure. Very much of the zeitgeist. Last week she was positively fierce on the subject of the metropolitan elite. And yet here we all are, sitting down to dinner, as elite and metropolitan and liberal a gathering as anybody could wish for, and she seems awfully at ease with us, doesn't she? Almost as if she was born to be a part of it herself.'

The pain seemed to flare up again, for the most fleeting of instants; then with downcast eyes she contemplated the slab of pâté a waiter had just noiselessly left in front of her.

'When I said that thing about Canadians,' said Martin, the words forming in halting steps, 'I didn't mean . . . that is, I didn't realise . . . '

'Don't worry,' said June. 'I never take national stereotypes seriously. Although, even if we don't have a great sense of humour, there is one thing . . . ' (And here she paused, parted her lips slightly, and licked them while fixing Martin with a strange, glassy stare) ' . . . that they say the Canadians are *very* good at.'

And this word 'very', as well as being spoken with great emphasis, was accompanied by something even more unexpected than the remark itself: a slow, effortful wink – one so laboured and unnatural, in fact, that instead of conveying anything in the way of amusement, or conspiracy, it merely looked like the wink of some kind of ghastly automaton, almost as if someone had attached an invisible string to June's eyelid and was pulling it from somewhere above her head like a puppet-master. The very sight of it chilled Martin to the bone, and for a moment distracted him from the alarming implications of what she had said. Coming back to that, however, he realised that not only had she addressed a sexually provocative remark to him, she had done so in a way that made absolutely no sense, relying as it did on a non-existent trope about Canadians being good in bed. (At least, he assumed that was what she had meant.) All in all, he had no idea how to respond, so he grabbed himself a bread roll – having ordered no starter – and buttered it studiously while hoping that the conversation would soon move into safer waters.

All went well for the next few minutes. Oliver had entered upon an intense discussion about genetics with the woman sitting opposite him (a well-known radio presenter), but Martin managed to inveigle himself into it despite his ignorance of the subject, and June was temporarily frozen out. Before long, however, another eruption of laughter from the middle of the table drew everyone's attention. This time it seemed to be Lionel who had made the joke – Hermione approving it so strongly that she rewarded him with a high-five which somehow ended, quite unnecessarily, with their fingers interlocked and intertwined for a number of seconds. This did not go unnoticed by June, and once again, when Martin caught her gaze, he saw that her eyes were filled with liquid sadness which, after springing up for one unguarded moment, quickly froze over into ice.

She smiled a brittle smile.

'That does look good,' she said, nodding down at the partridge which lay before him, newly arrived, uncarved and surrounded by green vegetables.

'I hope so.'

He began the delicate process of slicing into the meat and separating it from the crispy outer layer of skin. He was acutely aware that June was watching him as he did so, although occasionally she glanced back towards her husband and his young admirer, in whose adoring attention he was still revelling. Martin could feel that the situation was charged with strong, contradictory emotions, but he tried to block his mind to this and concentrate on the tricky task at hand.

After cutting off two regular, satisfyingly trim slices of meat, he glanced across at June and discovered something that was once again startling: namely, that she had altered her position, and was now sitting at right angles to him, her back to her neighbour. She seemed to have undone two or three buttons on her blouse and pulled the fabric slightly away from her body, thereby offering him a clear glimpse of her navy-blue bra and the flesh it contained. Martin took in the view quickly and then, shocked, looked up at June's face and found that she was staring at him intently, making no secret at all of the fact that she wanted him to see as much of her exposed cleavage as he cared to take in.

Perhaps I'm imagining this, Martin thought, as he broke out into a sweat. Perhaps she's just hot, and wants to allow some air to circulate.

But the restaurant was not at all hot. And in any case, June's next words were:

'Mm, doesn't that breast look delicious? What are you waiting for? Go ahead and tuck in.'

He had, in fact, been on the point of cutting off his first mouthful of the meat in question. Now he paused mid-incision, trying to formulate a reply to this invitation but lost for words. His eyes locked on to June's for a few moments, and then hers clouded with shame. She looked away, did up the buttons on her blouse and smoothed her hair back to hide her confusion.

'I'm sorry,' she said. 'I need the bathroom.'

In a clumsy and noisy movement she got up, pushed the table back and squeezed past him. Oliver and the radio presenter turned and watched in surprise; as indeed did the whole table.

'She all right?' Oliver asked.

'Yes, I think so,' said Martin. He chased some peas around the plate with his fork and tried to look as though everything was normal, but privately he was horrified: not just because Lionel's wife was coming on to him (there could be little doubt about that, now) but also because she didn't appear to have the first idea how to do it, and – worst of all – was mortifyingly aware of the fact. Her abrupt departure for the toilet made it obvious that she could see how disastrous her latest effort had been. Tonight, it seemed, Mrs Hampshire was determined to attempt the music of flirtation; but clearly she was tone-deaf, and she knew it.

And yet this was not going to stop her trying, even now. Further incredible attempts issued from her lips throughout the remainder of the meal. When Martin offered her some Brie from the cheeseboard, she opted for Cornish Yarg instead, saying that she preferred to have something 'hard and satisfying inside me'. Choosing vintage brandy as her *digestif*, she said that she 'always liked a stiff one at the end of the evening'. Each of these dreadful double entendres was accompanied by lingering looks in Martin's direction, followed immediately by averted eyes and blushes of shame, as if she could not believe either her own daring or her own ineptitude. Martin found himself simultaneously appalled by the spectacle, and fascinated to see how it would develop.

He did not wait long to find out. As the last remnants of food were cleared away, and Lionel's publicist discreetly settled the bill, Lionel announced that he, Hermione and two others would be moving on to the St George, one of the most exclusive private members' clubs in Soho. June was not mentioned, and while she seemed to accept this turn of events with equanimity (while being unable to keep her wounded, venomous eyes off the contrarian columnist, whose grip on her husband's arm now seemed to be unshakeable), Martin rebelled strongly against the idea that they should go without him. Against all the evidence, and all his better judgement, he could not quite relinquish the idea of ending the evening huddled in a cosy corner somewhere – anywhere – with the delicious Hermione. And so, while wriggling into his coat amidst the genial chaos of farewells and Merry Christmases, he said to Lionel, as airily as he could:

'I think I might come along and join you, actually. I feel like a nightcap.'

'Ah!' Lionel said. 'Are you a member?'

'No, but I thought . . . ' Martin tailed off. The truth was, he didn't know what he had thought.

Now Lionel smiled his deadliest smile – the one that was dashing and lethal at the same time, and could turn his female admirers to jelly. 'The trouble is, Martin – it's *very* exclusive, this place – even members are only allowed to bring one guest each. So Hermione will be my guest, and Marina will be Jack's. I'm really sorry, but that's how it goes.'

'Ah. Yes.'

In a last-minute display of faux-gallantry, Hermione glanced over at the stricken wife and said: 'Oh, but what about June? I mean, I don't want to . . . '

'That's all right,' said Lionel briskly. 'She hates the St George. Will you be all right getting home, darling?'

He turned to his wife and she gave a miserable nod. Then uttered the astonishing words: 'Martin and I can share a cab, then.'

Martin stared at her, speechless. Even Lionel seem baffled by this one.

'But Martin's in Muswell Hill, isn't he?' he said.

'So?'

'So how can you share a cab?'

'Why not?'

'In what conceivable universe is Muswell Hill on the way to Greenwich? They're in exactly the opposite direction. Unless you're coming from Wales.'

'Oh, we'll sort something out.'

And with that she took Martin's arm and propelled him out of the restaurant while the others looked on, dumbstruck. Before Martin could understand what was happening, she had waved down a black cab, and they were speeding northwards up the A1. She sat close beside him, breathing heavily, her thigh pressed against his, but she didn't speak. The warmth and conviviality of the restaurant were already left far behind, a distant, unlikely memory. After a minute or two the silence became unbearable.

'You don't have to come all this way with me, really,' he said. 'I mean, it's miles out of your way.'

'I want to,' said June.

Silence reigned again. The taxi driver's speaker crackled and his voice came through:

'Which end of Muswell Hill did you want, mate?'

'Corvick Terrace,' said Martin, leaning forward.

'OK. I'll swing left through Kentish Town, then.'

'Cheers.'

June looked across at him sharply.

'Cheers?' she said. 'That's not a very Martin-ish word.'

He laughed. 'Yeah, it's a bad habit. You know how it is – you change your way of speaking, depending on who you're talking to, I suppose . . . '

'I suppose you do. If you want to be all things to all people.'

Having said this, she looked him in the eye for a moment and then shifted her weight away from him, turning to look out of the window at the shops and houses as they slipped by in the dark. Their physical intimacy was over: there was a space of at least two feet between them now. Martin did not know what to make of the gesture. He waited for her to speak again. He waited a long time.

'I do love Lionel,' June said at last. The words came slowly, but clearly: her voice trance-like, almost robotic. 'I've always loved him, and always will. Ever since we met. He was on a book tour in Canada, just after his big success. I had a little radio show back then, on a station in Toronto. I gave all that up for him, of course. But I was so happy to do it. He was so charming, so British, so . . . *funny*. He's still funny, don't you think? Have you noticed how he always tries to make them laugh? That's how he was with me. I suppose I should have expected . . . After the show, that first time, he asked me out for a drink, and that was that. Five days later I was on a plane to London with him. I gave everything up. Haven't worked since then, not once. We had the children, they kept me busy, for a while. And then I found myself slipping into this role . . . his manager, his assistant, I don't know what you'd call it. Answering his email, filtering the invitations, putting his archive together so we could sell it to America. All because I believed in him, you see. I still do. He's a good writer, a very good writer. Maybe a great one. And his books are getting better, even if the reviewers don't think so.' She turned and stared at him. 'You reviewed him once, didn't you?'

Luckily, before Martin could confirm or deny this allegation, the taxi driver's speaker came to life again.

'You two warm enough back there? Only some passengers have been telling me the heating system's on the blink.'

'Yes, we're . . . ' Martin tailed off, not wishing to speak for both of them.

'We're fine, thanks,' said June decisively.

'Right-o,' said the taxi driver.

'Cheers, mate,' said Martin, before he could stop himself.

Silence was reimposed. Then June continued, in the same somnolent monotone:

'I don't know if he sleeps with them. That isn't the issue, really. It's the invisibility I can't stand. The way I become invisible to him. It's not about my age. It's not about my looks. At least, I don't think so. I've been trying to remember when it started. Or when I started to notice it, which I suppose is not the same thing. Probably about . . . ten years ago? When the kids were growing up and I was tired all the time and we hadn't fucked in ages.'

'I can hear every word of this, you know,' said the taxi driver.

'Then turn your speaker off,' said Martin.

'It doesn't make any difference. I can still hear you through the glass.'

June didn't seem to mind, in any case.

'Now look at me,' she continued. 'Tonight was the last straw. Putting his hands all over that slutty little troll like I didn't exist. And all I can do is sit there and make these horrible . . . these pathetic attempts.' Her voice shook slightly, as if tears were welling up, but she managed to steady herself. 'You're right about us. Canadians don't have a sense of humour. They can't flirt, either. They barely even know how to screw.'

'Well, I spent the night with a Canadian once . . . ' said the taxi driver.

'Will you please keep out of this?' said Martin. Then added, 'mate,' as an afterthought.

'I mean, what I really can't believe,' June went on, 'is that I chose you. *You*. What a dumb choice! Not just for the obvious reason . . . '

'The obvious reason?'

'The repressed homosexuality.'

'What? What are you talking about? I'm not a repressed homosexual.'

'Well if you're repressing it, how would you know? Anyway, I'm not talking about that. I'm talking about the review you wrote of Lionel's book. Horrible. Unforgivable. So vindictive, and personal and just so damn . . . self-satisfied. It was a personal attack on him and so it felt like a personal attack on me as well. That's how close he and I were at the time, you see: when I read that review, I truly hated you for it. And I thought I couldn't hate you more until you had the gall, the barefaced *nerve* to show up at our house and interview him, and then write that fawning, hypocritical piece. So that's it . . .' She stared ahead, her eyes now quite unfocused, quite unseeing. 'This is where I am. This is *who* I am. Sitting in the back of a cab with someone I despise more than pretty much anyone, and yet I'm so angry with Lionel that I'd probably suck your cock right now if you whipped it out and stuck it in my face.'

'Just remind me – did you say Corvick Terrace or Corvick Crescent?' the taxi driver asked, as he braked at a set of traffic lights.

'Don't worry,' said Martin. 'I think I should get out here.' And he did.

Without further comment, the taxi driver made a wide U-turn. He picked up speed as he drove southwards, jumping lights and weaving skilfully in and out of the sparse traffic.

'I'm so sorry,' June said, as he swerved to avoid a bicycle with no lights on. 'You shouldn't have had to listen to all that. It can't be nice to overhear it when your passengers are . . . losing their dignity.'

'You mean you, or him?' the driver asked. And then, when she didn't reply, 'Anyway, you were wrong.'

'Wrong?'

'About Canadians. Like I said, I spent the night with one once, and she was a right little firecracker.'

She looked up to see his gaze, mischievous and laughing, reflected in the driver's mirror. Then June smiled to herself, sank back in her seat, closed her eyes, and no more words were spoken on that long journey home.

TESSA HADLEY

OLD FRIENDS

—We have to wait, Sally said, and Christopher took it from her because that was his nature: not malleable, but subtly attentive to other people's necessities and prohibitions. Perhaps another man would have insisted on his moment in the sun of their passion, would have seized her and carried her off, but he was not another man. Anyway, any carrying-off scenario was bound to be messy, had to include the complication of the children, her children and Frank's – two boys and a girl, all handsome and characterful and opinionated, all with their mother's distinctive auburn hair. The older two were taller already than Sally and rather too prone, or so Christopher thought, to bossing her about. Not that she was a pushover: although she was as small and slight as a girl she was resilient, with extraordinary stamina. Other people thought Sally a sweet bland competent good woman, the perfect counterpart to Frank's noise and bluster and the whole exaggerated scale of Frank's personal operation, which drew in everyone else like a baggage train dragged after some showy emperor (he was a war correspondent for the BBC). Christopher, however, knew Frank's wife's quick, fierce look, her private judgement. Naturally she adored her children and thought them marvellous, which he didn't quite, so that he saw with clearer eyes than hers how she fell, in her relation to them, into a performance of deploring and forgiving and being put upon, and how the older two were hardening, as their glossy beauty ripened, into a sense of their entitlement to this. They were also Frank's children, after all.

So although Christopher and Sally loved each other, and although he believed they were perfectly suited – eager and diffident, serious, she fitted into the shape of his own serious nature like a nut in its nutshell – they would have to wait, just as if they were characters in an old story. He wasn't sure what they were waiting for, he didn't ask, he didn't want to press her in this place where all the difficulty, it painfully appeared to him, was hers. With women he had always been shy: legacy no doubt of the ghastly school he and Frank had attended together, though it didn't seem to have inhibited Frank. In his working life Christopher was boldly imaginative; against the grain of a family tradition which favoured PPE and the Foreign Office, he'd become an engineer with his own medium-sized business, manufacturing turbines for renewables. But he had found himself in an unknown, dreadful territory, falling in love with the wife of his old friend. All the falling in love he'd ever done before (he'd even been married for a few years, unsuitably but amiably enough, when he was very young) had been a child's play compared with the power, and the complication, of this.

If he hadn't known what he knew about Frank, and in fact if Sally hadn't confided in him, appealed to him, made the first move, he'd never have dreamed of doing anything but admiring her chivalrously from a safe distance, and thinking that she was wasted on his friend. But now he was involved, committed up to his neck – over his head, in fact: submerged in her astonishingly. So he had to trust that Sally knew what they must do next, or not do. He waited. And in the meantime they snatched what encounters they could, an afternoon here and there at his flat in town; it could never be often enough, and they had never, at least after their beginning, spent a whole evening alone together, not to speak of a night. He had a business to run, Sally had a family, and she also managed to do something or other part-time for the British Council (which was her cover story, too, when she came to him and left her mother, never undomesticated Frank, holding the fort at home).

Christopher's West Hampstead flat was so transformed by her visits that he could hardly recognise his old convenient refuge, and was uneasy spending time in there without her, preferring to drive back at night even when it was late to the anonymous box of a place he rented near his factory, in Gloucestershire. Certain indelible images seemed to be projected like home movies against that London flat's white walls: which were too vacantly receptive because he'd never got round to decorating and hanging up pictures as he ought to. Sally said she loved his flat, the emptiness of it, the unfilled blank spaces – they made her feel free. All the surfaces in her own life, she said, were written over and over in all directions, like an old letter.

The thing had begun on one afternoon of drama when Christopher had arrived for a visit at Frank and Sally's house outside Southwold on a hot Sunday in summer. It was a lovely old crumbling low stone farmhouse with deep-set windows, smothered on the side facing the road in a silver-limbed hoary ancient rambler whose roses burned intensely red in the strong light; but Sally said the garden was too much work and that she was often lonely here, would rather have lived in the city. How typical of Frank to cherish an ideal of a home in a lovely country place where he could charm and entertain, like the model of an

English rural romantic, flowing over with his own bounteous hospitality – and then to abandon his wife and children in it for months at a time while he was away working. On this occasion too Frank was going off somewhere, and he'd asked Christopher to come over to say goodbye, 'keep Sally's spirits up' after his departure.

They had all been out in the back garden when Christopher arrived, and the low rooms indoors, fragrant from the meat roasting with garlic in the kitchen, were dim and cool and restful; he could hear the children shrieking and splashing in the pool. Stepping into the glare again, through the French windows at the back of the house on to the sloping lawn, he seemed to catch the married couple just for one instant as they were when he wasn't present – seated tense with concentration on their canvas folding chairs, on the terrace Frank had energetically built one past summer, jingling the ice in their gin-and-tonics, intimately unspeaking, in the middle of something. For once Sally's lifted sharp vixen-face – for that was how he had thought about it since that day, now that he loved her: the velvety fine fur of her skin, russet colouring, slanting long muzzle-like lines of her cheekbones – had been unsmiling and naked, with no charming or placatory mask fixed in its place.

Then Frank had jumped up at the sight of Christopher: relieved, Christopher thought, by their being interrupted, as if that were exactly what he'd been invited for. Dropping a heavy hot arm across his friend's shoulders, Frank hailed him exuberantly; Christopher felt overdressed because Frank was only wearing khaki cargo shorts and flip-flops. His big brown belly shoved round and tight and unapologetic above his shorts like a pregnant woman's, and there were forceful scrabbles of black hair on his plump breasts and on his toes; he was one of those men who thrust his imperfect body shamelessly, even keenly, in your line of sight, with a winning, childlike, uninhibited unconsciousness, as if he'd never noticed he wasn't a cherub any longer. Christopher in his late forties was still straight and slim, six inches taller than Frank and with more hair, even if its fair colour had bleached to neutral; he was pleasant-looking, with a long face, chalky complexion, pale blue eyes under heavy lids. And yet somehow it was ugly Frank, with his sagging baby-face and the untidy bald circle like a tonsure in his black curls, who took everyone's eye, the women watched him and enjoyed him, and some of the men. They succumbed to his energy, and his self-love.

As soon as Christopher had arrived Frank was in his element, talking, talking; walking up and down the garden with some new flame-throwing gadget he'd acquired to kill weeds in the lawn, blasting at them perilously and leaving blackened patches, talking all the while in his loud, eager, confiding voice, punctuated with shouts of laughter: politics mostly, and gossip about personalities, and books – not fiction (only Sally, of the three of them, read fiction). It was their tradition that Christopher countered Frank with his quiet irony, his good information. He was the corrective to Frank's dogmatism, his quick-fix partisanship; it was to Frank's credit that he sought out his friend's dissent. The oldest boy, Nicholas, had come out of the pool after a while, wrapped in a towel and shivering with wet hair, drawn helplessly to follow the flame-thrower. After lunch – Frank had carved, wielded the knife in alarming proximity to his own naked belly as though he were serving up slices of himself, although Sally remonstrated with him mildly, asked him to put his shirt on, pointed out that she'd made the children get dressed decently before they were allowed at the table – Christopher helped Sally to clear the plates while Frank went to pack, hardly able to repress his jubilation at his imminent escape. –It's all right for you lucky blighters, he yelled downstairs. –Living the life down here in the country idyll. Some of us have to get back to work, do a reality check!

And then something happened in the pool: a change in the noise of the children's idling, a splash, and awful screams, brought the adults running down from the house. But all three children seemed to be all right at first, quarrelling and shoving at the pool's edge, streaming with wet, remonstrating with one another. –Corin's such a idiot, Nicholas was shouting. –Showing off as usual. Why can't he do anything properly? He's got no sense.

The younger boy began staggering about and pretending to puke, or half-puking, in what looked like a pantomime performance of drunkenness. –Is he putting it on? Sally asked, bemused.

–Really he was floating right on the bottom, Mum, Amber said. –It was his own fault. Nicky and me had to dive down to get him out.

–Don't fuck about though, Frank said to his children genially enough. –This is serious stuff. You're all right, aren't you?

When the little one dropped abruptly to his knees, still retching and choking, his eyes rolling up into his head, it was Christopher who scooped him quickly up and performed the necessary manoeuvres, laying him flat on his stomach on the grass and turning his head, making sure he didn't swallow his tongue, then pumping his frail shoulder blades so that he vomited up quite a quantity of pool-water, mixed with lunch. –My God, my God, Sally whispered in panic and sympathetic horror, crouching beside them, hardly daring in that moment to touch her own child, covering up her mouth with both her hands.

–But he's all right, isn't he? said Frank. –I mean, you can't get out of a pool and walk around and still be drowning, can you?

Once Corin was sitting up again and swearing, weeping,

hiding his messy face against Sally and sideswiping with a fist at his brother, Christopher agreed that everything was probably fine now, but said they still ought to take him to a hospital for checking out. Frank was visibly torn – he had a plane to catch. –You go, Christopher said. –It's only a routine, make sure the lungs are clear. I don't mind.

And so it was that he had spent all that afternoon and evening waiting in Southwold and District with Sally and Corin; Frank had dropped off his other two children, on his way out, to sleep over at a friend's house. Eventually the doctors cleared them to go home. Christopher carried the sleeping child up through the front garden from the car in the moonlight, and laid him in his bed while Sally pulled up the duvet tenderly to cover him; Christopher felt as if he'd trespassed for a moment inside the heart of a family life, which was something he'd always wanted for himself but not contrived to get. –You must be flat out, you poor thing, he said kindly to Sally once they'd closed the bedroom door behind them. –Can I get you a nightcap? Or would you like tea? Would you like me to stay?

He had truly only meant that he could kip down, if she liked, in a spare room: make quite sure that she and Corin were both all right in the morning. But the moment the words were out of his mouth he understood how they could be interpreted as a commitment to so much more than merely kindness; and Sally had turned to him, there in the dim light on the landing, burying her face in his shirt front with a mewing noise of self-abandonment, clinging to him, dropping her whole weight – which wasn't all that much – against him. –I would like you to stay, I would, she said. Of course it was partly the strain of her afternoon. –He didn't even ring, did he? To find out how Corin was. I left my phone on deliberately, all that time, even though you're not supposed to in the hospital.

Christopher tightened his grip cautiously around her, taking her weight. –Of course I can see, he said, –that old Frank could be quite a trial, to be married to.

–Oh, Chris, she groaned, you don't know the half of it.

Later in bed – they hadn't quite wanted to make love that first time, not in the same house as the sleeping child saved from disaster, as if that might be unlucky; so that Sally had stayed underneath the duvet and he had stayed on top of it, and the duvet had functioned as a kind of bolster, or a sword, between them, while Christopher held her in his arms to comfort her – she told him quite a lot about the half of it he didn't know. Although perhaps he knew, or could have guessed, somewhat more of it than he let on: that it wasn't only women Frank was unfaithful with, and that some of the boys he had were kids, they were really only kids, only just past the age of consent, and that he refused to get himself tested for anything, and that when he woke up with nightmares he needed Sally to comfort him like a baby. And that he'd never ever even once, not once, it was a joke, been there for any of the children's concerts or birthdays or parent evenings, even though he'd made such a huge deal out of sending them to all those private schools which they couldn't really conceivably afford. Because naturally there were chronic problems with money too. And as for his drinking, don't get her started on that. Frank's eternal absences, Sally said, were the least of her worries. They were the good bit.

And then, when Christopher and Sally had been loving each other clandestinely for about eighteen months, though after that first time they'd never even once spent a whole night together, Frank died reporting on the war in Syria: which you might have thought, looking at it cynically, must be the sort of thing they had been waiting for. It wasn't a heroic death, he wasn't shot or blown up or anything, though he might have been, he'd always pushed forward fearlessly into the worst places, despite his nightmares and his secret fears. But he got blood poisoning through a cut in his foot and died remarkably quickly, before anyone even really knew that anything was wrong, in some chaotic hospital on the Turkish border which had been turned upside-down by the war and had no antibiotics.

Christopher heard the news from a friend of a friend who rang him at his office in town. The strangest thing was that he'd already caught sight of Sally and the children that very same morning, before he got the call, just for a few seconds, quite by the most improbable chance – because in London who ever accidentally crossed paths with anyone they knew? He'd been waiting at a crossing on his way to a meeting when he saw Sally driving down Euston Road with all the children, tensely concentrated at the wheel of Frank's preposterous SUV, which was splattered in Suffolk mud. He knew she hated driving in London and after they'd gone past he'd even wondered, because there was no possible reason for them to all be there on a school day morning, whether he might have conjured them up out of his desire for Sally, like his hallucinations of her presence in his flat.

Something in the collection of their sombre, striking faces – beautifully alike as a donor's family lined up in graduated profile in a Renaissance altarpiece, all blue-white skin and rusty silky hair, gazing alertly forwards through the windscreen at the traffic – had troubled him even at the time. Lifted in the SUV up above the ordinary level of the street, they had seemed so inaccessible to him. He understood, as soon as he heard the news about Frank, that their bereavement had already fallen on to them, like a cloak – not of invisibility, but of apartness. He called Sally right away, but she didn't pick up, so he texted. 'When can we meet?'

–You've heard? she texted back, after a little while.

–I've heard.

–I'm in town, talking to the FO, she sent. –We have to wait.

They had Frank's body flown home and at his funeral, where of course Christopher was too – in fact he'd more or less organised it, Sally was in pieces – the distinguished, desolated family made a heart-rending picture, which went the rounds of all the media. You could hardly tell, until you looked carefully, that tiny Sally wasn't a fourth orphaned child. And after the funeral Christopher was often in their Southwold home for days and weeks at a time, helping Sally out, going through Frank's papers with her, and his clothes, though she wasn't good at throwing things away, sorting out probate and closing bank accounts, getting the house ready to put it in the hands of the estate agents. He always slept in the spare room. Once he tried to embrace her when the children were all away, Nicholas boarding at school now (it was what he wanted, and Christopher paid) and the other two at sleepovers. –I can't, Sally said apologetically, shaking her head, pushing her palms against his chest to keep him off, not meeting his eyes. –Not here. Not yet.

When a year had passed they began talking about buying a house together; Sally had said she hated the country but now it seemed she didn't want to move into London after all, so he looked in Gloucestershire and found the perfect place. But she still wasn't ready. –I don't know what to tell the kids, she said. – Not so soon, when they're still grieving for their father.

Christopher wondered how much the children were really grieving. They had been shocked out of their serenity and complacency, certainly; sometimes they were self-important with their loss, used it as leverage in their quarrels with Sally. But actually he thought they didn't miss their father hugely, as if they hadn't known him very well. They probably didn't miss him as much as Christopher did. He felt Frank's absence every day – the space in life where his friend's noise and his bullying exuberance were missing, and his warmth; and the waste of his death. The children didn't mind Christopher. Amber aged twelve in her cropped top, wound around with beads and painted with Sally's eyeshadow and lipstick, flashed her flawless prepubertal midriff at him. –Why don't you just sleep with my mother, Christopher, she drawled, –if you're so mad about her?

–Well I am mad about her, he said, blushing. –But it's not quite as easy as all that.

Christopher insisted eventually – for the sake of his own dignity, really, and his self-possession – that Sally come to talk it all out with him at his flat: which wasn't exactly neutral territory, haunted by the times they had spent there together. The place was still spartan, he hadn't done anything to it or bought any more furniture, hadn't wanted to change anything. When he asked why she wouldn't live with him she sat on the side of his bed with her head in her hands, fox-red hair falling forwards over her face. He dragged over a box of the books he'd never got round to unpacking and sat down on it, opposite to her, close enough to touch but not touching, watching her intently.

–It isn't the children really, is it? he gently said. –It's you.

–Chris, I can't leave the house. Frank's present in it everywhere. I can't leave him. I feel all the things I didn't use to feel. Think of his achievements! I'm reading everything he's written. Isn't it good? And I'm finding all these souvenirs and photographs, things from his childhood and boyhood, trophies and model aeroplanes and letters he wrote to his mother from school, all that stuff. I'm thinking about all those places he went in his adult life, sending back his reports – I never really asked, what was it like there? What was it *really* like? I'm cheated, by his leaving me this way. Because something's still unfinished between us.

–Between us? Christopher pressed her, needing to be sure.

–Between Frank and me.

And he knew that although by this time Sally had dropped her hands from her face and was looking right at him, she couldn't see him.

GILES FODEN

THE ROAD TO GABON

It must have been late autumn when Richard Rennison drove down from Notting Hill to Combe Britton to see Maudsley, poor man. Grey vapour swept towards the windscreen of the Lexus; it seemed to fold into it, as if the glass were absorbing a doubt about its own substance. When he came to the lanes, the boughs and leaves of the trees (forming in places arches which combined to create the effect of a tunnel) were dripping with a wet heaviness; and these leaves and boughs, too, appeared to be losing their edges, as if unsure whether they were part of that vivid organic life we call nature, or part of the coming night.

Night was part of nature, of course. But it also seemed to stand in his mind for some of those parts of humankind that humanity opposes to nature. As, driving, he thought about this division, it took the mental shape of the pixel grid with which digital designers manipulate images, each calibrated little cell making discrete what was in life continuous, and subjecting to rule what were in reality strange, irregular rhythms. Rennison, too, tended to make digital adjustments of this type before sending in his edit, though it was something Maudsley guyed him about, saying if a photographer were not *homo mimeticus*, who in the wide world would be?

He took a corner too fast, became aware that he needed to pay better attention to the road if he were not going to kill himself (on this or the next blind bend), and with that jolly admonition, and a lessening of pace, the tail of his thoughts returned to Maudsley. Teasing each other was part of the traditional pattern of their relationship, though that had changed in the past year, as Maudsley faced what he called his next big adventure.

For months Maudsley, who had long been Rennison's artistic benefactor, had been fighting cancer. He lived in one of the last big houses of southern England, on the borders of Devon and Somerset. On one or other of his previous visits, Maudsley had informed him this was the exact place where the colonial Norman influence on Britain had ceased, and that was why there were no other big houses in north Devon. He added that it was also here that the rocky detritus pushed by glaciers of the Ice Age had terminated, leaving a rubble of boulders and unaccountable geological specimens in the interminable mossy ridges that rose greedily about the house.

Maudsley was a stickler for punctuality, and Rennison had been anxious to make good time. The drive was always longer than he supposed. But apart from the usual bottlenecks around Bristol, where the tide of traffic never flows freely, he experienced no problems on the roads, arriving with a good ten minutes to spare before five o'clock, which was his appointed moment.

Approaching the familiar pillars of the gate, his field of vision criss-crossed by the wash of the windscreen wipers, Rennison felt himself assailed by a sense of poignant regret. He thought about the first time he had met Maudsley. It was in the early Nineties, when Africa was unfashionable in both finance and photography. Maudsley was the original man on a motorbike, chucking up his job in the City to ride across the continent, looking for private equity investments at a time when the phrase hedge fund had yet to soil anyone's lips.

A tall, ginger man approaching forty-five, Rennison got out of the car, feeling a chilly mist about his ears; he unlatched the gate, the iron of the hasp slippery and cold under his fingers.

They had first met on the long straight road that runs from the northern forests of Congo-Brazzaville into Gabon. Maudsley was leaning on his Harley-Davidson, his noble head inclined to one side as he stared avidly into the jungle, smoking a cigarette. There was a squashed snake on the road, which Rennison (rightly, as it turned out) assumed Maudsley must have run over.

Blowing wreaths of smoke into the sky-break above the road, the Maudsley of those days was impossibly brown and fit, his open-neck white shirt showing the line of his tan on his chest. When Rennison clambered from of his Land Rover, the back of which was filled with photographic *katundu* (as the boot of the Lexus now also was), he had laconically informed him that there was an outbreak of yellow fever in the gold-mining camp he had been visiting, and that Rennison had better go no further.

Maudsley's words to describe what he had found in the camp consisted mainly of disconnected ejaculations – 'singular'; 'most curious'; 'odd even for Africa'. The bodies that he found there, he'd said, 'were among the most nauseating I have ever seen, but inexpressibly significant in the way they sat about, lay about, as if death had surprised them'.

'Like I did this,' he'd added, hooking the stringy green body of the snake under the toe of one of his shoes and looping it into the trees.

Well, it wasn't yellow fever, it was Ebola, and Rennison did go further. In an innocence of desire to get his first big spread, he went deep into the rainforest and photographed those victims in their camp near Minkébé. The source of the virus was a chimpanzee killed in the forest, which had been eaten by the miners. Twelve people who were involved in the butchery of the animal had become ill. It was sombre images of these men, covered in mud as they sprawled in wicker chairs in front of their ragged huts, that first made Rennison's name – along with the vast, deliriously laddered pit itself and the nearby town of stores and whores where girls sold their bodies for a few grains of gold and Lebanese shopkeepers dispensed tots of white spirit and fried chicken for the same.

By the time his pictures of Minkébé were published, the outbreak had spread and become known to the World Health Organization. The fluke of Rennison's survival of it, itself the later subject of reports in newspaper profiles, added to his lustre as an artist – though he himself readily acknowledged it as one of those temerarious deeds done by those who are funking inside. That was the year he first won adventure photographer of the year and began styling himself 'Rennison', without a first name.

He walked across the spongy gravel towards Combe Britton, the roofs of which rose in tiers, as if having been conceived from the back. The effect was emphasised by a lift of dark hills above the chimney-tops. It had perhaps never been a house of good cheer.

He pulled the bell-cord, but it didn't work, he suddenly remembered, so he resorted to a massy knocker. After some minutes, the door opened. He saw Maudsley's hooded eyes and white face, slightly unshaven. While still a broad-chested figure, in T-shirt, jeans, cardigan and a sort of paisley kimono, he was a different man from the stylish, bronzed traveller Rennison had first known in Africa, so many years ago, his face always burnished from punctilious washing, razoring and moisturising.

The listless eyes flicked open more widely. 'You've come!'

'Yes.'

'I wasn't sure you would.'

'I said I would.'

'You've brought your kit?'

'Yes. I'll get it later when the rain stops.'

'It won't.'

Rennison heard the rain pattering on the gravel behind him – on the gravel and the turfy meadows and the furze-covered hills whence it tumbled in succession down into Simonsbath and the Lyn – as he followed Maudsley into the house, the door shutting loudly after, swinging on its own weight.

The owner of this big house lived alone. There was a gardener and a daily, but no woman's hand was soothing the passage of his illness – he'd only ever had model girlfriends, mistresses, now all paid off. Maudsley led him into a room where a fire burned. Its flames glinted on the Benin bronzes and other *objets d'art* which hung on the walls or stood like funerary monuments about the room.

A large box of kitchen matchsticks, half open, sat on the mantelpiece, the red head of each match seeming like that of a soldier lying down to be entombed.

'Have a seat,' said Maudsley.

Rennison lowered himself into one of a pair of well-rubbed, red leather armchairs as his ill friend, moving slowly, bent a neglected lock of frost-white hair above a sideboard and poured whisky into tumblers.

He brought one over to Rennison and flung himself into the other chair, the whisky slopping slightly in the glass.

'I am dying, Richard.'

'Don't say that.'

'Why not? It's true. Three months at best, the doctors say. That's why I wanted you to come and take my portrait.'

'It's the least I could do. Do you want to get it over straight away? I thought . . . the morning.'

'Rennison's golden hour? If we are lucky. This weather is infernally depressing. I think the mist, like the rain, is here to stay.'

'That's just your illness talking.'

'My illness, dear boy, is always talking. It's talking in my lungs, where tobacco played havoc for so many years, and now the doc says it's talking in my bones, too. Mets.'

'Mets?'

'Bone metastasis. The cancer cells flowing through the bloodstream like to settle in one's bones, apparently.' He took a sip of the whisky. 'Well at least I will go out at the top of my game. I closed all my positions last week. Pretty much the best returns of any fund this year, on both sides of the Atlantic. And that's what I wanted to talk to you about, as well as the portrait.'

'Your funds?'

'Yes, and being at the top of one's game. I think you have been slipping lately.'

It was true. Rennison had fallen into an easy routine of shoots for fashion chains and luxury hotels. All his life had been about taking photographs, and there had been many other award-winning highlights besides Minkébé: Mount Roraima and the Kavak caves in Venezuela; the clifftop church of Abuna Ymata, perched on a 2,500-foot-high rock face in Ethiopia; the *Noorderlicht* ship, frozen into the ice at Spitzbergen . . . But recently he had been staying more in his studio, managing his stock, and picking up lucrative commissions as his agent piped them through from ad agencies, on a 25 per cent commission. It made him feel queasy, as his own self-image was involved with a notion that he could scarce understand himself except in situations of authentic action – which shoots in the restaurant of the Dubai Four Seasons or lining up Boden models on the rocks of Polzeath were certainly not.

'There has been another outbreak at Minkébé. I think you should go back, revisit the scene of your first glory.'

'No way!'

'You need to. Think of the headlines. The culmination of a twenty-year journey in photography – a return to the source.'

Rennison's eye fell on the pattern of the ancient North African prayer rug which lay on the parquet between them. Among the themes suggested were portals, gardens and birds; also lovers, possibly – though not subversively, for the parts conjoined in the way man was meant to join with Allah, who was anyway protecting all under a Tree of Bliss, the boughs of which fell down along the border of the rug.

'I am not putting myself in the way of that kind of danger again,' he said. 'I was very lucky not to have contracted the disease. So were you. Or to have been shot by Monsieur Oueey and his friends.'

Monsieur Oueey was a pit boss who had flown into Minkébé while Rennison was doing the shoot, landing in an army helicopter next to that hellish hole in the ground. His security crew, who carried automatic weapons, had started threatening Rennison. They were about to remove his digital cards when Monsieur Oueey said, '*Laissez ce blanc, parce qu'il est aussi brave que nous d'être entré dans ce charnier! Qui sait, va t-il gagner sa récompense quand il retournera dans sa terre natale?*'

'I expect Monsieur Oueey is long gone, replaced by another thug. But I am quite serious, Richard. You should know that having no family I have left you most of my legacy – but only on condition that you go back to Minkébé.'

He gave this information very simply, without any typical English show of tactful evasion.

Rennison was almost too shocked to think what the money would mean. 'Why are you making me do this?'

'I am not making you. It's your own choice.'

'I have my own family now, Charles. My wife wouldn't let me do this for all the money in China.'

'You mean tea?'

'Yes, whatever. Christ, you might be ill, but you haven't changed.'

'I should hope not, but actually I have. What I have realised is that I have made a mistake in my life. When I was younger I regarded the world as a lever with which to exert my ego, and that is the basis on which I made my investments. Swimming against the tide, too. When I was going into Africa, Barclays, Standard Chartered and all those other blind bats were already thinking of pulling out. But you know, what I wish I had done was write. When I was up at Balliol, that's what I wanted to do, then somehow I drifted into the city and became a stockbroker.

'Then the Big Bang happened and I made a pile of cash and I thought, well Africa is the frontier of emerging markets so I'll go there and see what can be done by an individual. But I never wrote my book, just my notes from Africa, privately published . . . well, you have seen a few of those and now there are more. I have left some on your bedside table, as a matter of fact. Anyway, the point is, despite my successful slavings, I think I missed my calling; I don't want to see you doing the same, with all these ads for InterContinental and whatnot.'

A Malawian soapstone head, its scalp itchy white for lack of oil, regarded Rennison from next to the hearth. He felt a need to defend himself and began doing so warmly.

'I have to pay the bills. You haven't got kids, Charles, you don't know what school fees are like these days.'

'If you take this offer, you will never have to worry about a bill of any type ever again.'

'This is about as far from my plans as anything. I'm grateful, of course, but I have been offered a professorship of photography at Goldsmiths and I am minded to say yes.'

'Being a professor is an awful profession. Paid to talk. I bet Hirst – you know I have one of his – and all the other artists at that place grew as pale and sick as I am, hearing those bald heads talk, talk, talk at them for hours without being able to stop. Shall we eat? I've roasted a chicken.'

They went through to the kitchen. In contrast to the rest of the house, it was steely and modern, showing retractable taps out of which ready boiled water flowed, a fierce array of Swiss knife handles, and an Aga garlanded with pots on hooks, either side of a gargantuan hood for removal of fumes.

'I have had my coffin made,' said Maudsley, his kimono flapping as he shook a tray of roast potatoes with more vigour than Rennison would have expected from someone in his condition. 'One of those Ghanaian ones done in the shape of the profession of the deceased, you know?'

'No?'

'A fisherman gets a fish. A postman gets a postbox. Someone who sells SIM cards in a roadside shack, a mobile phone.'

'So what did you choose?'

'Well, that was the problem. You can hardly have a coffin in the shape of a bearer bond, well, I suppose you could but it would look a bit flat. I thought about what I loved most in my life and what came to mind was that Harley some bugger nicked off me in Maputo. But that didn't work, too messy with handlebars and pedals and so on, so I got one done which looks like the '63 Stingray

Corvette in the garage here, the one I took you out in when you were last down. Actually, we should do the portrait in it. I'd like that, if it's OK with you.'

'In the car?'

'No, the coffin. It's in a kind of glass mausoleum I have built in the garden.'

He went over to the window and flicked some switches. A rectangle of glass lit up between clipped yew hedges – and Rennison saw, inside the glass, a bright red shape with an open lid, surrounded by small white stones and a couple of cactus pots.

'That's what I am to be put in, when I go. I have made you my executor, by the way. There's no strings attached to that.'

Returning to the kitchen worktop, Maudsley laughed harshly, then began to cough like a cormorant. Once he had got his breath back, he said, 'Yes, that administrative pleasure you can have without going to Minkébé. But what do you say, about the other thing?'

'Let me think about it.'

They ate, and drank red wine, and Maudsley spoke in his thin, cracked voice about his former plans to revivify the African railways, now abandoned because the Chinese had got in on the act. Now and then he paused to spit into a blue handkerchief, saying that he feared each one of these seeds of catarrh would be his last. It was barbarous to expectorate like that during a meal but the man, once the very article of urbanity, was very ill and it was excusable.

After the meal, they retired to the room with the fire, which had become as smokily unwelcome as what followed, which was Maudsley's return to the topic of Minkébé. Renewing his campaign of persuasion, it was as if he was challenging Rennison, daring him to imperil himself.

The discussion left the photographer in an uncomfortable

mood, which pursued him up the wooden staircase to bed. That night, in damp sheets, in a room full of cold air, Rennison thought about what a fine person Maudsley had been in the old days, an authentic Odysseus piloting the excursus of capital into uncharted lands. The story of some of those adventures were recorded in Maudsley's *Notes from Africa*; several slim, blue-bound, privately printed volumes of these were stacked on the bedside table, under a lace-fringed lamp.

He wondered why he himself had been chosen to face the test which would win the millions that were the product of those journeys. They had met in many exotic places – in Mbeya once, when green flying ants covered every door, and among the stately royal palms of Mozambique, and amid the quaint glens of Kisoro in western Uganda, even under the jazz-filled roofs of Sowetan shanties – and each time given joint rein to the fancies that such places engender in visitors only.

But never had he expected to become the heir of the man whom even enemies recognised as the doyen of investment in these regions. And he had a lot of enemies, proudly playing at dinner parties a mobile phone recording in which a philanthropic Irish balladeer pronounced, in a broad Belfast accent, on 'that cownt Charles Maudsley'. Rennison reached for one of the blue volumes and opening it at random, read: 'The landscape of African investment is strewn with booby traps. The first thing to remember is that the expert notions are always wrong; you need to treat your investing brain to an enema, flushing out received ideas . . . '

He read on a little more, then closed the book and turned off the lamp, thinking about what Maudsley had said earlier that night, about wishing he had been a writer. Once before, during one of their meetings in exotic places, Rennison himself had said to Maudsley that he had wished he'd been an investor in Africa rather than a photographer of it. Maudsley had laughed and said don't be a fool man, art conquers all in the end. Was that it, was trying to prove that what this was all about? But the terms in which the offer was put, as a financial inducement, seemed to suggest the opposite.

For a few seconds, as he lay on the hard pillow, Rennison's private feelings – private from his wife Tabitha, sleeping miles away in Notting Hill, at least he hoped so – tended to the notion that so much money might be a great way to free him up as an artist; but they quickly bent back to the detestable, dangerous presence of the virus that potentially awaited him in Africa, however that same disease might be read back, over a period of two decades, to have been the thing which formed his sufficiency as an artist in the first place, gauge of a great future. As he tried to sleep, this interplay between art and money began to seem of a piece with a more extensive gallery of catastrophic fates that he feared were in salivatory anticipation of battening on him in the long *durée* between early middle and old age, louring like gargoyles on a cathedral roof.

His thoughts turned naturally to Tabitha. Tabby never wanted to hear about his trips, having no great curiosity about life beyond west London, and regarding the whole business of photography with a deep distrust. Perhaps she was minded to be complimentary, but it never seemed so. The preparations for an extreme shoot in a remote location she found especially irksome. For Rennison, just the thought of going away to a dangerous place involved readying himself to be traumatised in the name of art. And he had done it, he had gone through shattering moments to generate authentic situations in which the shutter closed, as he still thought of it, on the perfect image.

All this was hard to explain later. In the flow of dinner party conversation, people (not his wife) would ask him what it was like and he couldn't say, as the more successful the photograph, the more it seemed to turn back time, immunising him against the perils he had been expecting and sometimes undergone. On the days of his actual returns, Tabitha herself would most often regard the proffered images with a cold, vague complacency, before muttering crossly about some domestic oversight.

Once, he remembered, on his coming back from Yemen (where he had been in search of oryx on the Sarawat Mountains' western slopes), the topic of her displeasure had been the amount of canine excrement left in the garden because he had not taken Congo (as their black Lab was called, in honour of his own early productions) for a turn round the block on the morning of his departure. Rennison resented these duties. Tabby didn't work herself; there was nothing much active about her but her tongue, which seemed to mint every month a new way of being beastly about working-class people and foreigners. She got through nannies almost as rapidly as she bought new Emma Hopes.

Rennison did not sleep well that night, and he woke tired and cross. Washing his face with cold water – in one of those small porcelain basins, which along with pull-cord paisley curtains are often a fixture of these country houses – he wondered if the sleeplessness he had laboured under was a type of fear. As he brushed his teeth, he became conscious of a need for extreme wariness about Maudsley's offer; probably the best thing was to take the set of portraits and get himself back to London sharpish.

Coffee helped a bit and the fact that Maudsley had been wrong about the morning. It was clear and bright, a light fresh wind blowing down from Exmoor.

After breakfast, Rennison fetched his camera, tripod and other kit from the Lexus. They went out to the mausoleum: a strange, modernist feature in that otherwise old-fashioned garden of Victorian roses and raspberry canes. The Exmoor wind was blowing about the glass box, lifting leaves at its edges. Maudsley opened its door and let them in.

Made of painted wood, the coffin really was a smaller-scale reproduction of the garaged Corvette, in which Rennison had been given a ride on his previous visit, Maudsley swooping up and down the Devon lanes at such a speed as to put the fear of God into him.

Rennison erected the tripod, and affixed his camera to it, also setting up a silver-coloured, umbrella-like light reflector on the white gravel.

'Well,' said Maudsley, 'I suppose the only thing is for me to get in now, so that I am remembered this way alive when someone puts me in dead. That will be you, Richard, by the way.'

'You've got to be kidding. Aren't there undertakers for this kind of thing?'

'I have always wondered why they are called that,' Maudsley said, climbing into the cherry-red coffin with an action that seemed like a bound. 'I mean, what do they undertake?' His voice echoed under the canopy.

'Do you mind if I close the lid a little further?' asked Rennison, in the voice of a patient artist; he was checking the light meter in the green digital display of his camera, which at the touch of a button could be cumbered up with verifying numbers.

Four months later, Maudsley was in that coffin for real, and Rennison was on the road to Gabon. Tabitha had been remarkably encouraging about the plan, saying if he had done it before, why couldn't he do it again, in tones which suggested the expedition would really make a man to be reckoned with. Profoundly indifferent to danger as it was, her bravura attitude seemed to promise a new beginning for their marriage – a fresh start, a new channel of communication, a luxury of genuine intercourse such as he had never before really had with this thin, sharp blonde who had somehow become his wife.

At first, returning home from Combe Britton, Rennison had felicitated himself on resisting Maudsley's offer. But then news of his death came, and next the ponderous solicitor's letter outlining what he was to do if he were to inherit the estate, made all the more temptingly complicated by Rennison himself being sole executor of the will.

He sat in the vehicle with the engine idling – not a Land Rover this time, but a Toyota Land Cruiser, such as the Kurds, he remembered from one of his trips, called a Monica because of its full-bodied look. His plan had been to go first into the drinking shops and whorehouses of Minkébé town, begin with their infamies before entering the more hideous site of jungle infection, with its documentary prospect of imminent decay, of which the worst was blood flowing from victims' eyeballs.

Rennison was, not at all for the first time on this journey, driven to quit his route and seek refuge in the comfortable Michaelis hotel back in Brazzaville. There had been an Arabic woman there in high heels and a flowing caramel dress whose outlandishly seductive body had captivated him as he drank at the bar; he would have much rather taken her photograph – could have satiated himself upon its magnificence, in fact – than those of monstrous corpses, or the zombie-like near dead. But it had made him, the very thought of Minkébé, dreadfully nervous about everything, so he had not broached the idea with her.

Gripping the steering wheel with sweaty hands, he tried to imagine it – tried to see, in his mind's eye, all those wholesale human oozings in wicker chairs already red with mud which, along with Monsieur Oueey and his gold tooth and heavy-knobbed cane and pack of gunmen, had characterised the suite of photographs taken, over twenty years ago, by a nervous young man who'd get more money for his images than he ever expected.

He thought also about the pictures he had taken of Maudsley: they had given him an oddly babyish air, as if the garish image of the Corvette were not being presented (or represented) as a coffin but as a playful crib. He had photographed his subject in a dozen different attitudes in this receptacle – every position they could conceive of between them – but the impression of an infant was always the same.

The obesity of the jungle swelled around him, threatening to smother up the road in a curtain of rich green leaves and silence. But this road was not like other roads in Africa, rutted, impassable as a stony riverbed, or thronged with demands for cash from men with Kalashnikovs. It was straight, narrow, flat, with the blessedly attractive brush of central grass that the mind demands of the ideal country road; were it not for the threat of the jungle, wall-like and obvious, it was almost fine enough to convince oneself that one was on the right track for Eden.

If he wanted to pass on himself, he could; there was nothing stopping him, except for his desire to return to the slightly quickened notations of modernity that constituted Brazzaville, which apart from the Michaelis hotel was a brown, torpid place.

Still he sat, with the engine ticking on, reverberating dully through the cab, and seeming to echo palpitations in his chest. The spectre of the awaiting deaths haunted him before their exact perception, as if he was already looking at a double-page spread in the article he had arranged before having taken the shots. How could he go there now, into Minkébé, potentially sacrificing everything for a few images or many noughts in his bank account, whichever it was? Coming here struck him as a monstrous folly, testament to the savage nature of his munificent taskmaster, whose real nature he felt he had sentimentalised in life – and who now seemed to be stretching out, as it were, a clammy hand to exert his will from the grave.

Agitated by fear as he was, Rennison suddenly remembered a platform event he had attended at a festival in Saint-Malo, something to do with travel photography. Asked by the interviewer why he took photographs, he had replied that it was to pay the mortgage. A French photographer, also on the podium, had turned in shock to him and said this was a statement of artistic suicide, adding that if he was faking, it was just the kind of attitude he expected from an insincere Anglo-Saxon. At the time, Rennison had maintained that making art to meet the bills was nothing to be ashamed of, but now he was not so sure.

Giving a cry like an animal, he put his foot on the accelerator and drove onward a few miles, the air coming through the open window seeming an abomination of divine breath; then he stopped again. His chest hurt. Here he was, back in Africa, misled by the blandishments of a dead man and – oh, his chest really was hurting a lot, his heartbeat seeming to flutter to and fro within it like a batting eyelid. It was as if something that he had feared in his overly sympathetic imagination was now beginning to relish the process of taking hold of him bodily, grasping the heart that is real life more presently and vividly than any of his imaginings, which he now almost looked back on with a gilded yearning.

Here, where he'd stopped, the trees were waltzing shadows across the road; how late was it? had more time passed along this line of futility than he'd thought? Soon it would be time to don the protective white suit and mask he had packed, time to sweat from subject to subject, lugging his camera equipment between the impassive dead. Again he felt a malignant sense of anticipation, again his heart bruited irregularly in his breast, taking no more coherent order than the sight of matchsticks falling from a matchbox on to a tiled floor. He struck himself on the forehead, cursing his pusillanimous nature, then took to rubbing his chest.

He pulled himself together and drove on a little further – coming, he thought, to the exact spot where he had met Maudsley all those years ago; though he couldn't be sure. As he pulled on the handbrake, a fork of pain lodged in his torso.

It forked again, seeming to bend its prongs round his heart. The willing of viscosity out of that clenched organ finally put all the vulgar agencies of dread which had populated his imagination to flight, sending them back down the same invisible thoroughfares between mind and body from which they had mounted their campaign.

The agony spread. Steel thongs seemed now to garrotte his whole chest, in a pain at once punishingly physical and perversely abstract: it was like being strangled by the ineffable.

He opened the door of the Land Cruiser and half fell, half staggered out. He crawled to the edge of the road, feeling the sun on his back – not as sun, but as something which was trying to suck his heart up through his back, leaving a train of fire; it was as if a retreating star were trying to grasp back some of the light it had shed, millennia ago, before glaciers of which we know, before Britons, before Normans, before an age of empires, SIM cards, Monica Lewinsky, capitalism in its later phases.

It was a heart attack, he realised that rationally now, but suddenly he knew that nothing he possessed within reason was going to defend him against fatality. He looked up like a dog at one of the tall trees by the side of the road. He regarded its absolute, don't-give-a-shit inhumanity, and thought of the wood of Maudsley's coffin, before another bout of quivering pain cored into his chest like an augur.

A froth of spit began to bubble about his lips. He fell on to his face. His lips ate dirt. The dust of the road mixed with the spit of his mouth, became a paste. He rolled over, giving up his browned face to the mercy of the sun. But what the sun saw was the whiteness of death.

He raised his hands, scraping at the air with the tenacity of a climber. He heard a call of birds, and saw a flight of green parrots shoot up into the sky from the tree. Their wings made a noise like applause over the compounding solidity of his body, before disappearing in the direction of Brazzaville, as if they too wanted to leave Gabon an undiscovered country.

Then came a kind of lull or pause, that slowly began to be filled, but only by a dissonant, gong-like ringing in his ears, over one of which an ant had begun to crawl. The whiteness that the sun saw in his upturned face filled his own eyes, very bright, as if the commissioned article had been spiked, and all the coloured pictures were being snuffed from the page by clicks of the art director's mouse. Crawling back down the wire in staggered segments, like cars in slow traffic, the images he had not yet produced – and the self-image of Rennison also, somehow catapulted up into the figured face of the watching sun – began to disappear byte by byte, until the page was blank.

LYNNE TRUSS

TESTAMENTS

In the spring of 2010, a family meeting was held at Hoagland Hall, near to Devizes in Wiltshire. Presiding was the thirty-six-year-old newly encumbered 14th Earl Donington, christened Francis, but known since childhood to his family as Franco. Also present were Franco's wife Teresa, children Crispin and Anna, and older sister Harriet. His feckless younger brother Julian conspicuously failed to attend, but promised he would return from Patmos within the next month or two, once the punishing demands of his current song-writing project abated. While the three adults conducted their discussions in the old library at the rear of the house, with its view over the once-glorious (but now scrubby) parterre, the children, quietly, went exploring.

It was an exciting and productive meeting, concerning the future of the Hall. Julian would have done well to attend. Six months previously had occurred the sudden death of Franco's father, the 13th Earl, at the tender age of sixty-eight. While the customary observances had been quite sincerely made at the time of his departing (his offspring had wept, to their own surprise), both Franco and Harriet were agreed that the Earl's unexpected demise had been a terrific stroke of luck for them, and indeed for nearly everybody; it had been a calamity, in fact, only for the network of lowlier auction houses of the kingdom, where the loss of the Earl's reliable business would be keenly felt. His permanently open wallet and genial catchphrase ('What an absolute bargain!') had made him a very popular figure in the world of the provincial saleroom. But his capacity for squandering the family fortune on 'ephemera' had been a source of genuine concern to his more worldly children, which was why his death (by falling off the roof of the Hall, during a birthday party) was greeted with a large degree of both relief and opportunistic excitement. Of course, they had feared the tax bill. True, Franco had considerable personal wealth, accumulated through a combination of judicious marriage, luck in property investment, and a decade or more in stockbroking. This personal wealth on top of his inheritance might just suffice to save the Hall for the family, but only without taking his father's bizarre 'collections' into account. So, what a great day it was for them when Her Majesty's Revenue and Customs, after due consideration, deemed that, besides the house itself, the 13th Earl had left 'nothing of value'. Perversely encouraged by this news, the family met and produced a three-point strategy for going forward:

1. Franco and his family would live at Hoagland Hall, and in due course open it to the public.
2. The worthless collections (whatever they were) would be curated by Harriet and marketed to the visitors in some clever postmodern way.
3. Julian would always have a home there if he wanted.

After the meeting, the five of them (including the children) clinked glasses.

'Dad?' said ten-year-old Crispin. His father ignored him. Teresa noticed Crispin's frustration, but was unable to draw him into the conversation, because a grown-up (Harriet) had just had a thought.

'We must have a funny slogan!' Harriet yelled. Harriet had once worked as a publicist for a London publisher, so it was natural for the others to defer to her on matters of advertising.

'What do you mean?' asked Teresa.

'Dad?' said Crispin, again.

'Not now,' said Franco.

'I don't know,' said Harriet. 'I can't think. But, you know, like, um, *Like Castle Howard, but without –*' She stopped; she was racking her brain.

'I know, I know, I've got it,' said Franco. 'Like Beaulieu –'

'Yes?'

'But Without the Cars'.

Everyone laughed except Crispin.

'What is it, darling?' asked Teresa.

'I just wanted to say, Ma. Anna and I went upstairs and had a look at some of the stuff.'

Franco pulled a face. 'Your grandfather was a fool, Crispo,' he said. 'Is it really dreadful?'

Crispin lowered his voice. 'Dad, it is absolute *crap*.'

Five years later, Hoagland Hall was doing very, very well as a tourist attraction. It seems that the public had grown actually quite tired of the country-house model with costly reproduction period furnishings and minor eighteenth-century portraits. Given the chance to see the world's largest collection of unused Betamax tapes (in the old stables), or an exhibit of cheerful 1950s seed packets (in the ballroom), they merely took into consideration the outstandingly good five-star reviews of the tea room and thought, 'Why not?' It is the tea room that is, in reality, the most important attraction in any country-house experience; by way of research, Franco and Teresa visited many existing properties and were surprised by how crowded, offhand and dehumanising the tea rooms often were. Thus, the rather steep entrance fee for Hoagland Hall cunningly included a free pot of quality tea in the Orangerie Café, and also politically acceptable soft drinks for the children. This brought the punters straight in. Tea-shop manager Bethany – a caterer of rare brilliance – needed only to take it from there.

Julian came back from Greece eventually, but he sought no involvement in the running of the Hall. He was offered 'the cottage' on the estate, which had the benefit of being distant from the main house, and thus untroubled by the flow of visitors. 'I wish we could live in it ourselves,' Franco wrote in an email, disingenuously. 'But we just wouldn't all fit in when Anna and the Crisp are at home.' All three Donington siblings were familiar with the slightly derelict cottage from their childhood games in the park – and the idea of living in it had not appealed to Franco for a moment; he and Teresa were very happy with the bright upper floors of the Hall. Nor had it appealed to Harriet, who chose to buy a charming small flat above a fishing-tackle shop in the village. But Julian was enthusiastic about having a whole cottage to himself. 'Cheers, Franco,' he had written back. On Patmos, he had been living with a German woman who, unattractively, reminded him quite often that while she worked long hours as a cleaner to pay for all their food and accommodation, he strummed a guitar all day on a balcony. It was difficult to be creative under such conditions, and Julian had been seriously considering returning to England when, in 2014, the German woman found out that the Earl had died some time before, leaving her layabout boyfriend an inheritance. Furious, she grabbed Julian's guitar and tossed it into the harbour, where it sank, with bubbles, to the heartfelt cheers of several of the locals. At this point, Julian made his stand, by packing his stuff and leaving. His guitar, so they say, is still visible from the quayside as it rests on the rocky seabed below, such is the legendary clarity of the water around all the lovely islands of the Aegean.

'Will he eat with us?' Teresa asked, on the day Julian moved his meagre possessions into the cottage.

'I hope not,' said Franco. 'The kitchen's not bad down there, is it?'

'I've no idea. Bethany got it ready. She asked for money to buy some bits and pieces, and to get the chimney swept, and so on: was that all right, my darling?'

'Of course.'

Franco smiled. 'Look,' he said. 'You can just see the lights on down there. Through the trees.'

'Oh yes.'

They both gazed out.

'You won't expect anything of Julian?' he said, suddenly worried.

'No!' she laughed. 'No, I won't!'

'He's so hopeless.'

'I know.'

'Dad's favourite, of course, when we were little. Until he got so morally superior.'

'Younger children always have it so easy,' she said. 'He's not even a viable person, really; while you and Harriet are brilliant.'

*

It was true that Julian would never have seen the commercial potential in the 13th Earl's junk that Franco and Harriet had seen. Between them, they had done a magnificent job. Visitor interest was currently focused on the drawing room hung with fifty-two identical Green Lady portraits, in different states of repair, some of them with their original Boots the Chemist price labels (ranging from 25s. to 32s. 6d) still attached. (There had been a piece about the Green Ladies in the *Guardian* Weekend Magazine, which had certainly done no harm to business.)

'He couldn't have done any of it,' said Franco.

'I know, darling. Poor Julian, to have missed out.'

They both pondered, briefly, poor Julian, and what he had been missing.

A thought struck Franco. 'I wonder if I ought to go down to say hello. I haven't actually seen him for a few years, you know.'

From his tone, Teresa knew that the suggestion was not sincere. The last thing he wanted was for her to agree. She smiled.

'I think it's entirely up to you, darling,' she said. 'But he's probably very tired from the journey.'

'Yes, of course.'

'He probably just wants a bath and an early night.'

'Well, that's what *I'd* want, certainly.'

'And Bethany said she would wait there to show him everything.'

'Did she? Isn't she marvellous?'

It was when Julian had been in the cottage for a month or more that he and Franco expressed their first outright difference of opinion. Despite his long familiarity with Julian's high-mindedness (Julian was just two years younger, so they overlapped at both Winchester and Christ Church), Franco was still hurt that Julian took so little interest in the success of the Hoagland Hall family enterprise, seeming to regard it as beneath him. Julian's first tour of the place was a predictable disappointment; it turned out that the German woman on Patmos (despite expecting her boyfriend to pay his way) had been a highly persuasive New Age kind of person, doing astrological readings for the tourists and also holding firm views on karma, Eastern systems of medicine, and the incompatibility of spirituality and possessions. From this point of view, she and the priggish Julian had been very well matched. So, when he was first exposed to the heaps of stuff that were the Hall's famous selling point, he did not laugh or marvel, as Franco had hoped; he was genuinely shocked and offended. On seeing the veritable cathedral of old Betamax tapes in the stables (twenty thousand of them, acquired in batches by the 13th Earl over a period of fifteen years), Julian turned literally green. Franco pressed on, regardless. Julian's heightened sensitivities were his own problem.

'I know,' he said, with a chuckle. 'There's a conceptual art postgraduate at the Courtauld doing a PhD on it. She's contrasting it with Legoland. Wait till you see the Maclaren baby buggies. We've got seven hundred and fifty, all blue and white. It's phenomenal.'

Afterwards, Julian invited himself to dinner with Franco and Teresa, by way of apologising for his reaction to the exhibits; but it didn't come out like an apology, and it was the last time he came up to the big house. He brought lethal Greek liquor as a peace offering; after dinner, he lit up a Greek cigarette at table, despite Franco saying, 'I'd much rather you didn't do that,' and Teresa reflexively emitting a little scream.

'It was just the shock, Franco,' said Julian. 'The *scale*.' He spoke sweetly; he had drunk most of the Greek stuff himself.

'That's all right,' said Franco, as Teresa stood up and opened a window. 'Not everyone can see the wit in all this. It's something Harriet and I have to deal with every day.'

Julian frowned. It wasn't that he was missing any wit. He tapped some ash on to a saucer. 'Why do you think the old man went for Betamax tapes, then?'

Franco was ready for this. He had given countless interviews over the past years, after all. 'Because they were worthless, Julian. No one else wanted to collect them. It was just Dad with his hippie past making some point about materialism. When you think about it, Betamax tapes almost epitomise material ephemerality and worthlessness.'

Julian nodded. 'So you really don't think it's to do with Mummy?'

'Mummy?' Franco shot a glance at Teresa. He had predicted that Julian would disagree on principle with anything he said, but he had no idea what Julian was getting at with this one.

'Well. We had a Betamax machine, didn't we, when we were small?'

Franco, shrugging, said he couldn't remember. He didn't see how it was relevant. He felt uncomfortable. 'Lots of people bought Betamax machines.'

'But Mummy bought ours,' Julian said 'Don't you remember? She used to record things for us during term so we could watch them in the long vac.'

'Oh yes,' Franco said. Now that he thought about it, yes, he did remember how their mother – who had died from cancer when he was ten – had written to him at school sometimes about the episodes of *Blue Peter* that he wouldn't be missing, after all. There had often been a pile of tapes marked 'Franco' when he got home.

Julian took a final drag. 'And of course she pushed us round in those Maclaren buggies when we were smaller still.'

He pulled a face, as if to say, You know I'm right, don't you? And Franco said, 'I thought you came here to apologise?'

And then Julian said, 'How can you take this stuff at face value, Franco? Are you really so stupid? Remember when I had to explain to you that Mummy was ill?'

'Because she said she was OK! I was only ten!'

'And I was only eight.'

And then Franco said (and he wasn't proud of it), 'Oh, why don't you piss off back to Greece?'

After his departure, Franco gazed down to the cottage, seeing the lights on. He dared not admit to himself how angry he felt. That night, at 3 a.m., he slipped downstairs to look at the baby buggies in their artful ranks – ten rows of seventy-five – and was reassured. With only moonlight in the room, there was truly something beautiful about them; something happy and nostalgic. But they were still, most definitely, crap.

Julian felt bad about his behaviour at the dinner party. When he was relating it to Bethany in bed later that night, though, he was surprised when she pointed out that his smoking at the table had possibly been the worst part of what he'd done.

'Really?' he said.

'People don't do that, Julian,' she said. 'Or not without asking. Did you ask?'

'I can't remember. Shouldn't think so. But anyway, I don't think it was the smoking. He just hates it when I'm right. It's appalling, what they've done here. It's obscene.'

'I'd love to visit Greece,' said Bethany.

'I'd love to take you,' he said. And then he sat up abruptly. 'Let's go tomorrow,' he said.

Bethany laughed. 'You know I can't.'

The thing with Bethany, by the way, had started the very first evening of Julian's occupancy. She had waited for him in the cottage, having baked him a vegetarian moussaka, and warmed up the living room with a log fire. She was a woman who valued the high opinion of others; Franco and Teresa had recognised this trait, and trusted her with the tea room, with fabulous results. Franco was careful not to praise Bethany too often in front of his wife, as Teresa could be jealous of homemaker talents in other women (she didn't mind if they were beautiful). But there was, in fact, little danger of bad feeling. Teresa loved Bethany almost as much as Franco did. This lovely thirty-year-old woman was all smiles; she dealt with the public beautifully; she ran a charming staff of ten; and the fact that she had once been in a freakish road accident with her boyfriend (in which the boyfriend died) was something her adoring employers neither knew about nor suspected. Julian, by contrast, had discovered Bethany's secret trauma within a couple of hours of meeting her. It was just a knack he had. When buried misery was in his vicinity, he was a veritable human divining rod.

'A tree fell on the car,' Bethany said, as she collected his plate and placed it in the newly installed dishwasher. 'That's all.'

'That's *all*?'

'It was on the news,' she said. 'The car was crushed; it was a miracle I got out. His little daughter, who was in the back, she was killed too.'

Julian was confused by Bethany's casual manner in telling this. Was she being brave, or was she in denial? She kept rejecting his sympathy, either way.

'Oh my God. And you were driving?'

'Yes, but that was irrelevant. As I said, a tree fell on the car. It was random.'

It was true that it had been on the news. In the pictures, you could see a huge tree, in full leaf, horizontal, filling the width of the road, with glimpses of the crushed car underneath.

'But you must have blamed yourself.'

'Of course I didn't. Why should I?'

Julian frowned. It was tough sometimes, being the cleverest person in the room.

'You must have had counselling?'

'No, I didn't.'

'No?'

'Look, I don't really like to talk about it. It was five years ago.'

Julian couldn't leave it there.

'In Chinese medicine,' he said, 'they would say that a buried trauma like that would come out in your body – maybe in your hands. Have you had any strange tingling or paralysis or anything?'

Bethany pulled a face. 'I'm not Chinese,' she said.

Julian stopped pushing. He knew he was sounding judgemental. Which was why he decided, by way of changing the subject (and saving the occasion), to take the lovely Bethany to bed.

Franco started to wonder what it was like in the cottage. At night, when he was trying to sleep, he would picture certain aspects of the little house: the turn at the top of the stairs; the fireplace; his mother's watercolour pictures on the walls. He was thinking of his mother more and more since Julian had come home. There was a flash of a memory – a smell of disinfectant;

the treads on a wide flight of stairs; the squeak of rubber-soled shoes on a shiny floor. He never usually bothered about remembering his childhood because Harriet, being three years older, remembered it better than he did. He had always excelled at delegation. But now he realised he needed to ask Harriet a few things. For example, he had never considered it before, but wasn't it odd to have no known relatives on your mother's side? On the Donington side, there had been grandparents, plus cousins and great-uncles. But their mother's side had always been a blank.

As it happened, Harriet had been thinking about her mother, too. It had occurred to her to write a brisk potted history of the family for the second edition of the Hoagland Hall visitor brochure, and she had naturally focused on the more comical or grotesque aspects of the Donington inheritance, such as the 10th Earl's steaming success in the guano business. Of her father and mother, she had reported only the random but obsessive collecting habits of her eccentric father; she'd said nothing about his marriage. Anyone interested enough to research the 13th Earl online, however, would quickly be reminded of his notoriety in youth: headlines from the 1960s concerning the 'Donington Druggies' were accompanied by flash photographs of Harriet's youthful, leggy parents lolling on dark velvet cushions next to members of the Rolling Stones. Such pictures Harriet copied and dragged into folders on her computer. Another picture showed the more sedate golden couple in their thirties, laughing together in the grounds of Hoagland Hall with their three children: Harriet herself (aged six) standing next to Franco (three), and Julian cradled in his mother's arms.

Harriet had never been married. The truth of the matter was that she just didn't appeal to any kind of man, partly because she was always far too keen to impress men with her intelligence (which was not outstanding, in any case); partly because she was grossly insensitive to the feelings of others; but mostly because she had a strange shrieky posh voice which basically triggered an instinctive flight or fight reaction in more or less everyone she talked to. After studying art history, she'd worked for a couple of years as a publicist at a London publisher's, where the family name was a marvellous asset, but the shrieky voice unfortunately was not. It did not endear her to her colleagues, either, that at the end of her first month, she opened her payslip and said, screaming with laughter, 'Fucking hell, you couldn't live on that, could you?' On leaving the publisher's (by mutual agreement), she found it hard to find another berth, and moved back to Wiltshire, where she had lived ever since. From her London days, she still remembered a painful lunch with her father on the occasion of her 25th birthday, at a modest Greek restaurant near the British Museum. His behaviour had baffled her at the time, and it baffled her still. He hadn't even been drunk. He had just taken her hand in his and looked at her with tears in his eyes, as if about to declare 'I love you.' Instead of which he said, bizarrely, 'Your mother loved dolmades *so much*.' And then, when she had taken a breath to say something, he had placed his hand over her mouth and said, 'No, Harriet, please don't.'

Six weeks after Julian's return from Greece, Franco started to suspect that his brother was having an affair with Bethany. He didn't know whether to tell Teresa. If she asked him how he knew, he would have to admit that on most nights now he watched the cottage through a telescope from the top of the house; he had also followed Bethany. One day when he observed Julian strolling through the grounds in the early afternoon, clutching an empty plastic shopping bag (thus, on his way to the village), Franco actually ran down to the cottage and let himself in. Inside, it was exactly what he had expected: untidy but somehow elegantly so. Warm, with the smell of coffee, last night's coal ash, and freshly baked bread. Serious paperback books about the end of capitalism lay pointedly open on the arms of the only comfortable chair in the sitting room; Bethany's knitting basket was on the old settle; on the rustic kitchen table lay two well-thumbed issues of the *New Statesman* and also Julian's laptop, open at his Facebook page, where he had been – of course he had – sharing footage of the latest humanitarian crisis in the Middle East with friends around the world.

Franco didn't stay to look at anything else. All the high-mindedness on display in Julian's cottage made him simply furious. Of course, it was irrational for him to take it personally, but it was too late to change the habit of a lifetime. Julian had always been able to outrage him. When they had briefly shared a London house together in their twenties, Franco had one day reached for the box of teabags in the kitchen and found that Julian had defaced the picture on the box – of a charming Indian tea-picker lady in a sari – by scoring it with a blue ballpoint pen until he'd obliterated it completely. On the morning of Franco's wedding to Teresa at a romantic plantation house on a Caribbean island, Julian had, typically, made a point of visiting the local slavery museum, despite Franco begging him not to. Afterwards, Julian refused to say anything about what he'd learned there, in the interests of not ruining the day for everyone else – which naturally meant he still succeeded in ruining the day for everyone else.

Franco marched back to the house, where he was due to talk with Harriet. On the way, he met Teresa, who looked worried.

'Bethany's got a problem with her hands,' she said. 'She keeps dropping the individual pot pies.'

'What?'

'She says they're going numb. Apparently she's been suppressing a trauma.'

'Suppressing a what?'

'I know. Anyway, I told her to let someone else take over while she gets some rest.'

Franco's face filled with despair. Bethany was indispensable: how could anything happen to Bethany?

Teresa afterwards remembered her surprise at the strange way Franco took the news about Bethany. He spun on his heel and glared back towards the cottage. 'Julian!' he said.

It is now two years later. Julian's memoir, *My Father's Tat*, has been published to much acclaim. Its haunting baby-buggy cover was instantly iconic, and Julian has been compared in literary circles with no less an author than Edmund de Waal. It is no hindrance at all to his success that he is posh and humourless and morally self-satisfied; he is a huge draw at literary festivals, where he takes to the stage barefooted, in a white panama hat and linen trousers, carrying a couple of open beer bottles. It helps his mystique considerably that his beautiful wife Bethany suffers from a psychosomatic disability in her hands which has necessitated his moving into Hoagland Hall, despite his well-known preference for the tiny modest cottage in the grounds.

It was not long after Bethany's first pot-pie incident that Julian happened to bump into Harriet in the village and ask what she was working on. It was this event that apparently tipped the balance for him; made him take his historically important moral stand. After giving him coffee at the flat, she started to complain about the next curatorial challenge at the Hall: Julian might not know this, but along with the Green Ladies, the baby buggies, the Betamax tapes and the seed packets, it seems that their father had collected smelly old moth-eaten Afghan coats, which were both disgusting and a health hazard.

Julian had given his older sister a steady look and said, with significance, 'Afghan coats?'

'Yes!' she had shrieked. 'Can you BELIEVE it? Afghan COATS!'

She and Franco hated to be beaten by anything, she'd carried on. Hadn't they already worked wonders 'conferring value on the worthless'? But the Afghan coats were another thing altogether: they might actually need to be destroyed. It was only a matter of bunging them in the furnace, really. No one would ever know, and they certainly would never care.

'But you can't do that,' Julian had said.

'What are you TALKING about? Of COURSE we can!'

'No,' he said. 'You can't because I absolutely won't let you.'

What critics admired so much in *My Father's Tat* was the sheer emotional maturity of it. Julian described how he had returned from abroad to find his father's profoundly charged collections displayed in the family house as objects of ridicule by siblings blind to their true heart-breaking significance. They had always known that their mother had been a rags-to-riches model in the 1960s, but had they bothered to find out about her background working in Boots the Chemist selling mass-produced pictures of white horses leaping ashore through snowy white breakers, or women with long faces and weirdly verdant complexions? Did they not remember that their mother had been married at Chelsea Town Hall wearing an Afghan coat? That her only dowry had been some out-of-date packets of seeds? The insensitive older siblings did not come well out of *My Father's Tat*. At every stage they stubbornly resisted the obvious interpretation of the collections they had inherited: that their father had never recovered from his bereavement, and that the Hoagland Hall collections, far from being the mere raw material for larky monuments to ephemerality, were in fact powerful testaments to loss.

In the end, Franco decided to move his family back to London. He knew when he was beaten. He resumed his stockbroking and appointed an agent to oversee the business of the Hall. He didn't care if Julian lived there, because at least it meant that Bethany was all right. He still rejects Julian's interpretation of their father's tat; but his objections grow weaker. His only act of retaliation against Julian was to inform Bethany that experts in Chinese medicine (he consulted three) completely rejected Julian's absurd and amateur prediction that the trauma would come out 'through the hands'. But by then it was too late. *My Father's Tat* was winning prizes for non-fiction; Julian had been a guest editor on the *Today* programme; visitors to the Hall were issued with packets of Kleenex and guided in a new direction so that the baby buggy room ('Devastating' – The *Observer*) was the clear emotional climax of the tour.

It was too late, too, when the German woman wrote to Franco from Patmos, enclosing some documents that Julian had left behind. Franco received the little parcel at his office and at first was just bemused. The German woman was still livid with Julian, it seemed. When Julian had lived with her (she wrote), he had made her feel guilty for working all the time! Even though he had made no effort to contribute! He just played his damned guitar! (She used a lot of exclamation marks.) He had also broken things of hers, and when she was upset by this, he had accused her of caring about things more than she cared about people! Franco understood completely why, even years after Julian's departure, the German woman still felt these injustices so keenly.

And then, among the papers of Julian's, was a letter from the 13th Earl, their father. Written when Julian was in his twenties, it had been preserved unopened between the pages of *The Magus*, which is why it had taken the German woman such a long time to locate it. Franco sat down and looked at it with trepidation. A letter from his father was a rare enough object in itself; this one had been sent around the time when his father had begun his collecting. And Julian hadn't even opened it? Franco braced himself, and opened the letter resignedly. This would be the proof that Julian was right, wouldn't it? Here would be the authentic howl of the bereaved husband; the key to the true, shattering significance of . . . their father's tat.

But no, in fact it wasn't.

Dear Julian, (*it said*)

May I ask, first of all, did you receive the birthday cheque? I had no reply from you, but I have learned to read little into that, as I know you are above such everyday conventions. I merely note that the cheque was cashed with the usual alacrity, so naturally I hope the dibs are in the filial coffers as intended.

On the subject of thank-yous, I received the educational paperbacks you sent on the evils of materialism; they gave me an excellent laugh, and you will be pleased to hear that, as a direct result, I was at Tiverton on Friday and bought in the sale there an absolute mountain of meaningless crap! I can't tell you how liberating and weirdly life-affirming this was. Old video tapes, old pictures, all sorts of ghastly and worthless impedimenta. The first delivery is due this morning. So thank you from the bottom of my heart for – as always – showing me the way. There is a similar sale in Worcester on the 24th where I intend to sweep the board. They are advertising a job lot of 'baby buggies'. Does this mean a buggy of small proportions, or a buggy for a baby to drive? I sincerely hope not the latter, but can't quite picture the former. I suppose all will be apparent on the day.

I am sorry that Franco and Harriet will have the bother of throwing all the crap away when I am dead, but it gives me so much pleasure to imagine how much your eventual inheritance of such stuff will aggravate your finer feelings that I just can't resist carrying on. All of you children take things so deeply to heart! Your dear mother and I always agreed that no good would come of it. Lighten up, Julian, for goodness' sake. You only live once, old chap.

Yours affec,
Dad

AMIT CHAUDHURI

WENSLEYDALE

For love, all love of other sights controls,
And makes one little room an everywhere.
Let sea-discoverers to new worlds have gone,
Let maps to other, worlds on worlds have shown,
Let us possess one world, each hath one, and is one.

My face in thine eye, thine in mine appears . . .

I've always wanted to be a writer, baba. I want to express myself – there's so much beauty in small things. I don't have the skill, baba – but I love words! What if I hadn't been born into this family? If I hadn't been Sir Bikash's son, Sir Purnendu's nephew? Maybe I *could* have been a writer. There would have been no compulsion to read Economics. I was a simpleton. I loved Cambridge. I hated Economics. I didn't understand it. I didn't have the *courage* to tell my parents that my heart lay in life and not the burra sahib stuff that was *their* life. I mean the simple things. Sunlight on a January morning. I am sitting now in the sun.

*

I love winter sunshine. Soft and sweet. *Mishti.* The Bengali word gets it best, doesn't it, Amit? The Bengalis are not a sweet people, but they've devoted much superfluous energy to sweetness. Nolen gur, payesh, kheer et cetera. The sunshine is more palatable.

*

The sun is far away. By the time the rays reach Lower Circular Road and fall on the porch at the back where I'm sitting, they've – how should I say it, baba – become a kind of touch. Is it all right to put it like that, baba? I used to read the *Statesman* here. I mean till a few years ago. When Irani wrote his Caveat every day, and Calcutta Notebook teemed with the bustle of the city. Irani lost his marbles before he died. There was another journalist in the *Statesman* – very erudite – who went mad from time to time. Ranjan Sen, that's the one! I've moved to the *Telegraph* – I'm reading it as I sit here – impatiently. One thing I've noticed is that its Letters to the Editor is more plebeian than the *Statesman*'s. I guess that's to be expected. These are not literate times, are they, baba? Bad times. Sometimes Irani said something I felt I had to respond to. As you know. I sent you a cutting once – quite right. Mostly in agreement, but I also did write to register protest. They published my letters in full, baba. They'd put them on the top. I'm not a man of great achievements, but at least my voice was heard. My friends would read the letter and call me. There were times when I'd have a difference of opinion with Jyoti Basu. Let me add, Amit, that Jyoti babu and I liked each other. He'd drop in for dinner. He came unannounced once. He adored Chinese food. We ordered from Jimmy's Kitchen. Talked late into the night. The marvellous Uma was unfazed. She had a thing or two to say about politics – not necessarily what Jyoti babu liked to hear.

*

What are you up to this morning? Done with breakfast? Omelette? You don't have eggs?

I'm not disturbing you, am I, baba? *Do* come for tea again. Thursday maybe? You aren't off anywhere, are you? You're always travelling, baba . . .

*

Once you told me, *Travel is an education.* What did you mean, baba? I couldn't grasp what you were saying. I want to. You hate travelling, you said. I find the notion extraordinary. I would love to take a flight. To Spain. Where my brother lives. To Paris. I haven't seen England in over forty years. I miss strawberries. You're lucky, baba. Very lucky. Are you busy next Thursday?

*

Ideas come to me for stories. I don't think I'll have the gumption to write them, baba. You must be very disciplined. Do you write every morning? Extraordinarily disciplined. Me – I have nothing to *do*! But I *have* seen the world. A long time ago, but I think I've seen a dashed sight more than the people who come over for tea. Don't laugh, baba, but I've begun to make notes in a diary. For stories. Do you do that, baba? Of course, when I say 'write' or 'make notes', you know what I mean. I dictate to Uma. Like I did the letter I sent you about your novel. The words are mine – but that's Uma's handwriting. This morning she wrote two letters – one to the *Telegraph*, the other to a woman called Jacqueline who lives in Somerset – a friend of a friend's, who came to see us two years ago. We've written to each other since.

*

Jacqueline's great-grandfather died in Calcutta. McDermott or McDimmot. A lot of Scotsmen in Calcutta in those days. Building schools and colleges – jolly intrepid fellows! – succumbing to the heat. Did Tagore first hear 'Auld Lang Syne' in Calcutta or in London? Fascinating, baba. So she wants to visit the country again. Never been to Calcutta. I've asked her to tea. She said she'd bring me some cheese. Stilton. I love cheese, baba. It's the one thing you don't get here. Eating Amul is like biting into a salted eraser. Ha ha ha ha! Uma and I love things that – that *smell* a little.

*

You're right, Amit. I hear most things are available now – on the market. Though Uma says Johnson's has the most reasonable prices. You know – cheese, sausages, HP Sauce. No, I don't care for HP Sauce. Inexplicable predilection. Stranger than Marmite, which I spread on my toast once in Cambridge. Someone smuggled it into hall as a joke. An experiment. You've never tasted it? It looks like chawanprash, tastes nutritious. Uma says Johnson's charges less than the malls. Have you been to a mall, baba? What, every other day? They sound incredible. Johnson's is in the last aisle of New Market. I *adore* New Market. I haven't been in years. Uma goes every week. You're right, I *could* go. There are no steps. The stick would help – and Uma can hold me. But I can't sustain it. The trip to the drawing room to the bedroom to the porch at the back is sufficient.

You get Kalimpong cheese in the shops next to Johnson's. And Bondel cheese too – overly salted, rough brown discs, baba, white on the inside. Charming. Smoked, you know. We went to Bondel long ago. Outing to a lunch hosted by a friend. Manager at Dunlop. The dust and fumes we inhaled! It comes back to me when I eat the cheese. That Bondel smoke.

*

The house we live in – you say you like it. It isn't beautiful, but, yes – it has character. It didn't exist when I was growing up. This bit was the lawn of the mansion you see across the wall. Have a look when you come next. Yes, it belongs to the Nepalese High Commissioner. A man called Khatri.

It has an enormous lift, baba. Slow and ponderous. I spent

half my childhood in it. Going up and down. Top floor was my uncle's; first floor my father's. Sir Purnendu and Sir Bikash. Adroit men. A little too taken with the Raj, Bikash jethu. But serious men. Unlike their progeny – I include myself. Mostly duffers, our lot.

This house came up in 1940. When you're here again, please look at the picture of the man by the door to our bedroom. You can't miss it. Just turn your head left before you enter. My grandfather. He built the house next door.

*

My aunts played tennis on the lawn. But Bikash jethu's wife was a simple soul – made superlative chhanar tarkari and uchhe begun. All the joys of a Bengali household we were in danger of losing, she brought back. Renukadevi Bandhopadhyay. From a zamindari family settled in Balasore. Very graciously Bengali, though I did wonder if she could speak Oriya. She was shy, never held a tennis racquet. Sang kirtans in the evening – beautiful voice, baba.

*

Baba, you're sure that chicken tetrazzini isn't an Italian dish? You think it may be a Bengali invention? I can't say if we used to eat it at Firpo's – but at Sky Room, regularly. And those long glasses in which they served prawn cocktail. Strictly speaking it was shrimp, not prawn – but delectable. You had to be in possession of a long spoon to dip into the glass and salvage the dregs of Marie Rose sauce – or you had to be a crane.

*

Ha ha ha. You know the story. The fox invited the crane home for dinner and served soup in a bowl. He lapped it up in a leisurely way while the poor crane watched. Then the crane asked the fox to come over so that he could have his revenge. Birds are vengeful, baba. I'm transfixed by their animosity to each other when I'm on the porch. It was the fox's turn to go hungry when crane served soup in a long jug.

You had to be a crane to do justice to the prawn cocktail, baba. Or you needed the thin spoon. Or you went hungry.

*

Is there a chance the Sky Room might reopen? Amit? You discovered it in the Eighties, didn't you? Such a cocoon. It's been fifteen years since its doors closed, but that duffer Arvind Sharma – keeps inviting himself over for tea – said it's going to open under new management.

You think that's – ha ha ha! Too funny, baba. You're right. You're right! As likely as Netaji coming back and taking charge! Isn't that what we all want?

I see. Yes, I heard it was boarded up for years with a notice from the trade union. And that's gone. I see. Part of a new showroom. I see.

*

I have before me *The Namesake* – and *Atonement* by Ian McEwan. What do you think of Jhumpa Lahiri, baba? Not the person. I suppose you've met her? I see – in London and Calcutta. Striking woman. Those eyes! Uma and I would love to ask her to tea. I thought the style in the stories was quite – lucid. Lucid, yes. No, I can't believe you've stopped reading books! I'm a nobody – I sometimes read two or three books at a time. Stopped reading fiction! Why, baba? Ian McEwan? *The Cement Garden?* I must make a note of it. Uma's going to the club. She'll get it from the library. *St Mawr?* I *have* read *Women in*

Love – decades ago! Will you tell us about Lawrence when you come for tea next? When can you come for tea?

*

Lawrence Durrell. I read him twenty, thirty years ago. Acute sense of the foreign, baba. I felt I was in Egypt. I could *hear* the muezzin clearly. Of course, I *can* hear the muezzin. Four times a day. In the dawn I'm fast asleep. But from Lower Circular Road the mosques in Beck Bagan are audible. In the winter especially. Paul Bowles? Never heard of him.

*

Amit, we saw a film on TV. *The Hours*. Is it Virginia Woolf? Oh! I see. I *see*. How interesting!

What's *your* opinion? Of Virginia Woolf, I mean. Unhappy woman, wasn't she? Baba, can you tell me *exactly* what stream of consciousness is? Is it just free-flowing thoughts?

*

I got polio soon after I came back. Must have been '54. Don't know how. Put my right leg out of action more or less. Then my right arm. Which is why I can't really write without Uma. She's my amanuensis. Is that the word? Amanuensis.

My father took my brother and me on a tour before I returned to Cambridge. European tour. Vienna. Cable cars. The Alps. Pâté de foie gras. I love pâté. Then came back. With a Third from Trinity. Hated Economics, you see. Next year, fell ill.

*

The last time I went out was three years ago. I *know* you'd like to have me over for dinner, baba. It's the steps. I can't climb up the stairs. It's why I've stopped going to the club. Five steps at the entrance. I became a spectacle! The bearers lifted me up in the wheelchair. Mortifying.

So Uma goes to the club twice a week. Brings back a recherché something. Chicken pantheras.

*

I would love to be in Cambridge again. St John's Street. Gonville and Caius. The girls on bicycles. I wasted my time drinking with the boys. Too shy to say a word to a girl. Once we drove to Grantchester.

No, I can't say I felt anything like that. Racism, you mean? I was a callow youth, baba. When were you there last? You gave a talk at Sidney Sussex College? How *delightful*! You must have gone to St John's Street?

*

You hate Cambridge, Amit? Extraordinary. I'd forgotten you'd lived there. You say it's perfect for a two-day visit? *I* loved it – narrow streets widening into the quads at Trinity and King's. The revelation of grandeur. Trinity depresses you? My word. No, there were no malls or shopping centres in our day. I'm sure you're right about the redneck taxi drivers. Bill Gates is pouring money into the place, is he? I had no idea the region was so deprived. My word.

*

We'll see you at six on Friday, then, baba? Thank you. Thank you. That would be lovely. Thank *you*. The *both* of you. Your wife is lovely. Such hidden depths. She spoke so eloquently about the nineteenth century – I was utterly disarmed. Really.

I want to hear more from her. About Dinesh Chandra. Pyarechand. Michael. We are *so* illiterate.

*

We are your social life here? Ha ha ha. That's *too* funny. We're very lucky to have you in this wretched city, baba. I'm nothing – as you know. *Tuchho manush*.

There'll be two others on Friday. I must forewarn you. Mitra and Dutta. Related to me on my mother's side. Well-intentioned characters. I call them 'the detectives'. They look and sound like detectives. You'll see. I mean they rather ostentatiously try to look like everyone else. Difficult to remember later. Observe them at leisure. They will not know you. They do not read.

*

What is it you like *least* about being in Calcutta? You once said it isn't the traffic jams or fumes you find difficult – it's the pettiness. That's right – you came back because you were *missing* the traffic jams! Ha ha ha ha! This city's the place to return to if you're afflicted by that kind of homesickness.

*

Baba, I'm sorry. I'm terribly sorry. Could you possibly come *next* Friday? The cook's gone off suddenly. To his village. Says his older brother's ill. He does it every month. Drives us mad. No, we can't get a new cook. He's been with us for thirty years. We have to put up and shut up.

*

I'm so glad, baba. *Delighted* you like Uma's sandwiches this time. We were thinking of introducing a variation. She thought you'd like something more traditional – shingara! Then she changed her mind. You're right, you can have shingara anywhere. Yes, they *are* unique. She experiments. Adds a bit of yoghurt, I think, to the mayonnaise and cucumber.

*

Do you know, we hardly knew there was a famine? I was ten years old. I'd see them on my way to school. Emaciated wandering figures. Too tired to walk sometimes. They'd come to the gates with their bowls and say *Phan de ma*! Our lives went on as usual, baba. Yes.

*

Buddhadev babu! I don't know what to say about him. Very Bengali. Proud of his potted plants. Jyoti babu was Bengali too – but imperious. A bar at law and all that. Buddhadev babu – a fan of Lorca . . . I don't know. I don't know. They say the state will take a new turn under him. Do you think so? Do you think he's capable? Wants to bring in foreign investment. Can he? I know he's a good *translator.*

Yes, he came to tea on Wednesday. With his wife. Sweet, simple woman. Chatty.

*

I'm not a communist, baba. Yes, we did have a few Naxalites over in the Sixties. An education. The way they saw the world. Very exciting, their passion for total revolution. The blood rushes to the head, the adrenaline . . . I was a closet Naxal for a while. I'm very susceptible, baba. I love life. I want every person, ugly or handsome, stupid or bright, to live life to the full. The Naxals wanted that too. Then they got carried away.

I was much more mobile then . . .

*

Yes, the cook's OK, baba. He doesn't do a lot. He spends half the day in his room. Don't know what he does. I suspect he's a bit of a maniac for khaini. He and Gobinda come to the sitting room when there's a cricket match on; Uma lets them take charge of the TV.

Mostly the cook is at a loose end, baba. Because Uma will order dinner from Calcutta Club. Suruchi is splendid for Bengali food – just simple fare with unpronounceable names: you know, chhachda and rui machher kalia.

Thank you ever so much for sending over the chhana patal, baba. Very grateful. Uma says it's 'out of this world'. Her exact words. Chhana, and patal. Never the twain could meet, I would have thought. But it works perfectly. We were in a daze of chhana patal all afternoon.

*

It's very quiet. *Cholbe na, cholbe na!* Jyoti babu's legacy. He'd grumble to me about it. 'The cadres are out of hand and we have to keep them happy.' I don't even know what they're objecting to. Do you?

You'd think it makes no difference to me. I don't go out. But I abhor a deathly calm, baba – the grinding down of activity. Quite unlike the quiet of Sundays. Or the quiet of my childhood. So much more tentative and slower it was then. But bandh days! I feel the life ebbing from me.

*

You said the other day that you came back because you couldn't take the silence. Was it 1999?

Not the discrimination or the damp. It was the quiet you couldn't bear. Is that true? *Too* funny, baba! You missed noise?

Ah, the background hum. I see. I never thought of it that way. I prized the silence in Cambridge – never felt gloomy. I think we're educated in that way – we put a high price on silence, on privacy. Maybe we don't even realise we don't want to be alone. Impossible to be alone here, isn't it, baba? One is always part of *some* bloody thing. All these people inviting themselves over for tea.

How do you write, baba? Can you compose sentences with people around you? It's true, the French *did* write in cafes. You knew someone who did? Kolatkar? No, don't know him, baba. Extraordinary!

*

Hello.

Sorry, yes, it's me, baba.

Sorry. Yes. No, I don't have a sore throat. I'm well, thank you. I just change my voice a little when I pick up the phone. Quite right.

A long story, baba. I'll tell you another time. Stupid litigation. It'll bore you.

My great-aunt, baba. Don't know what possessed her – a recherché religious impulse. Penitence for that husband of hers. Left the house to a religious organisation. Ananda Seva Kendra. *This* house. The document has no legality, baba. But they use it to harass us. Ananda Seva Kendra. You'd think they'd have better things to do, the scoundrels – social work; singing bhajans to Hari. I mean, *we* could do with some social work. My pension is absurd, you'd laugh if I told you. I have sold two of my mother's earrings – thank God for her!

The Ananda Seva Kendra should do some seva for *me*.

Forgive me, baba. I've become very careful when I pick up the phone. You'll hear a different voice now and again. Yes, a croak, Ha ha. Meant to confuse them.

*

Hello.

Amit!

Forgive me.

Yes, of *course* you should come. We're dying to see you. Don't say another word. Thursday? Can you? I'd like you to meet Jacqueline. She's here. Remember I told you? Her grandfather's buried in Park Street or Park Circus.

*

You're going on Monday? That *is* soon. But Thursday should be possible, baba, shouldn't it?

Two weeks? We'll still be here when you're back, I promise. Ha ha ha.

You're sad, baba? Extraordinary! What I would do to go! London in the spring!

Oh, to escape the heat . . .

Yes, the mangoes will have arrived when you return.

What makes you sad?

Does it happen each time? The alienation you mention? Everything you love feeling alien when you go? Because you get into a funk each time, don't you?

You'll be back in two weeks, baba . . . True. True. The heart can't distinguish between two weeks and two years. Neither can the head, really. Sometimes I feel that it was last month that I went to the club.

I have a shameless request, baba. I'm sorry. Can you bring me some Wensleydale? Only if it's no trouble. Promise me you won't try if it's a problem.

SUSIE BOYT

PEOPLE WERE SO FUNNY

When she ran it through her mind there were three things lately that had made her stop and shake her head sharply and wonder if there wasn't something going on. Not a syndrome or anything, nothing with an actual name, it was just some small stirrings, not from every corner either, not yet, not thick and fast, but a gathering of little facts, facts or rather episodes with opinions attached to them which appeared to be speeding up and might just need her attention.

The 168 on the way to the hospital on Friday was struggling, making rude shuddering noises and sudden ill-tempered hypochondriac jolts. A man got on, rough in his appearance, his skin had too much texture, cross-hatched with scars, almost darned-looking. He was not exactly unsympathetic but undeniably he was falling to bits and flakes of him were settling on the plaid bus-cloth, on the bald and shiny shoulders of his jacket, on his shoes and he was – and there was no nice way of saying it – he was stinky. And he did that thing that people always do with a bus that is completely empty, he came and installed himself next to her. He spread his thighs so she had to make herself small. To have a stranger's leg rubbing against you in ancient suit trousers with stains dark and pale and loose skin and bits of crusted god knows what adhering to the folds in his face, on a windy Tuesday morning, when you were wearing a new pair of tights in a dark blue shade named 'admiral', well she was not sure she was equal to it.

'Hey,' he said with an extravagant smile. He had gone in his way all-out.

'Oh hello,' she answered unsteadily. That was her mistake.

'Nice day,' he said.

'Hmmm,' and then because she felt a bit sorry for him in his sorry state, 'the light's beautiful and the sky's such a lovely colour this morning.'

'Blue,' he said flatly.

It could not be denied.

'You know something?' He turned to her with an air of concern a bit too suddenly. His lips were dangerously close to her collarbone. She felt the sourness of his breaths. 'You're not bad looking, for your age, you should get yourself some decent clothes, make-up, do something with your hair. You dress like my grandma. What you scared of? Can't be *that* old.'

She was two weeks shy of thirty-one.

She switched off, willed him to go away, disintegrate, explode. She closed her eyes. It was something akin to vertigo that she felt. It was true that when she bought clothes the last few times, she had leafed through various catalogues thinking *that* might look inoffensive and efficient on the ward. Striped and checked things, cheering, muted end of cheering, not tactless, not banal. Her mother used to have a dress shop. She liked elegance, or rather she liked neatness which was really the absence of things. She liked her daughter 'put-together', everything in order, shipshape, house-proud. Even as a child Beth had been dressed like a forty-year-old woman: brass buttons, white collars, inverted-pleat skirts, ready at the drop of a hat for deck quoits on a luxury liner, or presenting a posy of violets to the Queen . . .

She came out of the lift on the 13th floor, the sleeves of her blue and white dress rolled and ready, her nursey white trainers squelching the new-mown-grass-look lino. She approached the bed where her mother lay sleeping under a green cellular blanket. A television suspended from the ceiling on a dark metal arm was playing softly. She crept into the chair next to her mother's bed. It was a hospital drama that was on TV, the surgeon, an old-school, chalk-striped, bow-tied gent was ill himself and trying to hide it from his colleagues who were beginning to pick up on his irrational behaviour. Beth took some fruit out of her bag, arranging it silently in the small basket on the tray table at the foot of the bed. Her mother could not eat solid food but she liked to have some fruit close to her. Like a pet, she said. A bit of life going on. Today she had black cherries and thin-skinned yellow grapes and there were two clean pin-tucked cotton lawn nightdresses, neatly folded.

A new woman was being brought to the bed that was diagonally opposite; a pair of nurses stood by as she unpacked her washbag and her handbag into the locker which slid a little, giddy on its wheels. She was helped into bed by a lanky son or grandson. She undid her pearls, gave them to him for safekeeping, which seemed daring. She asked if he had eaten and when he nodded, said he had had a baked potato, she closed her eyes.

Oh no! A couple of feet to the right of her mother's bed she spied some blood on the floor, five dark flower-shaped patches. God! She fetched a few wetted tissues from the toilets, sank discreetly to her knees, rubbing at the marks until they were gone.

The jagged outline of the blood took much longer to get rid of than the middle portion. She thought of her mother's lipstick adhering to the edges of her mouth after the saturated colour on the fleshy part had disappeared. She washed her hands thoroughly, spritzed them with hand sanitiser. Last month a small blonde girl wearing an orange hoody that said *LA County Jail* had come up on to the ward to visit and kept referring to the bottle of blue spray attached to the end of the bed as ham appetiser . . .

Beth wanted to say something amazing to her mother, something inspiring, the opposite of despair. 'You know there is a whole world out there or at least half a world in any case on the other side of the wall, you can see it from the landing by the lifts, through the picture windows and I'm not saying it's entirely composed of roses and starched tablecloths, or string quartets in hotel foyers and raspberry mousse cake on pistachio-coloured scalloped plates three times a day, but some of it is really something. Look at the yellow toy train pulling out of Euston Station! Look at that flock of seagulls, in an arrow formation, so carefree and deluxe! It's a world that is worth getting well for. Sometimes it is, anyway. Now and then. Dark blue mornings, green afternoons . . . You've got to believe it. Sort of got to. If you can. The moon even can be unbelievably beautiful, last night it was, and really slight, scant almost, just a tiny curved beam but it gave out so much light.'

There could be romance to their convalescence. That was what she wanted to convey. Beyond grief and mourning and the humiliations of age and poor health there were quite a few golden things to be unearthed. They could make up their minds to go after pleasure together, hail it like a taxi, grab it by the lapels. They could sit in chairs in the garden between the flowering currant and the sweet pea cages and remember things late into the evening. In a wheelchair at Manchester Square they could laugh, not unkindly, in the face of *The Laughing Cavalier. Sleeping Beauty*, they could save up for at Christmas, with Russian ballerinas; watch the rose-coloured dancers unfurl their limbs against the deep forest. You could not force people to decline in such a way, but you could open the doors to it, usher the best things on to the stage.

They had each other . . .

But in her dreams where it was often possible to say such things, to mount an argument for maximum life, her mother would raise her arms above her head and whisper weakly, 'Please don't shoot.'

Once when she was returning from a quick coffee with a school friend, her bus paused opposite the hospital and from the top deck she made out her mother lurking on the shallow hospital steps with a clutch of other smoking women, some of whom were attached by white wires to mobile drips. Her mother, unaccompanied by such a device, sucking on her cigarette, looked so forlorn. Her quilted satin dressing gown, salmon-coloured, farmed salmon, came over as fancy dress in its pavement setting, a seaside landlady from a hundred years ago. That night when Beth lay awake in bed with some bread and butter strips, she googled 'mobile drip stands' on her phone. The deluxe version had four hooks to hold containers and a five-bar base with castors making it stable and very easy to manoeuvre. It was actually quite handsome. Seventy-nine pounds did seem reasonable.

Her mother was still sleeping softly, the murmurs from the hospital series faint and soothing. Beth opened her book and, just as she began to read, the second thing, the thing that made her wonder, happened. A nurse approached, a new one she had not seen before. Beth rose and smiled across the patient. 'Thank you so much for all you're doing for us,' she said.

'Your sister's good as gold.' The nurse smiled too.

'Thank you so so much!' Beth said. She felt a bolt of pride spread about her.

Then – 'My – ? Oh.'

The third thing was nothing new, just something not quite right she remembered freshly from two years earlier. It had taken her a while to work it out.

The night her father lay dying her mother swore.

She was getting that feeling you got before you started a heavy cold, she told the nurse, she told Dr Clarkson, who had been their doctor since before Beth was born.

'Oh dear,' her mother said. 'This is the last straw.'

'Bad luck,' the doctor muttered tonelessly.

'Could you take my temperature please?' she asked. Dr Clarkson rinsed the thermometer in the sink in the adjoining bathroom, wiped it on a hand towel, but he did nothing more.

They were all in the bedroom at her parents'. It was the eleventh hour, the twelfth. Her mother was providing a running commentary of her symptoms, listing them on her fingers: the hot and cold feeling travelling up and down her spine, the beginnings of a headache, the salt and pepper sensation in her eyes.

They were at the stage with her father when you listen for the breaths, counting the gaps between them as they slow. His poor dry face, his frail body, were right at the edge of what they could endure. The air was hot, the atmosphere stiff. The radio was playing quietly, a drama about a cricket match, something like that, in a country village. Stumps, scones . . . Beth turned the dial round slowly until all the sound went out. The silence felt valuable.

It is about to happen, she thought.

'What would you advise me to do, doctor?' her mother was saying, fingers clasped to her pulse. She compared the heaviness in her legs to cold treacle.

The doctor smiled and shook his head. The nurse from the Catholic hospice actually snorted.

Beth slipped down to the kitchen, fetched some Echinacea and a vial of vitamin C, a brown bottle of paracetamol tablets and put them on a sandwich tray with a glass of mineral water.

'Not now.' Her mother shook her head in irritation.

'K.'

The doctor sat down. That had to be a sign. He was emotional, religious, Church of England, high end, and if you asked him how he was he tended to answer. One memorable time: 'Well I can't help wondering why I am drawn to taking on more and more patients rather than improving my relationships with my children. What is that, do you think?' He had four children, two of each, well-spaced. It was a rhetorical question she realised just in the nick of time.

Beth had a brother, Robin, in Florida, who was on a plane home for their father as they spoke. He was successful and glamorous in a square-shouldered, flawless, American way. He loved Miami. The air he said was 'milky'. She couldn't imagine what that meant. Soft? It sounded lovely in any case. She ought to visit him one day. Nowhere in the world, she had heard, she had read, would you encounter more glamorous women in the 100–110 age bracket. That was encouraging.

He had three small girls but it was painful to think of because Lauren, his wife, liked them very much away.

'I suppose the nurse can always stay on for me,' her mother said.

The nurse's face!

And then her father died and that was that and she left the room so that her mother could have some time alone with him, and then sat with him alone herself for a spell, unsure of what to say.

'It's OK, Dad,' she murmured every now and then as he was cooling. 'Doing well. It's all right. That's it. That's it now. Doing so so so so well. Lots of love.'

She felt strongly the throb of shyness in the room, a warm, loving embarrassment rising from him, from her, hovering above them, brightening the bedroom as the natural light failed.

Later that evening, she sat with her mother in the sitting room on the sofa. Her mother held a cushion to her chest.

'Could you eat something?' Beth asked.

'I don't think so. Not tonight.'

'Is there anything I can do for you?'

'There is something.'

'Sure,' she said.

'Will you stay?'

'Of course I will,' she said. 'I could stay all week if you like?'

'I was thinking more, permanently. Move back home.'

That she had not been expecting. She had a small flat in Hackney with her boyfriend Will who was a primary school teacher. 'Islington borders', her mother said. Beth was head of English at an academic girls' school. Exams were done and it was the start of the long summer break.

'I know you have your own life now, but I don't think I can see my way forward if you're not here.'

'Oh.'

'Please Beth.'

That was another story, hard to contain because it stretched and stretched and was not to be gone into here, not now – the headmistress who said you can always come back, *in some capacity*; the day she had packed her possessions at the flat and they had fitted easily into the boot of a Ford Galaxy – but the thing she was remembering, not ruefully but with a certain sense of things not being as they should, the third thing, was that as her father lay dying her mother had them all fussing that she might be getting a cold. It was a pressurised time, of course, and it was always impossible to be certain about reality as opposed to your sensations at such moments, and added to that it was essential in life to try to see round corners, to take things on the slant, but it struck her now that they shouldn't have been rinsing thermometers under taps and messing about with bottles of pills for her mother in his very last moments. It wasn't respectful.

'I am so sorry, Dad,' she whispered all the way back into the past.

Her mother was making tiny uncomfortable movements in her hospital bed. Perhaps she was in pain. She opened her eyes.

'Hi, Mum. How was your night? Looks like it's going to be a beautiful day.' The morning sky was blazing now, with streaks of pink laddering the blue.

'Hello dear.'

'Can I get you anything? I think the nurse will be over in a bit to take you for a wash and brush up and change your nightie and everything.'

'It's so nice to have you sitting there in the chair,' her mother said. 'I love to see you reading when I wake up. So civilised and comforting, you look like a painting.'

'Thank you!'

'Oh, you've brought me lovely fresh things.'

'Oh good. There was quite a nice thing on the telly I was watching earlier. It's very peaceful on the ward today.'

'You're such a good girl.' She lowered her voice, 'Janet, you know, in the bed next door, she said how come your daughter comes every day for hours?'

Beth reached for her mother's hand from the chair and they both closed their eyes and dozed for a bit.

'That doctor deserves to be struck off!' Her mother was livid.

'Oh no! What's he done?'

'It's what he's not done. Chiefly, his job!'

'That's terrible.'

'I am going to have to make a complaint. Can you find me a pen and some paper please?'

'Hang on. I've got some in here.' She fished in her bag for a red notebook she had bought at the hospital shop for writing down the doctors' remarks and instructions. She handed it to her mother. 'Sorry, let me find a pen that writes. Here you go. But what did he not do, the doctor, exactly?'

Her mother shook her head with heavy emotion.

'I'm too tired for all this,' she said.

'Poor Mum.'

'He says they can't do anything more for me. Says I've to go home.'

'Oh I am so so sorry.'

'Yes.'

'When do they say you should go home?'

'Asap, I think. Yesterday. They're ever so keen to get rid of me.'

'Oh no. They are beasts.'

Just then Beth spied Mr L her mother's oncologist finishing up with another patient. Although six foot four and solid and thick-set he had the consultant's knack of disappearing into thin air. She took her chance, chasing him down the corridor. If only it was Dr Clarkson. He didn't make you dive like a crazed goal-keeper just in order to speak to him. Will, her ex, had given her a Valentine's card once with a picture of a goalie on it, looking shy and pale and anxious and knock-kneed with the caption in black capitals 'You're a Keeper.'

Ha!

She sort of threw herself between Mr L and the bank of lifts, took a moment to catch her footing, find her breath. She tried to talk slowly and intelligently. 'Good morning, Mr L. Might you have a second, for a minute? And I do apologise for haranguing you. My mother says you have told her there's nothing more you can do for her here. Can we have a quick – about the kind of support she is going to need at home? And what's available because, and I hate to ask about timing but could we speak about that as well? We have to pace ourselves I suppose is what I am saying. If that is what we—'

He ushered her into a ward where the corner bed was empty, yanking the plastic privacy screen to make a little room. 'Well, let me tell you first that all the scans have come back clear. We can't find anything. I know she says she feels unwell and I am not absolutely ruling out the possibility of something emerging, some . . . *shoots* . . . but at this stage the best thing is for her to go home and we'll run tests again in three months' time.'

'No, I – Oh, I see. Right. Well, that's good, isn't it?'

He was already halfway down the corridor when he turned back to face her unexpectedly. She had forgotten to thank! 'Thank you so much for everything you've done for us,' Beth said quickly.

'A funny thing,' he put a thoughtful hand to his chin. 'Friend of mine, on call over the weekend, had a young man come into casualty in an ambulance, Saturday night, quarter past twelve. With a case of dandruff.'

'Oh no! How maddening—'

'We just can't operate like that.'

She was surprised to hear a doctor use the word operate in that way. She felt a strong desire to stick up for the young man with the minimal ailment. He was probably just lonely. Middle of the night – didn't know what to do with himself. It was a mental health situation he was presenting with I expect, she thought.

And then, almost as though he heard her thinking, Mr L spoke to her severely.

'A heart condition and loneliness are *not* one and the same. No. It isn't helpful to pretend they are when we have such limited resources. Even if we didn't.'

She was half amazed to hear herself answer, 'I do completely understand. But can't you see it might feel the same to a patient. And people can die of heartbreak. They really can—'

'In books!' he said. 'In books!'

'Well,' she said, 'maybe . . .' They were both laughing, she shyly and he, she felt, with a sense of how ridiculous the world was and how civilised it was to remember that fact when your work was life and death, undiluted, every day.

'You're the expert and I know what you're saying but' – that wasn't quite right, she tried again – 'Look I need to know how –' but that wouldn't do either, and finally when she found the words she needed (why was she always so slow!), 'But may I ask you,' that was the question, *yes*, 'why does my mother feel so dreadful all the time? Is it just the effects of the treatment last year? How do I keep her going is what I am trying to—' But Mr L had disappeared. She had a strong feeling that were she a man she would be treated to a higher level of *something*. She ran to the edge of the ward but there was absolutely no trace, not even an echo of steps.

God!

The next morning to be on the safe side Beth telephoned Dr Clarkson.

'How are things?' he asked.

'We are back at home but she's not right,' she said. 'Mr L said the scans show nothing. But she's a bad colour and she's weak. She can barely walk, she won't eat. She's definitely not herself.'

'I will pop in at lunchtime, shall I?' he said.

While he was upstairs with her mother she made him a ham sandwich, seeing as it was 12.26. She put a halved tomato on the side of the plate with some cucumber slices, cut a dill pickle into coins and fanned them out on a few gem lettuce leaves. 'Too kind,' he said, sitting down with her at the little kitchen table.

'And how are *you* doing?' he said, mid-sandwich.

'Me?'

'I wonder if a holiday might be in order. Change of scene. This has been going on for two years now. And your father before that. You have done amazingly but it must be taking its toll.'

'No, no,' she said lightly. She was smiling. *He* was too kind.

She had her routines. She liked them. 'No no,' she said again. A holiday? There was no need for actual hysteria. Besides it was impossible, he knew that.

'Do you good,' he said. There was a note of warning, was there? 'Could your brother be persuaded to come over? That would give her an enormous boost.'

'I'm just not sure he can get away but I could ask, I suppose.'

'In any case, day in day out, I just wonder if you might be running the risk of—'

'Well, I will certainly give it some thought.'

She would not.

Then things took a turn for the surreal.

'Thing is,' he said, 'you're young, you're intelligent, you're – and you're making sacrifices the value of which you just don't know. But you might one day and my worry is by then it will be too late. You mustn't let your high standards and your talents be – This could go on for years and years. You are doing a first-rate job with her care but is it really going to? I know you must feel an enormous pressure and I can't help thinking at your stage in life you ought to be – When you are older and you look back at things – There, I've said it,' he said.

Beth smiled frankly at the man.

'And of course I knew your father since we were children, as you know, and he would have never forgiven me if I just stood by and—'

'Please,' she said.

He stopped.

'I am incredibly grateful to you,' she said. 'We all are.'

She saw her note of formality wound his feelings.

'Not at all.' He pushed past her.

And in the middle of the night when Beth was turning everything over in her mind – 'Beth Beth! Can you come! Beth? Are you there?'

'Just coming,' she called along the landing. 'Putting my dressing gown on. God, it's cold. Just find my slippers.'

'Are you there, Beth?'

'Here I am! Poor Mum. Are you all right? Are you feeling rough? What can I get you?'

'Why do I feel so bad?'

'Oh I'm sorry.'

'I'm not right, Beth.'

'Well—'

'That hospital. The doctors are villains!'

'What did Dr Clarkson say?'

'Wants me to try antidepressants.'

'Does he?'

'Yes.'

'How does that feel?'

'I looked them up and do you know what the first side effect listed is?'

'What is it?'

'Suicide.'

'Oh dear.'

'Why would he want me to take something that inclined me towards suicide?'

'Well – that's a good question. But I suppose a side effect might only affect one in ten thousand, one in a hundred thousand.'

'Still, that is quite a lot of people.'

'I wouldn't try to talk you into it if you feel that way. It is alarming. It has to feel right. Shall I ask Clarkson if he has other patients who have tried them that we could speak to? Might be a place to start. Or is that — ?'

'Helen's daughter was given antidepressants for her anorexia and the first side effect listed was loss of appetite.'

'Oh no! Speaking of appetite, what would you like to eat tomorrow? Today, I mean. I am doing an internet order so the world is your oyster.'

'You are a darling.'

'Thanks. You're not so bad yourself.'

'Could you face making some soup?'

'Sure. Then I thought after lunch we could watch *The Lady Eve* with Barbara Stanwyck. The dresses are out of this world.'

'Perfect. Would you mind doing my nails for me as we watch?'

The following day at 7 a.m. her brother Robin telephoned. His tone was odd – faltering – as though he had bad news to impart.

'Thanks so much for all you are doing with Mum. I am so sorry you have to do everything.'

'Well—'

'It doesn't seem at all right or fair.'

'I am happy to do it. You have Lauren and the girls to take care of, anyway.'

'Well,' he said. 'It's very generous of you to see it like that. But I worry you don't have enough time to live your own life.'

'What do you think I do every day?'

'It's just – I don't know what I'm saying really.'

'No,' she said. And then, 'How are the girls?'

'Pretty naughty.'

'Well that sounds perfect,' she laughed.

'Yeah, maybe. I hope so. Funny being in a house with four females. All the hairbrushes – you wouldn't believe. The little ones let me do their plaits in the morning. Me! I love it. They're never that neat but they don't complain. Some of their friends have housekeepers who can do really fancy French plaits and mine are basic, but they're sturdy!'

'That's a lovely picture you paint,' Beth said.

'Thanks. With Mum, I mean, can I ask if it doesn't sound too – I mean do you meet people, go out and about sometimes with friends and have . . . times?'

Clarkson!

It was strange the way there was such a stigma, in life, attached to doing your duty.

'I do,' she said. By *times* she had an awful feeling he meant sexual intercourse.

People!

'Will still off the scene?' he asked.

Aha, she was right. 'Yep. That ship has sailed.'

'Shame,' he said, 'I did like him.'

'Yes,' she answered. 'Me too.'

'You wouldn't consider coming to visit us, would you?'

'I'd love to some time, it's just I am not certain if she'll ever feel up to the journey.'

'Ah . . . Well . . . it's an open invitation.'

'Thanks. I appreciate that. And they do say Miami is one of the best places on the planet to be an old lady.'

He made no answer.

'And there's no need to worry,' she said. 'I am completely fine. I'd say if I wasn't.'

'Thank you.' His voice which at the beginning of their talk had been thin and reedy now sounded half-drunk with relief.

She settled her mother at seven on Saturday night with cream of watercress soup and apple snow and a milky coffee on a flowered tray, and Ginger Rogers. She went out for ninety minutes to meet some old school friends.

'Sure you'll be OK now?'

'I think so, yes.'

'Will you phone if you need anything? It's less than ten minutes away.'

'I will,' her mother said.

She couldn't imagine the night she was in for would be preferable to staying at home. Her friends were so vehement in their complaints.

'What's the most maddening thing about Will?' they used to ask her. They sat back as she racked her brains.

'Sometimes when we go out he can be a little bit quiet.'

How they ladled on the scorn! She just didn't have extreme things in her life as they did, didn't need them, didn't miss them. It didn't make her, to herself, a bad person.

Now her life was a bit odd they seemed to find her more of a fascination. They were at pains to understand her world, attempting to apply things from her life to things in their own.

'Perhaps you are right and it is a tiny bit like you with the new baby, trying to keep a person alive. It is a responsibility, yes,' she said, 'as well as a privilege, of course. She doesn't sleep through the night, no, almost never! How's Archie doing anyway, has he got any new tricks up his sleeve?'

Her school friends were sympathetic, but they over-consoled. 'Oh you poooooor thing. That's absolutely terrible. What makes her think she has the right to—' There was an equation they tried to solve that wasn't helpful, as if anything you gave equalled a loss. They wouldn't view her mother's illness as collaboration, they only saw a renouncing and life passing her by.

Sometimes they spoke of her as though she were a victim of domestic abuse!

She didn't blame them. It was confusing. She had a blister on her lip that looked seedy. It told against her. She regretted that.

Next time though, she thought, she might say she couldn't get away.

One of the friends, Sheila, who was leaving early to attend her AA meeting, asked her if she would like a lift home. 'Give us a chance to catch up a bit.'

'Oh yes. Thank you. Great.'

At the lights at the junction with Gloucester Place, Sheila looked at her too kindly. 'What's up?' she asked, pulling over into a disabled parking bay so that they might talk.

Beth thought she might cry. 'I'm absolutely fine. Just a lot of pressure sometimes.'

When they got to her street and she was about to get out of the car Sheila faced her seriously. 'You think you might be like addicted to care-giving? It's made you lose your job, it's made you lose your relationship, it's made you lose your home.'

'It's not like that. Well, maybe a tiny bit but—'

'This may be hard for you to hear but there are meetings that support people with over-helping and co-dependency. Maybe that would be worth investigating.'

'Really? How interesting,' Beth said. 'You are kind. Thanks for the lift. Night!'

Then the following Friday at noon when her mother was in her bath, and she was setting a vegetable soup to simmer, three short rings on the doorbell.

It was her brother and Dr Clarkson and a nurse in a royal blue dress. An ambush.

'Fuck!' she said, apologising rapidly. Six eyes fixed on her a little too benignly.

Everything's all right now, the grown-ups are here, she almost seemed to hear them say.

She ushered them into the kitchen, thinking, thinking. She sat them all down. Now they were no longer standing in a row, they seemed tentative and hardly powerful at all.

'What can I do for you?' she said.

'I've come for a couple of weeks to visit Mum and give you a break. Will you forgive me?' her brother said. 'I didn't ask because I worried you'd say no. I will leave now if I've done something wrong.'

'No, no,' she reassured him, 'don't be silly.'

'I'm more than happy to stay in a hotel and pop in at times that suit you. Whatever seems best to you. I'm sure I've gone about everything in the wrong way. I know I can be clumsy and thick about stuff, I just wanted to see how Mum is and to see you and to see how you are and that's why I'm here.' He spoke calmly and with softness. 'I know you're doing amazing things and you're super-capable and everything like that and that you don't need me in any way, but I just didn't want you to think . . . '

'I myself, as you know, was wondering—' Dr Clarkson began cautiously but she interrupted him.

'Let's all calm the fuck down and have a cup of tea,' Beth suggested.

She never swore.

'Perfect,' her brother said.

'Beth?' her mother was calling from upstairs. 'Beth? Can I have a hand a second?'

'Shall I?' The nurse half rose. On seeing Beth's eyes she immediately sat down.

'You,' Beth said, 'you can make the tea.'

'I'll stir the soup, shall I?' Robin offered as she left the room.

She held her mother's underarms while she climbed out of the bath, closing her eyes for her mother's privacy, once she had a firm grip. Then she turned and grabbed a towel and held it out for her mother, folding it round her body from behind. She blotted her wisps of hair with a pink flannel and together they slipped her head into a white terry cloth turban.

'Do you need the loo or — ?'

'No, I'm good.'

While her mother rested for a moment, sitting down heavily on the lip of the bath, Beth said, 'Got some amazing news.'

'Oh?'

'Robin is downstairs.'

'Robin! Here?'

'Yes.'

'Oh, how lovely.'

'He just rang the doorbell out of the blue.'

'Just like that?'

'I *know!*'

'I thought it was the man with the Ensure.'

'Why don't I settle you in bed, in the pink cardigan, then I could send him up with the soup?'

'I think I will come down,' her mother said. 'Of course. That seems right. He has come all this way.'

'Wonderful,' Beth said. 'What would you like to wear, do you think?'

Very very slowly they came down. Beth out in front, going backwards down the stairs, arms braced to catch her mother if she fell. She had chosen a long green silk skirt and an ivory blouse with small embroidered ivory flowers. She added a bright scarf printed with phlox and hydrangea. It had been years since she had worn such festive things. Beth led her by the elbow into the kitchen. Everyone stood. Her mother blinked repeatedly as though the whole scene was some sort of mirage. There was a jug of fancy daffodils on the table, pale bone-coloured ones with faded orange centres. It was the first time she had been downstairs since the day she came back from the hospital.

Her mother greeted Robin like a prince, of course she did. She had always been courtly with her son. Her brother fielded his mother with strength and grace and honour. It was like a scene from the Bible.

Dr Clarkson made a brief speech, referring to Beth's care of her mother as a 'living, breathing work of art'. The nurse was watching her with captivated eyes.

Why did they assume that she would mind?

Did she mind?

Dr Clarkson suggested the nurse and Robin carve up the next two days between them if it suited Beth and the patient.

'Fine with me,' Beth said. 'If it's fine with you, Mum.'

Her mother nodded.

'There's a few things I'll probably write down for you, bits and bobs if that's OK.'

'Perfect,' Robin said.

The relief on Dr Clarkson's face showed how braced he must have been for upset and disaster. People were so funny. The way they assumed that rivalry and dismay were all there was. It was a pleasure to surprise them. She imagined Robin also was enjoying this – the way, as a family, they often defeated expectation.

Everyone was on their best behaviour and that always helped.

The nurse was on the basic side, prim and sullen-eyed. She wouldn't last long – they could do better – but she could sit downstairs and give her brother back-up if required. She was a good idea, really. And Robin would return after his two weeks, she might suggest ten days to him for two weeks was an awfully long time for Lauren to be by herself with the girls, but up to him, obviously. Anything was fine.

Her mother gradually came to life. Soon she was girlish and skittish and even sang some snatches of song. Pink lit her cheeks within the grey. She had started using slightly different turns of phrase lately, saying things like 'Bless him' when talking about a disgraced politician in the news, which was a little bit worrying. This liveliness felt like movement in the opposite way. Her print scarf fell down and her scars glowed but she did not seem to care. She is about ten minutes away from sheer exhaustion, Beth thought. The effort she was putting into the festivities might actually kill her, but – they could go back upstairs in a moment. There was so much joy in the room. Even the grim nurse, Beatrice her name was, had stopped frowning and confided to them that in her line she had to be vigilant about catching her soaps as people took advantage. They could all watch *Doctors* upstairs at three o'clock maybe, Beth thought. She would suggest it in a moment. The nurse needed a bit of cake to cheer her up, perhaps that was all. She could nip out and buy one. Keep the party atmosphere afloat.

Her mother and her brother were sitting holding on to each other, hand in hand in hand in hand, her mother's face almost neon with pleasure. Beth started laughing. It was a sort of celebratory hysteria that she felt. Christmassy or something, deep and brimming. Proper abandon. Her brother caught her eye and winked.

'Home is the hero,' she said and blew him a kiss across the table, extending her arm so fully that her fingers came close to his lips.

There wasn't an emotion at that moment which she didn't have.

A life looking after a loved one wasn't less of a life than any other sort. It might be the best of it. Why did ordinary family feeling shock people so? Did Dr Clarkson secretly wonder who would do it for him? He never spoke of Mrs Clarkson, and all the little Clarksons only seemed to cause him grief. Her mother once remarked 'Anthony Clarkson is half in love with you, Beth, I sometimes think.'

'Mum!' she had cried.

Dr Clarkson looked pale and one of his hands gripped the table. His whole body seemed to be saying, Why on earth am I still here? It was a question worth asking. The nurse was shaking her head as though she just didn't hold with merriment, or feelings or people or times, or anything really.

Strange.

It was their last April.

PHILIP HORNE

THE TROLL

I

He had waited and waited, the young man, at first happily enough, only a little on edge. Then, increasingly conscious that he cut a sorry figure among the gold and pearls and fine satin, the Italian cotton and designer silk, he became positively relieved at being left alone in the dark corner behind his damask napkin, glittering glassware and low-burning candle. The beautiful waiters and waitresses had briefly hovered, then given him up, perhaps after registering the slight crack in the face of his smartphone. Somehow he had forgotten how, each time, his pleasure in this avowedly celebratory occasion was shadowed by a vague unease. In his haste and agitation he had brought neither book nor paper; he was reduced to gazing at the tablecloth or the diners around, for whom, after their dismissive investigatory glances or long scornful stares, he had finally faded from view.

Until, at least, the smartphone rang out at top volume with the latest tone that Flora had surreptitiously decided to install for him. Heads swivelled disgustedly, and in his horror and rush to silence it he knocked the phone over the table-edge, tipping off a large wine glass in the process. He watched for an agonised second as they descended towards the shining floor of marble, granite, quartz – whatever it took to shatter them into a thousand pieces. The device was still howling away after the impact, behind a spider's web of brokenness, and he reached down to seize it, driving a shard of wine glass like a wasp sting up under his fingernail. As the staff moved forward disapprovingly to restore order – though not yet, as he feared for a second, to eject him unceremoniously from the restaurant, an idea that he could see had flickered across their minds – he stanched the bleeding with the damask napkin and took the call. It was Gloria.

It should not have come as such a relief, the knowledge that he would have another hour to wait alone, thanks to some complication of snow and missed connections and cattle on the line. As instructed, he ordered bread, olives, sparkling water and, rather self-consciously, a bottle of champagne. And he requested too a sticking plaster and, when the olives arrived, plump and spicy and pungently Roman, something that was an inspiration of his own, a pad of paper and a pen.

The slim-hipped waitress moved off with a charming, interested smile, reassured no doubt by the champagne order, and he began to write.

It should be one of those things that perks you up and compensates for the lonely life of the writer – a mark of recognition by a colleague and ally, an act of generosity by an old friend, a break from the treadmill, a chance to review the state of things, and of course the new work. *N'exagérons pas*, I'm doing well, I've pulled myself together after that bad patch – and even if this one is found to suck I really think the next will rise to, well, a new level of something or other. Is it just because I keep falling short that these feasts – which have become symbols of the act or fact of publication – now seem to stick in my throat; so that I've come to regard them with as much joy as a visit to the dentist?

Little has exactly changed since all this began – since that time five years ago when she and I, and Norman, who mustn't be forgotten, were Bright Young British Novelists (that is, under forty).

We were in Rome in 2011 for the British Council, giving glittering readings and workshops, signing dozens of copies of our books, eating magnificent meals and drinking prosecco as if we were journalists. It was late April, but felt like a perfect English June. And we were in a *palazzo* that someone had vacated for a week, or a *piano* of a *palazzo*, with the full works – scagliola floors, frescos on the ceiling, a balcony overlooking our very own piazza, even a Guercino, with a bit of that lovely blue he does, quite sexy, *Joseph Fighting Off Potiphar's Wife*, I think, though it may have been a copy, or 'school of'.

Poor old Norman was at one end – they'd created an extra bedroom when they converted it – and she and I were in cavernous chambers at the other, one at each corner. She had a four-poster that would have accommodated a family of seven – she called me in to see it with screams of delight. Not the manner to which any of us were accustomed back home. It went to one's head, rather, the *dolce vita* – drinking so freely, being luxuriously warm, living in a palace, getting all that attention when one's more used to being ignored in the newsagent's.

It's a little grotesque, that I was there reading from my 'sensitive' first novel, *Cleavings*, about all these supersensitive people in a postgraduate house outside Durham and the tiny stirrings and vibrations in the air around them, their antennae tingling as they manoeuvred around each other – and that I didn't notice at all what was, as it transpired, going on under my nose. My personal image for what lurked beneath the surface, unimagined by me, comes from San Clemente, which the three of us visited with our lovely minder. Below the basilica built in 1108, which had seemed ancient enough in itself, dominated by a lovely golden mosaic of the Triumph of the Cross, with Christ surrounded by doves, they discovered a church from the fourth century, hushed and primitive; and then, below that, a pagan temple with a sacrificial altar bearing a carved image of Mithras slashing the throat of a bull. At the bottom of it all runs a gurgling subterranean river, no doubt to carry away the blood. For me, that somehow stands for all I had missed about my co-Bright-Young-BNs.

Firstly, that the author of *The Salford Chronicles*, Norman Higgs – although thoroughly married and indeed already progenitor of a couple of kids – had developed a major crush on Gloria, which she'd been rebuffing with some well-aimed jabs to his soft underbelly, that is, his ego (at the time I simply took these for fairly routine feminist objections to his stolid Northern sexism). She referred a few times, even in front of him, to his plentifully sprouting bodily hair, which curled out of the shirts he wore open-necked in the Roman sunshine. Poor Norman didn't have a medallion, but she kept saying she would buy him one. And maybe he thought that meant she did fancy him, despite his girth. He didn't hear her say that whereas he thought he was Ted Hughes he always made her think of Les Dawson.

But secondly, and more seriously, I failed to register that Gloria, the author of *The Brides of March*, who was funny, and kind of attractive in a rather wild way, but not really my type – she loved the Brontës and *Saturday Night Fever* more than Henry James and *Ma nuit chez Maud* – had developed a thing for me. Perhaps I missed this because I had a very nice girlfriend at home, or rather *had* had one – we crashed into a major row before I came away and our future was worse than uncertain; so I wasn't really in the mood for romance, despite the setting. But we'd been having fun. Gloria was a great reader – she knew how to amuse the audience in a way that lifted their spirits after they had been depressed by Norman. The combination of torrid sex scenes (in several kinds), dark-edged farcical incidents and offhand slaughter in *The Brides* (all of whom were widows by July) went down well in Fellini's Roma. She and I would have running jokes, and exchange little smiles, especially when Norman was being more solemn than usual, and she made a point of kissing – on both cheeks – in the morning and evening, and taking my arm at odd moments. But I didn't see much in it, thinking this must be what we bohemians did, so what happened took me unawares.

To cut to the chase, or even, I suppose, to the kill. On our last night we gave a final reading, followed by a final reception on the rooftop terrace at the Council with a buffet and much drinking and hilarity. Norman, Gloria and I were dropped at the door of our *palazzo*, slightly unsteady from the free-flowing wine, and I realised I might not be back this way for a while. (In fact, I haven't been since.) I said I would take a stroll on my own through the streets of Rome before turning in. Gloria looked disappointed, whereas Norman, tipsy as he was, perked up.

I was gone some time. I didn't have a clever phone then, and only a scrumpled little free tourist map, and, having had one prosecco too many, wasn't very good at orientation. Plus, the real point seemed to *be* to get a little lost, to lay oneself open to the place. I wandered through the streets of

Rome in the warmth of the night with a luxurious sense of possession, past the Spanish Steps, where I thought of poor Keats; down, somehow, to the Trevi Fountain, where like everybody I thought of the voluptuous abundance of Anita Ekberg; over to the Pantheon, where I thought of the pagans, the Christians and the big blank eye which glares down on everyone from above; then across to the banks of the Tiber, where I looked at the Castel Sant'Angelo and thought about Tosca and her death-plunge. Then, feeling overcome with tiredness – it was 2.30 in the morning, and it all caught up with me – I headed back along the riverbank past the grand, rather overpowering Napoleonic Museum in the Palazzo Primoli to our own not unimpressive *palazzo*. I felt like a mild conqueror of the city, in my own small degree. I suppose, actually, you could say it was the high-water mark of my life. Unless somehow this new book reverses what I've come to think of as the long ebb.

I was already desperate for sleep, and was hoping as I tiptoed up the great staircase that Gloria and Norman were safely in their beds. I fumbled for the code and punched it in, eased the big door open, removed my shoes and stepped lightly to the bathroom without turning on the lights – enough illumination came in from the street. There was something magical about the great, gleaming, pointlessly spacious *salone* as I glided across it. I brushed my teeth and splashed my face and slipped into my warm, darkened room with relief – then simply threw off my clothes and climbed into the grand bed, which was, I recalled, though I couldn't see it, ornamented in gilt like a royal barge. I lay there almost soberly, as my barge moved from the brink, savouring in the blackness – the shutters were shut – this last moment of an extraordinary passage of time.

Suddenly I passed from cushiony self-satisfaction to rigid alarm. There was low breathing coming from the pillow next to mine. Had I got the wrong room? No, I wasn't that drunk. I reached for my granny-phone and its dim light showed me – very close – the face of Gloria, asleep beside me, looking innocent, almost childlike in repose and, to be honest, quite attractive. *She* had obviously been the worse for wear – she'd matched me glass for glass, despite her small frame. Maybe she had just mistaken my room for hers.

But then her eyes opened, and she smiled in a way that showed it was no mistake. 'Come here,' she whispered. She pulled back the covers to show a slim but sinuous body. I was hesitating, unsure what to do, when she slid closer to me and her warm skin came into contact with mine. I should perhaps have behaved like Philip Marlowe, but Gloria was no murderous Carmen Sternwood, I reflected, and I liked her, and she was a sort of guest, though an uninvited one, in my bed. I could have said I was gay – that might have been the one acceptable escape clause – but it didn't occur to me, and I imagine wouldn't have been convincing. In Lord Lucan's circle – not that I model my conduct on theirs – there was a phrase, '*boff de politesse*', to describe what a gentleman does for a lady when the alternative would be painfully embarrassing for both. This was more than that. On the other hand, I confess, it was rather less than a *coup de foudre*.

Afterwards we lay there in silence for a long time. It wasn't at all clear what this meant – to her, or actually to me. She lay on my chest – she wasn't heavy, and strands of her long hair were coiled in all directions, covering me – and seemed very happy. I tried to think of this as the perfect Roman ending.

Perhaps we'd have talked about it all and cleared the air, but a noise – a chair violently scraping on a fake-marble floor and someone muttering 'Bugger!' – broke in on us. We both laughed under our breath. Norman was on the move – presumably going to the fridge for a glass of water. But no, we heard him padding across the *salone*, and then closer and closer. It occurred to me with horror that he was drunkenly set upon waking me up and having a heart-to-heart – in which he would tell me what he really thought of me and my work at length, instead of making sour little barbed remarks – as he had been doing – and harrumphing in the background when I did my readings.

The footsteps paused outside my door, but there was no knock. He was listening. We both held our breath. Then the low slap of flesh on stone could be heard again – went further, to Gloria's door. Silence again – he was listening there. Then a low knock. Then a louder knock. 'Gloria!' he whispered – then louder, very Mancunian, '*Gloria!*' There was the sound of a handle turning, and he evidently stepped into her room. Plaintively, 'Gloria?' Then, 'Oh!' At this, I'm afraid we both giggled. He evidently heard. Because he said '*Oh!*' again – much more darkly.

Now he padded back across the corridor and stood outside my door, breathing audibly. It felt in the dark and the quiet as if he was standing beside the bed, glowering down at us. He seemed angry, hurt, maybe about to become violent. We lay there in tense silence, suppressing giggles, but also just a little afraid. He must have stayed there for a minute. Then the heavy footsteps moved away.

'Fee fi fo fum,' said Gloria, when we heard his door finally click shut. 'He'll grind your bones to make his bread if you're not careful.' We laughed, in relief – and also because, for once, life had come up with a fitting finale, in the key of farce, for an episode already memorable in itself.

We didn't have that conversation in Rome to clear the air, which is why . . . But she's here. To be continued?

2

'Hello, darling. Give me a kiss. There, that's better. My God! That journey was a *nightmare* . . . not so much the delay, which is usual – good, I see you got a bottle of champagne as I told you, did you leave any? Oh good! No, it was the *people*! Snap-chatting, *Fifty Shades of Nondescript*, *Femail* all round. Diehard Faragistes, philistines, rich and arrogant or poor and resentful . . .' Gloria's arrival caused a stir, as always, and Will half enjoyed the attention now – he got so little anywhere else – even though it was only reflected curiosity.

'My little village is such a haven from all that,' she went on. 'Fake news hardly penetrates. Well, that's not quite true, I suppose. They do like stories about suicide-bomber refugee pre-teens, and they still talk about Defra having deliberately infected herds with foot-and-mouth . . . I know, they're not all soulmates. But I have a sort of coven, who are lovely. My "friends" and "followers", you know . . . ' Will was distracted by a thirtysomething woman at a nearby table taking a surreptitious photo on her phone – of Gloria and therefore of him – and, it appeared, excitedly posting it at once. ' . . . Anyway, yes, it *is* good to be back in London – and to see you. Oh, another bottle of champagne, please. No, really, this is on me. It's so good of you to meet me, as always – this is my treat. That's the deal, my dear.'

In her cascading black asymmetrical garments and with her large dangling earrings, delicate silver nose-stud and mane of black hair, Gloria looked the part of a glamorous best-selling author – just as Will, in his low moments, imagined he looked the part of a failure. She was still talking.

'I just loved the new one. *Fine Print* – it's tremendous, my dear. I think you're on to something new. Not just the title – so clever, and a step on from *Cleavages* and *Unbucklings* and *Nobody Much* and that other one with the title that's too long – but the story. I mean, this time you've *got* one! It's your version of the *Faust* story, isn't it? But in the age of unlimited credit. So clever. You'll sell the TV rights, I wouldn't be surprised. Ah, thanks, yes, open it now – let's raise a glass to its success – and to you! Is it today it's published? Tomorrow? Excellent.'

They drank to his book – and he insisted on drinking also to her new one, *Passion Faced*, a story of *amour fou* between a young widow and the director of a crematorium, which was already selling ferociously. They talked about their various projects, and things that had occurred since their last meeting.

But the longer she talked the more he felt in a doomed way that she was just sparing him, and that there was something she had no choice but to mention. In fact, it felt like a mercy when it finally came out. This time, at least, it was only a question – as Will had half expected.

'Has our hirsute friend broken cover yet? Sorry to mention him, but you know very well that every time you've come out with a novel he's been there under the bridge clutching at your ankle, trying to stop you getting past.'

This was the Troll, as they'd come to refer to him, a shadowy but unavoidable figure who, starting with Will's second novel *Bucklings*, had posted reviews on all good websites, under the web alias of Otto Stroller, a 'Top Reviewer' – hence their nickname. He had fired his first salvo from the undergrowth some time back. Happily, on this occasion, Will could answer Gloria's query in the negative. The troll hadn't pounced; yet, anyway. She expressed relief, but seemed struck by the fact that this somehow didn't seem to lift Will's spirits.

The return from Rome – five years ago now – had been awkward. Norman had been thunderously sullen all the way, hung-over but also brooding abysmally, and they'd sat uncomfortably in a row of three on the plane, reading each other's books: well, Will and Norman read Gloria's, Gloria read Will's, and no one read Norman's. Will had later forced himself through *The Salford Chronicles* – an epic survey of Salford history extending from the visit of Bonnie Prince Charlie, through William Huskisson's death in the first ever railway accident, and Buffalo Bill's Wild West Show, to the Blitz, all seen through the eyes of the heroic Huggins family. It had a rough energy, but Will winced at the portrayals of patronising Southern intellectuals which punctuated the book. At least it had been written before Norman met Will, so Ambrose St John couldn't be him.

A few days after they got home Gloria had started sending Will emails clearly conveying that she assumed their relationship, as if that was the word for it, would carry on. He had been paralysed with the awkwardness – had left most of them unanswered, and sent brief occasional replies over which he agonised, of a cordial but evasive kind that he knew very well buttered no parsnips. She was up in the wilds of Yorkshire – the success of *The Brides of March*, and of its TV adaptation, allowed her to buy a small cottage, not to mention a cream Porsche which she texted him an image of – so a casual meeting was out of the question, since because of his teaching commitments, and routine of visits to his ailing mother, he seldom got away from London. After a month or two she stopped sending the emails.

But when *Bucklings*, in which Will's main characters had moved down to London and were struggling ineffectually in the worlds of publishing and literary journalism, appeared just under a year later, they saw each other again. She'd sent him a message asking to read it in manuscript – and had been very supportive – and insisted on buying him lunch in Mayfair, at a place where the food was, she pointed out, authentically Roman. And at that first lunch, she had drawn his attention to Stroller's vitriolic tour de force, which she had come across in a conspicuous place on Amazon.

It started by sketching the privileged ivory-tower milieu from which Will was said to have emerged, then accused him of being a complacent, vacuous pseudo-avant-gardist who thought he was Henry James but lacked the intellectual scope or moral substance, let alone the narrative interest, of James Herriot. It ended by meditating on how he could be persuaded to put an end to a career which was an embarrassing disaster and brought shame on the name of literature. This would save his readers from the sensation of taking an endless bus journey through some dreary London suburb where every stop seemed the same as every other – which Stroller suspected might have been responsible already for a suicide or two, and certainly some cases of severe depression.

Who was Stroller? she had asked. Was there anyone from his university time who had it in for him? He was a bit stunned, but when he had scratched around in his past, the only real candidate was his contemporary and college-mate Mark Lord – who had got a 2.1 when Will got a First, and who felt that difference the more sharply because of the expectations of his academic parents. Will had stayed on at Cambridge for his PhD, while Mark to get funding had to go off to Lampeter – where he had stuck, full-time, among the sheep, with a Welsh wife and children. An academic friend who knew them both and had done some externalling in Lampeter had confided to Will that in his cups Mark confessed to his loathing of Will, an emotion he had apparently expatiated on for over an hour. But that had been a couple of years back.

Gloria was sceptical anyway. Surely, she had said, there was a prime suspect, who had a motive that they were both very aware of – one who, moreover, even looked rather like a troll. She revealed that Norman was not only in the habit of sending her rather plaintive yearning texts, he occasionally drove over from Salford to pay a visit – though she did her best to avoid him, and when he cornered her he was self-pitying rather than threatening. He would hint that if she relented he would be prepared to leave his growing family for her. And he would mutter darkly about Will, she said, especially since *Bucklings* had been nominated for the Vere De Vere Prize (which, however, it would not go on to win).

At her subsequent lunches with Will she had reported additional discoveries: for one thing, that Stroller had reviewed other works very favourably – including hers, and, actually, Norman's own. If Norman *was* Stroller, that wouldn't be unprecedented. Poe had reviewed himself more than once, hadn't he? As they went on, the reviews took the form of a series of open letters to Will pleading with him to stop writing, to spare his readers the tortures of boredom and disappointment his works inflicted.

But 'Honestly, you mustn't worry so much about it', she had said, even though he had just told her he wasn't worried. 'I know a lot of people would find this disheartening. And I see that you can't very well ignore it, because, after all, he *is* doing this in just the place where the most readers will be deciding whether or not to buy the book. But, you know, "Hobgoblin, nor foul fiend, Can daunt his spirit . . . There's no discouragement Shall make him once relent His first avowed intent To be a pilgrim." OK, so there's someone who has it in for you. So what? Man up! Defy him . . .'

Towards the end of that first lunch she had revealed that she was staying in a discreet little boutique hotel round the corner, and insisted that he come back with her for a third bottle of champagne. He had thought they were on a new, non-sexual basis. But when he didn't immediately say yes, he saw a pain and vulnerability in her eyes, and it neutralised his reluctance, so that he couldn't refuse. She wasn't really giving him a choice, anyway. 'It's the least you can do,' she had said. He wasn't attached to anyone at the time, and he *was* fond of her – so he wavered, and he was lost.

What followed was excruciating, so much so, to tell the truth, that he was unable to play his part, something that had never happened to him before. He had staggered out into the chill of the evening, feeling humiliated and ashamed – and as full of pity for Gloria as he was for himself. The look of sad bafflement on her face as he had kissed her goodbye would come back to him at unexpected moments and almost reduce him to tears.

Each succeeding year, for *Grey Man* (which she called, laughing, *Faceless Nonentity*), about a young writer in the grip of depression, and then *We Did Not Know What Was Happening To Us* (which she called *The Gormless)*, where Will's main characters lost their jobs, homes and spouses and their ambitions were crushed, she had offered the same invitation. But through those previous lunches he had gently but firmly refused to come back with her to those burgundy silk sheets, pleading the appointments that he had consciously made to keep him from succumbing. And now, in any case, he was with Flora, who definitely wouldn't understand the concept of the *boff de politesse* – they were getting married next year. This time Gloria seemed rather alarmingly lively – he even wondered if she were on some medication – but all the way to and through pudding their talk was pleasant enough, with no further mention of Stroller.

Then, as they reached the liqueurs – she always insisted on Amaro, the name of which she said perfectly combined bitterness and love, because it was so close to *amare* – she suddenly recalled something. 'Oh, sorry! I should have said this earlier. *Good* news, I think. One of my "followers" who knows I know you tweeted me this morning a link to an early review of your book in the *LLR*, but I didn't have time to look. Maybe the tide is turning for you!' She pulled out her iPad and deftly brought it up. It was called, ominously, 'Small in Every Way' – and as Will craned over the table to see, his heart sank. Under the title was that name – Otto Stroller.

This time, somehow, the Troll who had been a nuisance under the bridge had got inside the castle – the *LLR*, for God's sake, about the only serious mainstream literary review left – and graduated to the rank of full-blown ogreish gatekeeper, raising the drawbridge and hurling down boulders on the would-be interloper Will. As he read on, there was no respite. This was Stroller's most effective blow yet, by some way. It was malign, and hyperbolic, but he had pitched it as a manifesto for big ambitious novels against small intricate ones, and it made hideously compulsive reading, which some would certainly find funny – 3,500 words of satirical caricature of his whole world-view and manner and idea of himself; not fair, but not easy to shrug off. Parts of it made even Will laugh. He was filled with sudden despair. Would he never escape? Would his publisher even keep him on after this? Sales had been getting low on *Grey Man* and *We Did Not Know What Was Happening To Us*, and how could *Fine Print* do better now? The Troll called it *Terms and Conditions*, saying this was a perfect name for it, since the T&Cs were the kind of thing people never bothered to read. Will should have seen that coming, he thought; indeed, maybe his unconscious was in league with the Troll, setting up his mockeries. The worst of it was, because of the timing all the other reviewers would read this before they filed their own copy – and contempt, he had learned, was among the most infectious of emotions.

'Look, Will, my dear, don't cry, for goodness' sake.' He wasn't crying, actually, but when she said this he was shocked to realise he was on the verge of it, as he registered how upset he had allowed himself to appear. 'Let's keep this in proportion, darling,' she went on. 'How could Norman have got himself into the *LLR*, I wonder? That's terrible. But people will know it's just malicious – no one will take it seriously. Look, let's save the afternoon: just come back to the hotel with me. I know about Dora, and she sounds marvellous – but we don't need to let that stop us. I won't breathe a word. We can just shut out the world for the afternoon. One more time. I'll take you under my wing.'

Will was struck by something she had said, and put his head in his hands. She put her hand on his shoulder and waited. Something was troubling him. He remained silent for a full minute.

Then, 'I'm sorry, Gloria,' he said. 'I just don't think I can keep on doing this. It's very kind of you, but I think I've just got to go. Let's leave it there. This is hard to take.'

But he didn't move. He sat there for a moment, biting his lower lip. 'And in fact, there's something *I* should have told *you* earlier – something a bit upsetting, in more than one way. I heard something from my agent – it's not been made public yet – and . . .Well, the Troll *can't* have been Norman as we thought. Because Norman is dead. He was at some book festival in Australia six weeks ago, and had a row with the organisers after his reading, so they didn't keep in touch after he left. Apparently he was driving from one place to another and stopped to go for a long run in the outback. Remember how he was always getting lost in Rome? Eventually someone noticed the car abandoned in the car park. They just found him a couple of days ago, what was left of him – in a hollow. Horrible.'

Gloria's face contorted. 'That *is* horrible. Good God, poor Norman. And his *family*. The children . . . That's ghastly.' She stared into space, and took a gulp of Amaro. 'But surely he must have written the review before leaving the festival?'

'No,' Will said quietly, 'the proof copies only went out three weeks ago. Remember? It couldn't have been him.'

She looked uneasy. 'What about your other friend, what's his name? – Mark, then? It must have been him, after all.'

'Well, I don't think so. You see, I ran into him at the British Library a couple of months back, and we went for lunch, in spite of everything. He told me that he'd come to think that Wales was the best place he could have ended up – he's a big fish there now, and he's got funding for a long period of research leave to write a book that sounds as if it will be really good. That's why he was in London. I told him about my troubles – you know, writing block, my sort of breakdown, all the hostile reviews, money worries, the short-term contracts – and he said he'd had completely the wrong idea about me. He actually apologised for having thought we were rivals. And I must say I believed him. We cleared the air, and got on really well. So he's ruled out too.'

A strange look came over Gloria's face. 'So who do you think the Troll is?'

'I simply couldn't say,' Will replied, gently.

3

That peculiar expression on Gloria's face came back to Will two months later as he climbed over the stile on his way to her village, which he had never visited before. She had seemed stricken. That rather airless dark corner of the Mayfair restaurant felt impossibly remote to him as he made his way through the breeze-tossed late-morning sunshine of the Dales in spring. She had confusedly checked the time, called for the bill and paid, bundled together her things and departed, all without any further conversational niceties – as if she couldn't wait to get out of there.

He was early, having made a point of allowing time to walk the five miles of countryside from the nearest station. A taxi would have been too abrupt; this meandering rustic path gave him time to think. As he reached the crest of the last hill, he was granted a view down over the village in its wooded valley, seemingly unchanged since – well, at least the 1950s. It was beautiful, and he couldn't hold back tears. Sitting down on a tussock in the luminously green grass, he shut his eyes for a moment.

Now he was going to meet Gloria's friends for the first time, he realised, a thought which gave him a moment's pause. What might she have said to them about him? Probably nothing, despite what he now couldn't but assume about the authorship of those reviews. The world didn't revolve around *him*, as he kept being reminded – and he could just tell people he was an old friend.

The tolling of church bells carried up to him there on the wind, and he looked at his phone to see the time; having been early, he had dawdled and was now on the point of being late. So he jumped to his feet and strode down the field towards the point where the path entered a dark, tangled copse – full, though, of birds, singing for their lives.

The bells had stopped while he was still in the middle of the wood, but the ancient grey-stone church – ivied, squat-towered, hunched in a ring of sheltering woods that in midwinter would have been sinister but now were illuminated by bright sunshine – still hadn't closed its doors. The last few people were drifting in, and Will slipped inside with them. The door, which faced south, was then left open, so that sunlight poured in and was reflected off the old, worn slabs – as well as coming in through the high windows, many of which were plain glass. Somehow the faith had been kept going for centuries in this tiny settlement, amid snow, floods, war, poverty. The peacefulness of it consoled him.

He couldn't at first find a place, but a rather impatient female usher led him down the length of the narrow nave, past rows of faces on either side, to a pew awkwardly near the front. It was a comfort that the church was clearly so full of love for Gloria. He was only just settled when a hush fell, and the coffin was carried in by four sturdy women, one of whom was crying audibly. He looked down, struck by the reality of the ending of this life that had touched his. Surely, he thought, with a chill – and he realised it was something that had been at the back of his mind since he heard the news – Gloria's death couldn't be anything to do with him?

As he looked up again, he had the illusion – it must be an illusion – that everyone was looking at him – or had just turned away, in order to avoid meeting his look. Whether or not this was the case, he suddenly felt very self-conscious. Almost everyone there was a woman, it seemed, except for a few accompanying males, and it felt almost as if he had broken some taboo. This was Gloria's 'coven', then.

The tributes, by two women of roughly Gloria's age, her best friend and her agent, praised Gloria's bravery, her imaginative genius, her generosity, her mischievous sense of humour. Her loss in such cruel circumstances would be devastating – but her books, which had changed their lives and those of millions, would live on. The critics, and her rivals, had never been fair, resenting her high sales and attaching the grotesque label of 'women's fiction' to work that would always have the power to transform and enrich. She had never, one speaker said, had much luck with men, had thought too well of them and been repeatedly deceived – choosing cold, self-centred charmers who had abused her kindness. Only her father, and her gay best friend from college, had not let her down. A sigh of sympathy, and indignation, ran through the congregation. 'Well, they'll be sorry now,' the friend declared.

A couple of people glanced in Will's direction. A shiver swept over him. His agent had simply told him Gloria was killed in a car accident, and given him the time of the funeral. He had come because he felt he must, and because he wanted properly to grieve for her – but now the woman vicar began to speak, and as he listened he realised from the way she skirted round the subject that almost everyone present believed that Gloria had intentionally driven her cream Porsche off the road and into that fatal gorge.

He sat on in the church as the others filed out into the

sunshine. It was achingly sad, the thought that her death might have been something meant, not just a hideous accident. He looked over to the door. Silhouetted against the sun was a middle-aged woman with short hair and glasses, standing there and looking intently in his direction. He could not make out her face, but her posture was – well, baleful. It now crossed his mind: what might Gloria have said to them about him in her wounded state? He foresaw that there might be difficulties at the reception.

When he came outside, no one was looking at him, at least, and he just stood there, at a loss. There was one woman, however, of about his age, definitely unbaleful, with a kindly face, who had evidently been weeping during the service. She was on her own, having arrived late, and now smiled dimly across at him. She came over through the graves, saying, 'Hello, I'm Jill, I'm one of Gloria's oldest friends. I don't think we've met . . . ' Relieved, Will smiled back at her and shook her hand. 'Hello,' he said, and told her his name.

She didn't say anything. In fact, she looked as if he had kicked her in the stomach. Her face crumpled. 'I'm sorry,' she muttered, and turned and ran, desperately, clumsily, out of the churchyard. From behind the stone wall came sounds of gasping, retching, sobbing. A couple of other women went out to help her.

It was like a hideous dream. Will just looked at his feet. He sensed that all round people were staring at him, whispering his name, outraged by his presence. Some were crying, overcome by the mixture of grief and violation. But he could not move.

At last, one of the women who had been helping Jill re-entered the churchyard and marched up to him. It was evidently something that required enormous courage on her part, but she felt she had to represent the collective spirit. He recognised her stance: she was the baleful one. 'You should never have come here,' she hissed at him, heroically. 'We all know what you did, all Gloria's friends – it was unforgivable. She forgave you – but don't think that we can. She was such a sweet person. Please just go now, and never come back. You think you can get away with this? Let me tell you, we all want justice for Gloria – and you'll be sorry.'

The words struck him like an unexpected rugby tackle: Will felt faint, and he heard a buzzing in his ears. But he had to get away, so, unsteadily, he made his way to the church gate, amid a murmur of disapproval. At the gate he paused, holding a stanchion for support.

One of the men present, a stocky, mild-mannered-looking man in his thirties, came over, his face unreadable. Will thought for a moment he was going to offer to intercede, to hear what Will had to say for himself. But then a fist walloped him on the side of the head. He fell to his knees with the force of the blow.

He stumbled away, his ears ringing, back into the dark wood, up the hill, under skies that were now full of grim clouds portending rain. He half walked, half ran for a couple of miles, putting as much distance as he could between himself and the church. In the downpour, he missed his path; then, slipping and sliding in the mud, he found his phone was gone – it must have fallen out of his pocket when he was knocked down. So, wet, lost, ashamed, confused, grieving, he wandered for miles that day and into the night, sometimes weeping for Gloria, sometimes for himself, sometimes for Norman; sometimes laughing bitterly at everything. He should have gone back for the phone, but which way even *was* back? It was after dark when he reached the station, and well after midnight when the train finally pulled into London.

By that time, another web review of *Fine Print* had appeared. It was there in his inbox, sent by a solicitous friend, when he checked, as he somehow couldn't help doing, before sleep, or what should have been sleep. It lacked the playfulness and finesse of the earlier assaults, but was quite jagged enough to reopen old wounds. The first of many bearing the byline, 'Ottoline Stroller', it ended,

> *This soi-disant author seems to think he has talent, and for a while the world was fooled into thinking so too. Fortunately,* Fine Print *dispels any uncertainty: it shows conclusively that he is simply not worth the candle – he's coldly self-obsessed, blindly sexist, institutionally racist, and his uninteresting 'experiments' are cases for the Journal of Negative Results. This 'Print' is not only not 'Fine', I'm wasting my time and yours in even discussing it. He is, in fact, not a zero but a minus, mean-spirited and abusive – and not just of our patience. I usually give books I don't like to charity. In this case that would be irresponsible, so I have fed his oeuvre instead to my wood-burning stove, where, as I type these closing words, it at last achieves some value by giving off a little smoky warmth.*

As Will climbed into bed, Flora turned over, tutting gently, and returned to her deep slumbers. He lay there beside her, eyes wide open, strange strands of memory in his head, shivering, watching an icy future yawn before him. He had gone wrong somewhere; would never get across the bridge as many others seemed to do, would wait and wait, beside the abyss, unseen in the darkness – or rather, unseeing, he would be forever unforgivingly scrutinised by burning, hostile, anonymous eyes, dead eyes, from which there could be no getting away.

JOSEPH O'NEILL

THE POLTROON HUSBAND

Five years ago we sold the Phoenix house and bought land in Flagstaff and built a house there – our 'final abode', I called it. Jayne objected to this designation, but I defended myself with what I termed an 'argument from reality' – which was also objected to by Jayne, who said I was using 'an argument from being really annoying'.

'Are you saying this isn't going to be our final abode?' I said. 'And don't talk to me about hospices or nuthouses. You know what I mean. This is the last place you and I will call home. This is our final abode.'

I looked up 'abode'. It refers to a habitual residence, of course; but it derives from an Old English verb meaning 'to wait'. The expression 'abide with me' can be traced back to the same source. An abode is a place of waiting. Waiting for what? Not to be a downer, but I think we all know the answer. When I shared my research with Jayne, she said, 'I see that your darkness is somewhat useful to you, but it's a bit intellectually weak.' This delighted me, of course.

The final abode is on a wooded, intermittently waterlogged double lot on South San Francisco Street, near the university.

The neighborhood was quite ramshackle when we moved in, and to this day it hosts a significant population of indigent men. They come to Flagstaff with good reason, in my opinion: the climate is lovely in this desert oasis seven thousand feet above the sea, and there are good social services, and the townsfolk are good-hearted, I would claim, although it must be noted that the city only recently decriminalised begging. I took part in the protests against the law. Jayne, whose politics on this issue are the same as mine, was disinclined to man the barricades, so to speak. We, the protesters, chanted slogans and held up placards and marched along Beaver Street, where some of us got into good trouble, to use the catchphrase of my hero, John Lewis: we sat down in the middle of the road and symbolically panhandled. I was among those sitting down but not among those randomly arrested and dragged away by the cops, much to Jayne's relief.

Our house, very cleverly laid out by a local architect, consists of five shipping containers raised several feet from the ground. Half of one container functions as a garden office and the other half functions as a covered footbridge over the stream that runs through our land: previously you had to negotiate a pair of old planks. The covered bridge was my idea. It makes me stupidly proud when visitors pause to enjoy the view through the bridge's window: the small brown watercourse, the translucent thicket. It is extraordinary how many of the design problems we encountered led to solutions whose positive dimensions exceeded the negative dimensions of the original problem. And how fortunate we were to find this magical overgrown downtown woodland in the first place. Road traffic is imperceptible from the house; and when the maples and river birches are in leaf, we cannot be seen by anyone walking by. It is a wonderfully private, precious urban place.

*

One night, Jayne grabs my wrist. We are in bed.

'Did you hear that?' she says.

'Hear what?'

Jayne is still holding my wrist, though not as tightly as before.

'Shush,' she says.

We listen. I am about to declare the all-clear when there's a noise – a kind of thud, as if a person had collided with the sofa.

Jayne and I look at each other. 'What was that?' she says. She is whispering.

We listen some more. Another noise: not as loud, but also thud-like.

'It could be a skunk,' I say. We have a lot of skunks around here. Skunks are born intruders.

'Is it downstairs?'

It's hard for me to give an answer. Although the house has two stories and numerous dedicated 'zones', to use the architect's word, only the bathrooms are *rooms*, that is, spaces enclosed by four walls and a door. Otherwise the house comprises a single acoustical unit. This can be confusing. Often a noise made in one zone will sound as if it emanates from another.

Now there is a sudden louder noise that must be described as a cough. Something or someone is either coughing or making a coughing sound. It's definitely coming from inside the house. I think.

'I'd better take a look,' I say. A little to my surprise, Jayne doesn't disagree. I turn off my bedside light. 'Let's listen again,' I say.

For several minutes, Jayne and I sit up in bed in the darkness and the quiet. We don't hear anything. Actually, that's incorrect: we don't hear anything untoward. If you listen hard enough, you always hear something. The susurration of the ceiling fan. The faint roar of the comforter.

'I think it's fine,' I finally say.

'What's fine?'

'It was nothing,' I say. 'We're always hearing noises.' That's basically true. Often, at night, a racket of clawed feet on the roof produces the false impression that animals have penetrated the abode.

'Let's call 911,' Jayne says.

I don't have to tell her that our phones are downstairs, in the kitchen, plugged into chargers. I say, 'Sweetie, there's no need to worry. Nothing has happened.'

'Shouldn't we check?' she says.

What she's really suggesting is that I'm the one who should check – that the checker should be me. I should get out of bed and go down the stairs and find out what is making the noises. My feeling is that this isn't called for. Those noises happened a long time ago, is how I feel about it. I feel like they are historical facts.

Jayne says, 'I won't be able to sleep.'

I wouldn't say that she says this loudly, but she's definitely no longer speaking in what you'd call a low voice.

Jayne says, 'I'll just lie here all night, wondering what those noises are.'

I don't know what to say. For some reason, I feel very exhausted.

Jayne says, 'Honey, it's not safe.'

I hear her. She's arguing that, even if we could fall asleep, it would be unsafe to do so in circumstances where we've heard thuds and coughs of an unknown character and origin. I say, 'You're right.'

I don't move, however. I stay right where I am, in bed.

It's important to examine this moment with some care and, above all, to avoid simplistic psychological conclusions. In that moment, which I clearly recall, the following occurred: I was overcome by a *dreamlike inertness*. I was not experiencing fear as such. I have been afraid and I know what it is to be afraid. This wasn't that. This was what I'd call an *oneiric paralysis*.

Thus I could intuit that my wife was looking at me, yet my own eyes, open but unaccountably immobilised, were directed straight ahead, toward some point in the darkness: I lacked the wherewithal to turn my head and return her look. Her bedside lamp lit up, presumably by her hand. I sensed her climbing out of the bed. She appeared at the foot of the bed. There she was visible to me. She fixed her hair into a bun and put on a dressing gown I didn't know existed. She was as beautiful as ever, that much I could take in. She said, 'I'll go down myself.'

Here I became most strongly conscious of my incapacitation – because I found myself unable to intervene. But for this incapacity, I would surely have pointed out that she was taking a crazy risk. I would have reminded her that Arizona is teeming with guns and gunmen. I would have proposed an alternative to venturing alone downstairs. In short, I would have stopped her.

To be clear, my inability to speak up wasn't because I'd lost my voice as such. The content of my thoughts amounted to a blank. I was the subject of a *mental whiteout*.

My beloved left the sleeping zone. I heard her footfall as she went down the stairs.

My symptoms improved a little. I found myself able to move my feet over the border of the bed – though no further. I could not escape a sedentary posture. I *perforce* awaited the sound of whatever next happened.

Which was: a soft utterance. Certainly it was a human voice, or a human-like voice. Then came a pause; then a repetition of the first utterance, equally soft; and then what sounded like a responsive utterance. I heard a movement being made, a movement I associated with an act of clumsiness. Then came a series of sounds made by bodily movements, it seemed, then another, slightly longer speech episode involving one voice or more than one voice, I couldn't tell for sure. What was being said and being done, and by whom, and in which zone: all of these matters were beyond me. I was on the bed's edge, that is to say, still bedridden. This state of affairs persisted for a period of time that even in retrospect remains incalculable: soft utterances belonging, it seemed, although I could not be sure, to more than one speaker; pauses; the sounds of movements human or animal; and my own stasis. At any rate, there eventually came a moment when the light in the living zone was switched on; and very soon after that, I heard the distinctive exhalation of the refrigerator door being opened, and the splashing, or plashing, of liquid being poured into a glass. Here, my motive powers returned as mysteriously as they had abandoned me. I got to my feet and went down.

Jayne is seated at the kitchen table with a glass of milk. She has taken to drinking milk regularly, for the calcium: one of her greatest fears is that she'll lose bone density and end up stooped, like her mother.

'Good idea,' I say, and I pour myself a glass of milk, too, even though my bone density isn't something I lose sleep over. I sit down across the table from her.

Jayne is on her smartphone, scrolling. I wait for her to send a text or make a phone call, because she normally doesn't pick up her gadget without a purpose in mind. She keeps scrolling, though, almost as if she's just passing time.

I've never seen her in any kind of dressing gown before. This one has an old-fashioned pattern of brown-and-green tartan. She looks good in it. 'I like your dressing gown,' I say.

'Thank you,' she says. 'I thought it might come in handy.'

I survey the surroundings. I see nothing amiss or unusual. Nor can I smell anything out of the ordinary.

Jayne finishes her milk. 'I think I'll go back to bed now,' she says.

'Yes,' I say. 'It's late.' I go up with her.

In the morning, we follow our routine. I make scrambled eggs and coffee for two; we consume the eggs and coffee; and we retire to our respective work zones: I to the garden office, where I do the consultancy stuff that occupies me for about five hours, six days a week; Jayne to the studio, which is her name for the zone of the house dedicated to her printmaking activities. We are both very busy on this particular day and work longer and more intensely than normal, and at midday we separately grab a bite to eat. In the late afternoon, I check in on her.

'How's it going?' I say.

'Good,' she says, all vagueness and preoccupation. She is standing at her worktable, her palms black with ink. She wears the green apron I know so well.

I peek over her shoulder. 'Very nice,' I say.

Jayne does not respond, which is to be expected.

'For tonight, I was thinking steak,' I say.

'Yay,' Jayne says. She loves steak, if I make it.

So I step out and get the meat and cook it. I open a bottle of red wine. I serve the meat with grilled asparagus and sautéed potatoes.

'You don't like the steak?' I say. Jayne has only eaten a mouthful of it. Otherwise she has finished her food – including two helpings of potatoes.

She says, 'I'm not that hungry.'

'Not hungry?' I say.

'Maybe I'll have some later.'

I say to her, 'What happened last night? When you went downstairs.'

Jayne says, 'You were right. It was nothing.'

I say, 'I heard voices. I heard you talking to someone.'

'You did?' she says.

'You're saying those voices I heard were nothing?'

'You tell me,' Jayne says.

'You were there,' I say. 'I wasn't. You tell me.'

'Where were you?' she says. 'In bed?' Now she is eating her steak.

I say, 'You're hungry now?' I say, 'Who were you talking to?'

Jayne says, 'Are you sure you weren't dreaming?'

It must be said: I'm furious. 'Can I get you anything else?' I say. 'A glass of milk?'

I didn't press Jayne further. If there's one thing I'm not, it's an interrogator. I decided to bide my time. Jayne, who is a great one for marital candor and discussion, would open up to me sooner or later. Meanwhile, I held off telling her about my side of things; in particular, the bizarre condition to which I fell victim on that night – a *catastrophic neural stoppage*. My story went hand in hand with her story. I couldn't tell her mine unless she told me hers.

Three months have passed. Neither of us has brought up the subject.

The nocturnal noises have not reoccurred, it should be said. There have been noises of the usual variety, of course, but none that have caused a disturbance. I may have played a role in this.

It has always been the case that, when Jayne and I finally call it a day, she goes upstairs while I linger in order to lock up, switch off the lights, perform a visual sweep, and generally satisfy myself that everything is shipshape and we can safely bed down. Lately, however, I have taken to staying downstairs after my patrol, if I can call it that. I sit in my armchair. All the lights have been turned off except for the lamp by the chair, so that I am, in effect, spotlighted, and clearly visible to any visitor. I remain seated for a period of time that varies between half an hour and a whole hour. I don't do anything. I remain alert. I offer myself for inspection.

'Are you coming up?' Jayne called down when I first began to do this.

'Yes,' I answered. 'I'm just seeing to a few things.'

'OK, well, come up soon,' Jayne said. 'I miss you.'

A short while later, she was at the top of the stairs. 'Love, I'm going to go to sleep soon,' she said.

'You do that, my darling,' I said. 'Get yourself some shut-eye. You've worked hard.'

'Is that new?' she said.

'It's my dressing gown,' I said.

The dressing gown had been delivered that morning. It bothered me, when I began these vigils, that I lacked appropriate attire. To watchfully occupy a chair was a pursuit that belonged neither to the day nor to the night; neither to the world of action nor to the world of rest. Specifically, I wanted to remove my clothing at day's end and yet not sit downstairs dressed only in pajamas. The solution was a dressing gown.

Shopping for a dressing gown isn't straightforward. Not only is there the danger of ordering a bathrobe by mistake, but there's also the danger of buying something that will make you ridiculous. After a considerable effort of online browsing, I got one made of dark-blue silk. I chose well. I enjoy slipping it on and fastening the sash and – because this, too, has become part of the ritual – wetting and combing my hair so that, unforeseeably, I am more spruce than I've been in years. I'm very much a jeans and lumberjack shirt kind of guy.

'It looks nice on you,' Jayne said. As was now the norm, she too was wearing her dressing gown. She added, laughing, 'In a Hugh Hefner kind of way.'

Was this an entirely friendly qualification? I couldn't tell; an unfamiliar opacity clouded Jayne in that moment. And when she got me monogrammed black slippers for my birthday – 'To complete the Hef look' – the same cloud suddenly returned. Still, I wear the slippers happily. And whenever I finally turn in, Jayne is always awake or half-awake, and always rolls over on her side to hold me, and always asks, 'Is everything OK?' It is, I tell her.

When I'm in my chair, I automatically compare any weird noises to those that disturbed us that night – the thuds, the coughs. The comparison has not yet yielded an echo. I also replay in my mind what I heard when Jayne went downstairs, which sounded to me like a conversation between Jayne and another person, even though it may have been nothing and certainly came to nothing; and I find myself again looking forward to the day when Jayne will finally reminisce about the incident, and will at last disclose what happened to her during those interminable moments when I found myself in a *veritable psychic captivity*, a state which I'll finally have the opportunity to describe to her – although, because Jayne is given to worry, maybe it would be best if I protected her from learning about a biobehavioral ailment of such troubling neurophysiological dimensions. It wouldn't be the first time I've kept something from her. I've never told her that, when she and I first met, I had reached a point in my life when it would comfort me to look around a room and figure out exactly how I might hang myself. Jayne is my rescuer from all of that.

It's quite possible that she has forgotten all about the night of the noises. Certainly, the alternative scenario is highly improbable: that hers is a calculated muteness; that she is keeping the facts from me on purpose. It would be most unlike Jayne to do such a thing. She can't abide tactical silences. Moreover, this particular silence would serve no purpose that I can see; therefore it cannot be purposeful.

Meanwhile, I've become quite the expert in what might be called bionomic audio. For example, I've learned that the chatter of skunks can resemble the chirping of birds. This sort of knowledge doesn't just offer itself on a plate. It requires a physical deed. Several times I've stepped out of the abode, armed only with a flashlight, to investigate a noise. One night, while reconnoitring a scuttling in the bushes – it could have been a lot of things: the raccoon may be spotted in Flagstaff, and the grey fox, and the feral cat, and certainly the squirrel – I found myself in the middle of the woods without even a flashlight. It's true that a 'woods' is a sizeable wooded area and that we're actually concerned with a copse here, but to me it seemed as if I was in the middle of a woods in the middle of the night, even if was only about ten o'clock.

It was very dark. Our block has no streetlights, and the nuisance of light trespass doesn't affect us in the slightest. We have only one next-door neighbor, and her property, hidden by brush and oak trees, has been scrupulously disilluminated in compliance with the dark-skies ordinances for which Flagstaff is so famous. I recently looked into installing motion-sensing security lights around the house, only to immediately fall down into a deep, scary pit of outdoor lighting codes. In any case, Jayne was opposed to the idea. 'You'll just light up a bunch of rodents,' she said. She also said, 'I refuse to live like a poltroon', which made me smile. I love and admire her fiery verbal streak.

A 'poltroon', I read, is an 'utter coward', which I knew. I

didn't know that the word probably descends from the Old Italian *poltrire*, to laze around in bed, from *poltro*, bed. Interesting, I guess.

Where was I? In dark woods. But once my vision has adapted to the absence of light, of man's light, I am in bright woods. It is a paradox: dark skies, precisely because they're untainted by the pollution known as sky glow, are extraordinarily luminous. A strong lunar light penetrates the high black foliage and falls in a crazy silver scatter onto the underwood; and it's quite possible that starlight also plays a part in the woods' weird monochromatic brilliance, which has a powerfully camouflaging effect in that every usually distinct thing, each plant and rock and patch of open ground, appears in a common uniform of sheen and shadow. This must account for the strange feeling of personal invisibility that comes over me. I lean against a tree – and am tree-like. I find myself calmly standing sentry there, part-clad in my mail of moonlight, and doing so in a state of such optical and auditory supervigilance that I perceive, with no trace of a startle reflex, the movements not only of the forest creatures as they hop and scamper and flit, but even, through the blackened chaparral, the distant footsteps of someone walking on San Francisco. When my phone vibrates, it's as if I've pocketed a tremor of the earth.

'Love?' Jayne says. 'Love, where are you?'

I inform her.

She says, 'The woods? You mean the yard? Are you OK? You've been gone for half an hour.'

I turn toward the abode. An upstairs window offers an enchanting rectangle of warm yellow light. Otherwise our abode partakes of the dark and of the woods.

I assure Jayne that all's well. A bit of me would like to say more – would like to let her know about my adventure in the silver forest.

'Come inside, love,' Jayne says. She sounds worried, as well she might. She is a woman all alone in a house in the woods.

'I'll be right there,' I say. 'Sit tight. I'm on my way.'

APPENDIX

SUBJECTS FROM JAMES'S NOTEBOOKS

What follow are the subjects the writers have taken as the basis or inspiration for their stories, not always complete, as they have often seized on part of the 'germ' and grown their story from that. Some of the subjects, as readers who are led to look at James's notebooks will find, carry on down roads untravelled – untravelled both by James himself, who didn't write them, and certainly by these new adventurers.

Where James uses phrases in French I have glossed them at the foot of the page.

PAUL THEROUX *Father X*

Jan. 28th 1900. Note at leisure the subject of the parson & *bought* sermon situation suggested to me by something mentioned by A[rthur] C[hristopher] B[enson].* My notion of the unfrocked, disgraced cleric, living in hole &c, & writing, for an agent, sermons that the latter sells, type-written, & for which there is a demand.

* James's friend Benson (1862–1925), a poet, critic and scholar most noted now for his *Diary*, was the son of Edward White Benson, the Archbishop of Canterbury, who gave James the subject for 'The Turn of the Screw'.

COLM TÓIBÍN *Silence*

34 D[e].V[ere].G[ardens]. Jan. 23d 1894.*

I failed the other day, through interruption, to make a note, as I intended, of the anecdote told me some time since by Lady Gregory,† who gave it me as a 'plot' and saw more in it than, I confess, I do myself. However, it is worth mentioning. (I mean that I see in it all there is – but what there is is in the rather barren (today,) and dreary, frumpy direction of the pardon, the not-pardon, of the erring wife. When the stout middle-aged wife has an unmentionable 'past,' one feels how tiresome & charmless, how suggestive of mature petticoats & other frowsy properties, the whole general situation has become.) At any rate, Lady G.'s story was that of an Irish squire who discovered his wife in an intrigue. She left her home, I think, with another man – and left her two young daughters. The episode was brief and disastrous – the other man left her in turn, and the husband took her back. He covered up, hushed up her absence – perhaps moved into another part of the country, where the story was unknown; and she resumed her place at his *foyer*‡ and in the care and supervision of her children. *But* the husband's action had been taken on an inexorable condition – that of her remaining only while the daughters were young and in want of a mother's apparent as well as real presence. 'I wish to avoid

* James took a lease on a spacious fourth-floor flat at 34 De Vere Gardens, Kensington in November 1885, moving in the following March.

† Lady Isabella Augusta Gregory née Persse (1852–1932), Irish playwright, translator, critic, and in 1899 co-founder with W. B. Yeats and others of the Irish National Theatre Society.

‡ **foyer:** hearth, fireside

scandal – injury to their little lives; I don't wish them to ask questions about you that I can't answer or that I can answer only with lies. But you remain only till they are of such and such ages, to such and such a date. Then you go.' She accepts the bargain, and does everything she can, by her devotion to her children, to repair her fault. Does she hope to induce her husband to relax his rigour – or does she really accept the prospect that stares her in the face? The story doesn't say: what it does say is that the husband maintains his conditions and the attitude of the wife, maintained also for years, avails in no degree to attenuate them. He has fixed a particular date, a particular year, and they have lived de part & d'autre,* with her eyes upon this dreadful day. The two girls alone have been in ignorance of it, as well as of everything else. But at last the day comes – they have grown up; her work is done and she must go. I suppose there isn't much question of their 'going out'; or else that it is just this function of taking them into the world, at 17, at 18, that he judges her most unfit for. She leaves them, in short, on the stroke of the clock, and leaves them in a bewilderment and distress against which the father, surely, shld. have deemed it his duty to provide – which he must, from afar off, have seen as inevitable. The way he meets it, in Lady G.'s anecdote, at any rate, is by giving the daughters the real explanation – revealing to them the facts of the case. These facts *appal* them, have the most terrible effect upon them. They are sensitive, pure, proud, religious (Catholics;) they feel stained, sickened, horrified with life, and they both go into a convent – take the veil. That was Lady G.'s anecdote. I confess that as I roughly write it out, this way, there seems to me to be more in it – in fact its possibilities open out. It becomes, indeed, very much what one sees in it or puts in it;

* **de part & d'autre:** on both sides

presenting itself even as the possible theme of a rather strong short novel – 80 000 to a 100 000 words. Jotting roughly what it appears to recéler,* or suggest, I see the spectacle of the effect on the different natures of the 2 girls. I see a kind of drama of the woman's hopes and fears. I see the question of the marriage of one of the girls or of both – and the attitude, là-dedans,† the part played, by the young men whom it is a question of their marrying. I see one of the girls 'take after' her mother on the spot. The other, different, throws herself into religion. The 1st one, say, has *always known* the truth. The revelation has nothing new to teach her. Something doubtless resides in such a subject, and it grows, I am bound to say, as one thinks of it. The character, the strange, deep, prolonged and preserved rigour of the husband – and above all his responsibility: that of his action, his effect upon his daughters. His stupidity, his woodenness, his pedantry of consistency, his want of conception, of imagination of how they will feel, will take the thing. The absence of imagination his main characteristic. Then the young man – the lover of one of them, and his part in the drama, his knowledge in advance, his dread of it. He is the lover of the girl who goes into religion. The other one – reckless, cynical, with the soul of a cocotte,‡ has another tie: a secret relation with some bad fellow to whom, say, she gives herself. And the mother – and her lover? What becomes of her? The lover, say, has waited for her? – or the husband relents after he has seen the ravage made by his inhuman action and is re-united to her on the ruins of their common domestic happiness. x x x x x x x x x x x x x x x x x x

* **recéler:** contain

† **là-dedans:** in the matter

‡ **cocotte:** tart, harlot

Colm Tóibín's story mainly draws on the next passage, used by him as an epigraph, which promptly follows the other, and seems to have been written on the same day.

Another incident – 'subject' – related to me by Lady G. was that of [the] eminent London clergyman who on the Dover-to[-]Calais steamer, starting on his wedding tour, picked up on the deck a letter addressed to his wife, while she was below, and finding it to be from an old lover, and very ardent (an engagement – a rupture, a relation, in short,) of which he had never been told, took the line of sending her, from Paris, straight back to her parents – without having touched her – on the ground that he had been deceived. He ended, subsequently, by taking her back into his house to live, but *never* lived with her as his wife. There is a drama in the various things, for her, to which that situation – that night in Paris – might have led. Her immediate surrender to some one else, &c, &c, &c. x x x x x x x x x

It reminds me of something I meant to make a note of at the time – what I heard of the W.B.'s* when their strange rupture (in Paris too) immediately after their almost equally strange marriage became known. He had agreed, according to the legend, to bring her back to London for the Season, for a couple of months of dinners – of *showing*, of sitting at the head of his table and wearing the family diamonds. This, in point of fact, he did – and when the season was over he turned her out of the house. There is a story, a short story, in that. x x x x x x x x x x x x

* Unidentified: seemingly none of James's friends and acquaintances with these initials: Welbore St. Clair Baddeley, Wolcott Balestier (American), Walter Berry (American), William Wilberforce Baldwin (American), Walter Besant (happily married), William Blackwood (lived in Edinburgh), Sir Percy William Bunting (happily married), Witter Bynner (the dates don't work) . . .

ROSE TREMAIN *Is Anybody There?*

Rose Tremain's tale takes off from two notebook subjects recorded twenty years apart.

Jan. 22d [1879] Subject for a ghost-story.

Imagine a door – either walled-up, or that has been long locked – at which there is an occasional knocking – a knocking which – as the other side of the door is inaccessible – can only be ghostly. The occupant of the house or room, containing the door, has long been familiar with the sound; and regarding it as ghostly, has ceased to heed it particularly – as the ghostly presence remains on the other side of the door, and never reveals itself in other ways. But this person may be imagined to have some great & constant trouble; & it may be observed by another person, relating the story, that the knocking increases with each fresh manifestation of the trouble.

Rome. *Hotel de l'Europe. May 16th* [1899]

Note the idea of the knock at door (petite fantaisie)* that comes to young man (3 loud taps &c) *everywhere* – in all rooms & places he successively occupies – going from one to the other. '*I*' tell it – am with him: (*he* has told *me*;) share a little (though joking him always) his wonder, worry, suspense. I've my idea of what it means. His fate &c. 'Sometimes there *will* be something there – some one.' I am *with* him once when it happens. I am

* **petite fantaisie:** little fantasy

with him the 1st time – I mean the 1st time *I* know about it. (He doesn't notice – I do; then he explains: 'Oh, I thought it was only –.' He opens: there *is* some one – natural & ordinary. It is my *entrée en matière*.)* The dénoûment is all. What *does* come – at last. What *is* there. This to be ciphered out.

JONATHAN COE *Canadians Can't Flirt*

[1879] A subject.

The Count G. in Florence (*Mme T.* told me the other night) married an American girl, Miss F., whom he neglected for other women, to whom he was constantly making love.† She, very fond of him, tried to console herself by flirting with other men; but she couldn't do it – it was not in her – she broke down in the attempt. This might be related from the point of view of one of the men whom she selects for this purpose & who really cares for her. Her caprices, absences, preoccupations, &c – her sadness, her mechanical, perfunctory way of doing it – then her suddenly breaking it off & letting him see that she has a horror of him – he meanwhile being very innocent & devoted.

* **my entrée en matière**: my introduction; where I come in

† Klara, the widow of the Russian political exile Nikolai Turgenev (1789–1871), a distant relative of James's friend the novelist Ivan Turgenev, lived in Paris with her daughter Fanny and two sons. The Florentine Count and his American wife may possibly be Alberto Guido della Gherardesca and Giuseppina (Josephine) Fisher, whom he married in 1873.

TESSA HADLEY *Old Friends*

Oct. 22[d] 1891 (34 De Vere Gdns.)

What of this idea for a very little tale? – The situation of a married woman who during her husband's lifetime has loved another man and who, after his death[,] finds herself confronted with her lover – with the man whom, at least, she has suffered to make love to her, in a certain particular way. The particular way I imagine to be this: the husband is older, stupider, uglier, but she has of course always had a bad conscience. I imagine a flirtation between her and the younger man, who is really in love with her, which she breaks off on becoming aware that her husband is ill & dying. *He* is kind, indulgent, unsuspicious to her and she is so touched by his tenderness and suffering that she is filled with remorse at her infidelity and breaks utterly with her lover. She devotes herself to her husband, nurses and cherishes him – but at the end of a short time he dies. She is haunted by the sense that she was unkind to him – that he suspected her – that she broke his heart – that she really killed him. In this state she passes 6 months, at the end of which she meets again the man who has loved her and who still loves her. His hope is now that she will marry him – that he has gained his cause by waiting, by respecting her, by leaving her alone. x x x x x x x x

GILES FODEN *The Road to Gabon*

[Rome, 1899]

The coward – *le Brave*. The man who by a fluke has done a great bravery in the past; knows he can't do it again & lives in *terror* of the occasion that shall put him to the test. *Dies* of that terror.

LYNNE TRUSS *Testaments*

[Lamb House, Rye. September 1900]*

Note on some other occasion the little theme suggested by Lady W[olseley]'s account of attitude & behaviour of their landlord, in the greater house, consequent on their beautiful installation in the smaller & happy creation in it – beyond what he could have dreamed – of an interesting & exquisite milieu.† Something in the general situation – the resentment by the bewildered &

* James signed a lease on Lamb House in Rye, Sussex, a Georgian house he had been admiring, in September 1897, and after renovations moved in the following summer. In 1889 he bought the freehold.

† James's friends Sir Garnet Wolseley (1833–1913), 'victor of the Ashantees' in the first Ashanti War of 1873–4, from 1895 to 1899 Commander-in-Chief of the British Army, and his pretty, sympathetic wife, the former Louisa Erskine (1843–1920), moved in 1898 into the Farm House, on the Glynde estate in Sussex – to which Lady Wolseley applied her resources of taste. The 'landlord' – proprietor of Glynde Place and the smaller Farm House a hundred yards away – was Rear Admiral the Honourable Thomas Brand, whom James had met, and who was evidently bemused by the success of their new arrangements. James visited the Farm House in 1900, he wrote to a friend, 'with a good deal of envious & surprised perception, moreover, of the way the little house, originally so thankless, justifies itself when peopled with the proprietors and their treasures. She has a rare mind for things & the arrangement of them.'

mystified proprietor – of a work of charm beyond anything he had conceived or can, even yet, understand. It's a case – a study [of] a peculiar kind of jealousy, the resentment of supersession. The ugly hopeless, helpless great house – the beautiful, clever, unimitable small one. *The mystification – the original mistake.*

AMIT CHAUDHURI *Wensleydale*

Vallombrosa.* July 27th. 1890.

Subject for a short tale: a young man or woman who, in a far Western city – Colorado or California – surrounds himself with a European 'atmosphere' by means of French & English books – Maupassant, Revue des 2. Mondes† – Anatole France, Paul Bourget, Jules Lemaitre, &c; &, making it really very complete, & a little world, intense world of association & perception in the alien air, lives in it altogether. Visit to him of narrator, who has been in Europe & knows the people (say narrator is a very modern impressionist painter;) & contrast of all these hallucinations with the hard western ugliness, newspaperism, vulgarity – democracy. There must be an American literary woman, from New

* James was staying, as he wrote to his brother William four days earlier, in what he called a 'perfect . . . paradise' – 'Milton's Vallombrosa, the original of his famous line, the site of the old mountain monastery which he visited and which stands still a few hundred feet below me as I write'. (*Paradise Lost*, I, ll. 302–4: 'Thick as autumnal leaves that strow the brooks / In Vallombrosa, where the Etrurian shades, / High overarched, embower . . . ')

† The advanced French literary monthly, founded in Paris in 1829. In Ch. IV of his memoir *Notes of a Son and Brother* (1914), James says that 'there could perhaps be no better sample of the effect of sharpness with which the forces of culture might emerge than, say, the fairly golden glow of romance investing the mere act of perusal of the *Revue des Deux Mondes*'.

England, 'pure & refined,' thin & intense. The sketch, picture, vision – à la Maupassant. The point that, after all, even when an opportunity offers to go over & see the realities – go to Paris & there know something of the life described – the individual *stays* – won't leave: held by the spell of knowing it all *that* way – as the best. It isn't much of a 'point' – but I can sharpen it; & the situation, & what one can bring in, are the point.

SUSIE BOYT *People Were So Funny*

April 25th 1911 (95 Irving St.)

And then there is the little fantasy of the young woman (as she came into my head the other month,) who remains so devoted to her apparently chronically invalid Mother, so attached to her bedside and so piously & exhaustedly glued there, to her waste of youth & strength & cheer, that certain persons, the doctor, the friend, or two, the other relation or two, are unanimous as to the necessity that something be done about it – that is that the daughter be got away, that she be saved while yet there is time.

PHILIP HORNE *The Troll*

November 18th 1894 (34 De Vere Gdns. W.)

Isn't there perhaps the subject of a little – a very little – tale (de moeurs littéraires*) in the idea of a man of letters, a poet, a novelist, finding out, after years, or a considerable period, of very

* **de moeurs littéraires:** of literary manners

happy, unsuspecting & more or less affectionate intercourse with a 'lady-writer,' a newspaper-woman, as it were, that he has been systematically débiné,* 'slated' by her in certain critical journals to which she contributes? He has known her long & liked her, known of her hack-work &c, and liked it less; and has also known that the *éreintements*† in question have periodically appeared – but he has never connected them with her or her with them, and when he makes the discovery it is an agitating, a very painful revelation to him. Or the reviewer may be a man & the author anonymously and viciously – or at least abusively – reviewed may be a woman. The point of the thing is whether there be not a little supposable theme or drama in the relation, the situation of the two people after the thing comes to light – the pretension on the part of the reviewer of having one attitude to the writer *as* a writer, & a totally distinct one as a member of society, a friend, a human being. They *may* be – the reviewer may be – unconsciously, disappointedly, *rageusement*,‡ in love with the victim. It is only a little situation; but perhaps there is something in it.

JOSEPH O'NEILL *The Poltroon Husband*

[Lamb House, Rye. September 1900]

Alice§ related a day or two ago another little anecdote, of New England, of 'Weymouth' origin, in which there might be some

* **débiné:** pulled to pieces, picked apart.

† **éreintements:** demolitions, eviscerations

‡ **rageusement:** ragingly

§ Alice Howe Gibbens James (1849–1922), wife of James's elder brother William James (1842–1910), the psychologist and philosopher, was born and mostly brought up in Weymouth, Massachusetts.

small *very* good thing. Some woman of that countryside – some woman & her husband – were [waked] at night by a sound below-stairs which they knew, or believed, must be burglars, and it was a question of the husband's naturally going down to see. But the husband declined – wouldn't stir, said he wasn't armed, hung back &c, & his wife declared that in that case *she* must. But her disgust & scorn. 'You mean to say you'll *let* me?' 'Well, I can't prevent you. But *I* won't –!' She goes down, leaving him, & in the lower regions finds a man – a young man of the place – whom she *knows*. He's not a professional housebreaker, naturally, only a fellow in bad ways, in trouble, wanting to get hold of some particular thing, to sell, realise it, that they have. Taken in the act, & by *her*, his assurance fails him, while hers rises, & her view of the situation. He too is a poorish creature – he makes no stand. She threatens to denounce him (he keeps her from *calling*,) & he pleads with her not to ruin him. The little scene takes place between, & she consents at last, this first time, to let him off. But if ever again – why, she'll [do] *this*: which count[s] all the *more* against him – so, look out! He does look out; she lets him off & out, he escapes, & she returns to her husband. He has heard the voices below, making out, however, nothing, & he knows something has taken place. She admits part of it – says there *was* somebody, & she has let him off. *Who* was it then? – he is all eagerness to know. Ah, but this she won't tell him, & she meets curiosity with derision & scorn. She will *never* tell him; he won't be able to find out; & he will never know – so that he will be properly punished for his cowardice. Well, his baffled curiosity *is* his punishment, & the subject, the little subject, would be something or other that this produces and leads to. Tormenting effect of this withholding of his wife's – & creation for him, by it, of a sense of a relation with (on her part,) the man she found. There is something in it; but for very brief treatment, for the simple reason that the poltroon of a husband can't be made to have a consciousness in wh. the reader will linger long. ———— x x x x x x

CONTRIBUTORS

Susie Boyt was educated at St Catherine's College Oxford and University College London where she specialised in the works of Henry James and the poetry of John Berryman. She is the author of six acclaimed novels and a much-loved memoir and has written a weekly column for the *Financial Times Weekend* for the last thirteen years. Her latest novel *Love & Fame* appeared in the autumn of 2017 from Virago. Her edition of *The Turn of the Screw and Other Ghost Stories* was published by Penguin Classics, also in 2017. Susie is also a director at the Hampstead Theatre in London.

Amit Chaudhuri is the author of seven novels, the latest of which is *Friend of My Youth*. He is also a critic and a musician and composer. He is a Fellow of the Royal Society of Literature. Awards for his fiction include the Commonwealth Writers Prize, the Betty Trask Prize, the Encore Prize, the Los Angeles Times Book Prize for Fiction, and the Indian government's Sahitya Akademi Award. In 2013, he was awarded the first Infosys Prize in the Humanities for outstanding contribution to literary studies. He is Professor of Contemporary Literature at the University of East Anglia.

Jonathan Coe was born in Birmingham in 1961 and is the author of eleven novels, including *What a Carve Up!*, *The House of Sleep*, *The Rotters' Club* and *Number 11*. His biography of B.S. Johnson, *Like a Fiery Elephant*, won the Samuel Johnson Prize in 2005.

Giles Foden is Professor of Creative Writing at the University of East Anglia and the University of Limerick. After growing up in Africa, the UK and Ireland, he held the Harper-Wood Studentship in English Poetry and Literature at St John's College, Cambridge. In 1993, he became assistant editor of the *Times Literary Supplement*. Between 1996 and 2006 he worked on the books pages of the *Guardian*, during which period he published *The Last King of Scotland*, which won the 1998 Whitbread First Novel Award and was released as an Oscar-winning film in 2006. He is the author of three other novels and a work of narrative non-fiction. He was one of the judges of the Man Booker Prize in 2007 and of the IMPAC Prize in 2014. His writing has appeared in the *New York Times*, *Granta* and *Esquire*, among other publications.

Tessa Hadley has written six novels, three collections of short stories, and one full-length critical study, *Henry James and the Imagination of Pleasure*. Her novel *The Past*, published in the UK in 2015, won the Hawthornden Prize; a collection of stories, *Bad Dreams,* was published in 2017. She publishes short stories regularly in the *New Yorker*, reviews for the *Guardian* and the *London Review of Books*, and is a Professor of Creative Writing at Bath Spa University. In 2016 she was awarded a Windham-Campbell prize for Fiction.

Philip Horne teaches at University College London. He is the author of *Henry James and Revision: The New York Edition* (Oxford University Press, 1990); and editor of *Henry James: A Life in Letters*, Dickens's *Oliver Twist*; and James's *The Tragic Muse* and *The Portrait of a Lady* (all Penguin), as well as of James's *Autobiographies* (Library of America, 2016). He is the founding General Editor of the *Complete Fiction of Henry James* for Cambridge University Press, for which he is editing James's *Notebooks* and *The Golden Bowl*.

Joseph O'Neill is the author of four novels, most recently *The Dog*. A book of his short stories, *Good Trouble*, is published in 2018. He teaches at Bard College.

Paul Theroux, novelist and travel writer, was born in Medford, Massachusetts – the setting of Henry James's story, 'The Ghostly Rental'. He is the proud owner of the 24-volume New York Edition of the *Novels and Tales of Henry James*, and has written the Introduction to *What Maisie Knew* (Penguin). He is the author of *The Mosquito Coast*, and *The Great Railway Bazaar*, and many other books. His most recent travel book is *Deep South: Four Seasons on Back Roads*, and his most recent novel, *Mother Land* (2017).

Colm Tóibín is the author of nine novels, including *The Master* (a novel about Henry James) and *House of Names*, and two collections of stories. His work has been translated into more than thirty languages. He is a contributing editor at the *London*

Review of Books, Irene and Sidney B. Silverman Professor of the Humanities at Columbia University and Chancellor of Liverpool University.

Rose Tremain was one of only five women to be selected for *Granta*'s original twenty 'Best of Young British Novelists' in 1983. Since then, her novels and short stories have been published in twenty-seven countries and won many prizes, including the Whitbread Award, the Prix Femina in France and the 2008 Orange Prize for Fiction. Her fourteenth novel, *The Gustav Sonata*, was published to wide acclaim in 2016. It won the National Jewish Book Award for Fiction in the United States and has been shortlisted for five other awards, including the South Bank Sky Arts Award for Literature 2017. She was made a CBE in 2007.

Lynne Truss is the author of several novels and works of non-fiction, including *Eats, Shoots & Leaves*, a bestselling book on punctuation. Her only other foray into the world of Henry James was a comic-Gothic short story for a Glyndebourne collection, in which an over-imaginative woman named her two rescue cats Miles and Flora, and lived to rue the day.

Michael Wood is professor emeritus of English and Comparative Literature at Princeton. His most recent books are *Hitchcock: The Man Who Knew Too Much* and *On Empson*.

ACKNOWLEDGEMENTS

This book would have been impossible without help and encouragement from many people. I can't name them all, but my warm thanks go to: Susie Boyt, Jonathan Coe, Caroline Dawnay, Giles Foden, Tessa Hadley, Joe O'Neill; to Charlotte Knight and Frances Macmillan at Vintage, as well as David Purvis and Nick Skidmore; to Nick Hornby, David Lodge and John Sutherland; to Paul Auster, John Banville, Julian Barnes, William Boyd, J. M. Coetzee, Mark Haddon, Kazuo Ishiguro and Rose Tremain; to Matthew Beaumont, Gert Buelens, Jonathan Crewe, Quentin Curtis, Susan Halpert, Oliver Herford, Richard Holmes, Simon Johnson, Adrian Poole, Peter Swaab, René Weis, Michael Wood and Marino Zorzi and Rosella Mamoli Zorzi; and to Sarah Burton and Sarah Baxter at the Society of Authors. As always, Judith Hawley and Olivia Horne have been a vital support throughout. Acknowledgement is due to Bay James for kind permission to reproduce the image of the notebook page (in the sixth notebook) from which Giles Foden has drawn 'The Road to Gabon'; likewise to the Houghton Library, where the notebooks are housed (as bMS Am 1094); and to Penguin Books, for permission to reprint Colm Tóibín's story 'Silence', which first appeared in his collection of stories *The Empty Family*.

penguin.co.uk/vintage